THE CLOUDED MOUNTAIN

Elizabeth Daish

This first world edition published in Great Britain 2000 by
SEVERN HOUSE PUBLISHERS LTD of
9–15 High Street, Sutton, Surrey SM1 1DF.
This first world edition published in the U.S.A. 2000 by
SEVERN HOUSE PUBLISHERS INC of
595 Madison Avenue, New York, N.Y. 10022.

British Library Cataloguing in Publication Data

Daish,   Elizabeth
    The clouded mountain
    1.Love stories
    I. Title
    823.9'14 [F]

    ISBN 0-7278-5528-X

All situations in this publication are fictitious and
any resemblance to living persons is purely coincidental.

Typeset by Hewer Text Ltd
Edinburgh, Scotland.
Printed and bound in Great Britain by
MPG Books Ltd, Bodmin, Cornwall.

THE CLOUDED MOUNTAIN

Recent Titles by Elizabeth Daish from Severn House

EMMA'S WAR
EMMA'S PEACE
EMMA'S HAVEN
EMMA'S FAMILY
EMMA'S CHRISTMAS ROSE
EMMA'S JOURNEY

AVENUE OF POPLARS
CATRINA
THE CLOUDED MOUNTAIN
RYAN'S QUADRANGLE
SUMMER ROMANCE

One

T he stewardess smiled down at Carl Paterson, thinking that he was the most attractive man she'd seen in the last dozen flights. He smiled back and ordered wine to help down the nondescript meal on the plastic tray, then eased his shoulders back as if the seat were designed for a midget and his broad shoulders just weren't at home in the confines of the cramped upholstery. He drew in his long legs as the drinks trolley came down the aisle.

He glanced sideways at the girl sitting with him. "You'll have wine." It wasn't a question but Bridget Mark nodded, hoping that the travel pill and alcohol wouldn't explode together, but she was far too chastened by her own carelessness and the lack of communication with the man at her side to dare suggest that she'd prefer orange juice. "Sorry we aren't even in Club Class, but my secretary is to blame for that," he said, grimly. "I'd forgotten how I hate this kind of travel."

The wine came in small bottles with plastic beakers, and the stewardess eyed Bridget with speculation as if she couldn't believe that a man like Mr Paterson would want to travel with a girl who was so obviously ill-at-ease, pale, and dressed in such uninteresting clothes.

She knows I am only a minion, Bridget thought unhappily. Who would think any differently? Even the fake-fur jacket was an embarrassment now as it was too bulky to put under the seat with the travel bag, and there was no room for it in the overhead locker as two students, with packs that were far too untidy and flimsy to put in the luggage hold, had taken all the

1

room in the lockers above the seats. The jacket was stuffed down by her feet and she hoped that the floor of the aircraft was fairly clean.

Carl Paterson handed her a full beaker and smiled. It wasn't the warm smile he had given the stewardess as she brushed past his leg in her tight skirt, but it was a better effort than any that Bridget had got from him so far.

"You look a bit pale round the gills. Here, drink this and eat up all your nice supper," he said, stirring the contents of his own plastic tray as if intrigued by it all. She tried to eat but her throat was dry from the travel pill and the fear of the situation into which she had been plunged. She drank some wine and tried to appear calm.

He picked up the jam slice from his tray then put it back again. "I wonder how they achieve this? Do you make pastry? If so, I hope it's better than this."

"I make very good pastry," she replied and resolved to take no further notice of his slighting remarks. I didn't want to come with him, she thought resentfully, and drank some more wine.

"Well, well, who knows? We may find you have other unexpected talents during this week together."

She bit her lip and couldn't decide if she disliked his irony more than his amusement, but said firmly, "I hope you'll find I am efficient, sir, but you must remember that I am not your secretary and I am not used to everything in Herald Enterprises as yet."

"I'm sure you'll do your best. Most of the work in Switzerland will be to do with my new procedures and the patents of my equipment, not the usual routine back in the office. It's very confidential, but I can't imagine you chatting up the opposition or becoming involved in shady industrial espionage." He laughed as if he found the idea of Bridget Mark as a spy very amusing, and Bridget blushed and tried not to react and say something really cutting.

"I know," she replied. "Brian Greene told me how confidential it all is, but as I know nothing of the technicalities of software and computers, I can't be much of a risk, can I?"

"I'm sure that Brian is right. He's the best Personal Assistant I've had in years and he assured me that I could trust you in everything." He grinned, as if at a private and slightly malicious joke that was very amusing. "In fact he had to admit that you were the only girl he could suggest to fill this emergency, and who I could trust to take with me as my secretary for a whole week, so I take his word for it." His blue eyes sparkled. "I wonder if he was thinking of the secrecy of my work or my moral welfare? I think I feel safe on all counts, Miss Mark."

She stared into her glass and felt her colour rising as the sarcastic voice stung her and she knew that her temper was being tested. If he wants a little mouse he can have one, she thought. The sooner that this week is over the better I shall like it. She gave an inward sigh. We aren't even there yet! He has only the memory of me putting down his briefcase for a minute at the airport, even if I didn't really leave it unattended, to give him any idea of what I can or can not do. She glanced at his profile. And he's not the kind to forget such a stupid lapse of duty, she thought.

The pastry was dry and she found it impossible to swallow so she abandoned the effort and sipped more wine. She coughed. "I'm sorry," she murmured.

"If you'd made that pastry I suppose you'd have thrown it to the pigs," he said. "Or whatever you have in that remote part of the world where you live."

She turned to look at him, her eyes bright with anger and unshed tears. "We don't keep pigs," she said, shortly. Was he deliberately trying to goad her into making a verbal indiscretion to add to the other misdemeanour? Was he taking a delight in trying to put her in the wrong all the time? Too late she saw that his eyes were now gentle and he was really trying to put her more at ease.

"I'm sure you don't," he said quietly. "I was just thinking

that you probably come from a fairly rural background. Scotland, isn't it?"

"Yes." If it was possible, she felt even more deflated. Just when she had summoned the courage to stand up for herself if he said anything more that was wounding, he had foiled her by being polite. I know he thinks I was dragged up in a cave or somewhere equally unsophisticated but he needn't think I'm ashamed of my background, she told herself.

"I thought so. You have the slightest trace of accent. Just enough to place you," he went on. "Have you lived south of the border for very long?"

She forced herself to look at him again and to her surprise found real interest in the now serious blue eyes. "My family live in the Highlands and my father is a minister of the Kirk." He nodded as if to encourage her to say more. "I came down to stay with a cousin in London while I applied for a place in a physiotherapy school. There were no immediate vacancies so I enrolled in the same business course that Jean was taking. I took several exams and came to Herald Enterprises four months ago."

He smiled and Bridget lowered her gaze. So now, she thought, he knows that I am a country bumpkin in the big city, just as he suspected. I wonder how much satisfaction he gets from being right all the time?

"I love Scotland. I used to climb there when I was a student and we went for weekends away in camp. Once, we climbed in Glencoe for a whole week. It rained most of the time but the climbing was fun."

"That was dangerous," Bridget said impulsively. Her disapproval gave her courage. Everyone at home knew the dangers of climbing in certain areas in the wet, especially if that period followed a dry spell, as heavy rain washed away the dry earth holding the rocks firm and made the rock-face unstable. It could be very treacherous in such conditions.

"You are right," he admitted slowly. "I was very silly. It pays to listen to the locals when it comes to climbing, or when sailing in unfamiliar waters. On the last day, I climbed a fairly easy chimney, but I failed to take all the right precautions that had been routine when the surface was dry and simple. The rock was slippery and I fell and broke a leg, and put my shoulder out. They said I was lucky to be alive." He eyed her with interest. "Have you given up the idea of being a physio? I have the greatest regard for them as they made my leg workable after the accident. It no longer troubles me, although the shoulder does at times."

"I have my name down for a future vacancy but I'm undecided," she said.

"What made you want to do that?"

"An aunt was a physiotherapist and she taught me a lot of the minor treatments and that made me want to learn more," Bridget said simply.

He looked interested. "In a strange way I enjoyed being in hospital, although I hate everything to do with surgery. I had no idea that any girl could work as hard as the nurses did, and I admired them all." He laughed in an embarrassed way, as if unused to confiding in strange girls who he didn't really like.

Bridget held out her cup for more coffee and stirred in a little milk when the stewardess came round with refills. Carl Paterson sipped his, staring before him as if he had forgotten her existence, then realised he hadn't stirred the drink and that his plastic spoon had fallen to the floor.

"Have mine," she said.

He shifted restlessly in his seat as if confined. "Thank you, Miss Mark." He pulled a face. "I can't go on calling you Miss Mark for a whole week. You do have a first name?" The irony was back again. "I call my secretary Sandra all the time I am away with her on business and she calls me Carl, but never in the office as it leads to a false kind of familiarity." He saw her mouth tighten. "Very well, if you find it impossible to call me Carl, then call me what you like, but never 'sir'. Do I get to know your first name?"

"I'm Bridget, s— Mr Paterson." In her confusion, and to

5

hide the fact that she had almost immediately nearly called him sir, after he had forbidden it, she blurted out, "But my family call me Bridie." She blushed. What a stupid thing to say, as if inviting the very familiarity that he deplored. He was a man who would use her secretarial skills for a week and then send her back to the office where she usually worked and never saw him from one week to another. He need never think of her again once they returned from Switzerland.

"Bridget will do very well while you insist on calling me Mr Paterson," he said and smiled. "Bridget from the manse."

The trays were cleared and the lights dimmed. It's too dark to work, Bridget thought, wondering why Carl Paterson was not expecting her to take notes while on the plane as she had expected him to do, but he folded back the tables and said, "Better relax for half an hour. There's no real rest on this flight but there will be a lull before they bring round the duty free."

She took the hint that he wanted to be quiet and sank back in her seat and closed her eyes. Suddenly she was utterly weary. The rush and excitement caught up with her now that everything was peaceful and she drifted into a twilight of half-sleep in which images formed and dispersed, like shadows on water. She remembered the mountain at the back of her home in Scotland and the many times she had looked up at it, hoping to see the top, only to see it wreathed in cloud. The cloud made it a magical place, like Olympus where the gods of Greek mythology had their homes. Beyond the clouded mountain anything could happen; or was it like looking for the end of a rainbow? She sighed. For her there was no end of the rainbow, only a life bogged down by her own lack of confidence and the natural generosity that allowed others to take advantage of her good nature.

In her half-sleep she smiled ruefully, recalling the events that had led to her being on this plane with this wonderful, terrible man from the penthouse office block, the holy of holies at Herald Enterprises.

Mrs Dean, the office know-all, had been pushing her trolley

along to the next section, collecting waste paper to be taken down to the shredder. She paused by Bridget's desk and shook her head. "You want to stand up for yourself, dear," she said. "It's the willing horse that gets the heaviest burden."

Good old Mrs Dean, Bridget thought. At least one person in this God-forsaken firm can give my ego a boost and know that I really do work hard. The woman looked at the overloaded pile of work on the desk, put there just an hour before she was due to leave for home. "The more you do the more they'll expect." The woman wandered off, her sharp eyes missing nothing of what went on in the head office of Herald Enterprises.

"What's biting you?" Sandra, the personal secretary of Mr Carl Paterson paused to glance at the disconsolate face of the quiet girl, before disappearing into her own smart little office. "Ouch! Even my boss can't expect all that to be done today, before you leave. You'd be here until midnight!" She riffled through the papers. "Do this and this. Not that, it isn't urgent. Do that or they'll be screaming for it in the morning, but leave the rest. Say quite firmly that it was impossible to fit it all in today." She laughed. "He'll accept miracles if he can get them without too much hassle, but even he is human at times, believe it or not!"

"Are you all right?" Bridget saw that Sandra looked flushed, putting a hand to her head and closing her eyes for a second.

"Yes . . . I mean no. I've a splitting head and, to tell the truth, I feel lousy. Have you any aspirin?"

"You don't look at all well. Are you sure it's only a headache? You could be running a temperature."

"I am, but I have to clobber it tonight, whatever it is. Mr Paterson is off to Switzerland tomorrow and I have to go with him." She gave a weak smile. "At least neither he nor Brian can expect all that work to be done before he goes, and when he's away the workload isn't as heavy, so you can relax. There really isn't a rush to get that lot done."

"What a lovely break – to go to Switzerland," Bridget said enviously. "Do you know, I've never been further than Normandy, and that was by ferry."

Sandra made a face. "Don't you believe it. It's not a lot of fun. Everyone here thinks I've got it made, but there's more to life than a well-paid job, however satisfying the work. Oh, I know I have a lot of perks and a good time generally, but I have to keep up a high standard all the time with Carl Paterson. He expects nothing but the best, and when I go away with him I work harder than ever without the benefit of all our equipment and our records handy. *And* I have to be polite to dreary industrialists."

She took the tablets that Bridget handed to her. "Thanks a lot. Trust you to have the right thing handy. You really do think of everything, as always. Push yourself more and you'll do well here."

"Can't you get home before the rush hour?"

"Not a hope. There are loads of papers to take with us; some very confidential and I must get them packed in a briefcase, tonight." Sandra walked away, her shoulders drooping and her steps listless.

Bridget went back to her desk. It was just possible to do the paper that Sandra had placed in one tray. She worked steadily for fifteen minutes and then the buzzer on the desk startled her. "The top floor, Miss Mark," a voice said. "Mr Paterson's private office."

Bridget put her papers in a neat pile and picked up a pad and ballpoint pen. What could he want with her in the palatial suite in the penthouse? If he wanted this work done then the least he could do was leave her to get on with it. She relaxed. It might be Brian Greene, his PA who would be taking over tomorrow when Carl Paterson left for Switzerland.

She had been to the penthouse once before when Mr Paterson had wanted notes made of a speech he had to give to the Chamber of Commerce, so she remembered which door to approach. She shrugged. That last time was when she was

8

leaving for lunch and he had been annoyed because his own typist and secretary were out at the same time and he had had to make do with whoever Brian Greene could get hold of. Whatever was needed now would mean more work before she left the office.

The pile of the carpet thickened as she left the corridor and entered the foyer of the penthouse suite. Bowls of flowers and jardinières of exotic plants added to the opulence and she saw that the heavy teak door to the inner office was half-open, as if impatient for her arrival. She hurried forward, her shoes making no sound on the carpet. She raised her hand to tap on the door, then paused, realising that the door was not left open just for her, but possibly had been flung open by the man now speaking into the telephone.

Words came clearly and the deep voice of Carl Paterson was impatient. "You know I have to take someone and that someone must be efficient. I can't go to this particular congress without a really efficient and discreet secretary. I also need someone to be with me at dinner and whatever damn fool function they arrange for the delegates. If I have to attend those things, at least give me a female who is over five foot nothing, isn't built like a bus and hasn't crossed eyes!" His voice dropped into a quiet and terrifying whisper. "Find me someone, Brian, before I get the tiniest bit annoyed!"

The phone was slammed down and Bridget tapped nervously on the door. The cross voice told her to enter. "You wanted me to take notes, sir?" He stared at Bridget as if he had never seen or heard of her before in his life. "You buzzed my desk, sir," she went on. "At least, someone from this office did." She stood before him and tried to appear cool, but found his sheer dynamism almost overpowering.

"I have to go to Switzerland," he said as if to himself. The deep blue eyes seemed to see something far away. "I have to go tomorrow to one of the most important congresses of the year, perhaps of the decade, where I shall attend all the meetings and make all the right noises to secure a number

9

of contracts and make waves in several directions, and what happens?"

She shook her head, wordlessly, and he seemed to register her presence for the first time.

"I'll tell you what happens. My efficient, attractive and very bright secretary, Sandra, chooses this moment to have 'flu!" He glared at Bridget. "I, or rather the firm, pays that girl a princely salary and when I need her most she lets me down!" He gave a hollow laugh and tossed a folder down on to the desk. "And now, they tell me they can't find a replacement. Do you know how many females we have on the staff of this enormous firm?" She shook her head again. "Neither do I, but surely among those teeming chattering crowds there is one girl who could help me now? I find it ridiculous."

"Not everyone knows your routine, sir, and the trade agreements are not generally known in the lower offices."

"I suppose you're right. Sit down." He looked tired. Bridget flipped over the pages of the notepad and he sat straight in his chair. "I want a few notes on separate cards. You know the thing – pointers for me when I give a vote of thanks. You did it once before, if I remember correctly."

"I used the smaller, thin cards," she said. He waved her to the neat stationary receptacle so that she could select what was needed, and then began to dictate. They worked for ten minutes before the white internal telephone at his elbow burped discreetly. He leaned back in the swivel chair and nodded to her to answer it.

"Mr Paterson's office," she said. "Yes, I am Miss Mark." She put her other hand on the desk as if to steady herself. "I'm sorry. What did you say?"

"Give it to me," growled the man at the desk, and took the handset from her. "I haven't all night. Is that you, Brian? Right, tell me the worst. Who is she? And I warn you, that if you haven't found me someone who is efficient, who knows my ways, and knows which fork to use for meals, and who isn't entirely repulsive, I shall fire you. I don't care what excuses you make." He listened to the pained voice at the other end of the line. "Hell, Brian, is that the best you can do?"

Carl Paterson swung round in his chair and saw Bridget. He did a quick double-take as if just realising that she had heard every word he said. The pale girl with the expression of growing horror was frozen to her seat. "OK," he said in a milder tone, "If you say so. I can settle details myself. Sandra did manage to book the flight?" He frowned. "Oh, hell. Not even Club Class? What was she doing? OK. I'll manage."

He tossed the phone towards her, and Bridget caught it before it hit the floor. His smile was brittle and filled her with cold dread. "Well, did you get that? You are Miss Mark, one of our bright new young females?" She nodded miserably. "Well, smile girl, we are off to sunny Switzerland."

"But I can't!" began Bridget. Utter panic welled up inside her. "I can't do that. I couldn't pack in time and I've a date for tomorrow evening."

"Well, it's time you learned to pack fast. As for your date; is he involved with this firm?" She nodded. "Then he will be delighted to forgo a romantic evening with you in the interests of his future career."

Bridget stared. "I've never flown before, sir."

"You don't have to pilot the thing," he said, impatiently. "And your date will have to restrain his passion for a week, won't he?"

She nodded. The smile was frosty and didn't reach the blue of his widely spaced eyes. He looked fierce, exasperated and disconcertingly handsome.

On the few occasions when he had come down to the main office, people like Sandra and Brian Greene had been there and the atmosphere had been fairly relaxed, and when she had taken the notes in his office, Brian Greene had been there to give her confidence, but now, to be near him alone, in his present frame of mind, it was like sitting on the crumbling edge of a dam about to burst.

11

"When do you want me to be ready to leave, sir?" She set her face into a negative expression, knowing that he was looking her over and making judgements. At least I can't do all that work that landed on my desk, she thought. They can whistle for that!

But the thought gave her no comfort. She knew that under stress her face was pale and gave no hint of the warm and humorous personality she showed to her family and close friends.

"Leave here early tomorrow – I'll order a car take you home. Do you live far from the office?" She wrote her address on one of the cards and he glanced at it. "Right. The car will collect you to take you to the airport for eight p.m. You must check in by nine." He looked at the sober tweed skirt and high-necked woollen sweater that she had put on in a hurry that morning as the June day was surprisingly cold.

"You'll need light clothes. Switzerland will be warmer than it is here. You'll certainly need thinner things in overheated hotels," he added. The warm sweater had been comfortable earlier but now she knew she looked all wrong and was far too hot in it. Carl Paterson gave a short laugh. "No wonder Sandra catches cold. She never wears enough to keep warm." His irritation was tinged with amusement and Bridget knew that he was comparing her manner of dress with the fairly way-out clothes that Sandra wore to the office.

How can I live up to her? she thought. Sandra was blonde and vivacious, with a toothbrush-advertisement smile – the complete opposite to the girl trembling in the huge office, even if her eyes were huge and dark, with golden lights in their depths, her figure under the shapeless sweater good, and her skin clear. She brushed her hair away from her face with a nervous gesture. He seemed to have forgotten her again. "May I go now, sir?"

"Not yet." He scribbled a note and handed it to her. "Let Brian have this before you leave tonight so that he can arrange your transport tomorrow. He scribbled again. "This will

12

release the briefcase now in security which you will bring to the airport with your own luggage. It must not be left unattended for a second, do you understand? I shall see you at the airport . . . You do have a passport?" She inclined her head. At least that was to his liking! "I shall be near passport control or in the bar. Collect your ticket from me and we shall sit together on the plane."

For a moment, her heart warmed towards him. How nice of him to make sure thay sat together so that she would feel less uneasy.

"Bring those cards with you and we can do some work during the flight," he said.

Bridget went back to her desk with her mind a whirl of conflicting emotions. If she had been informed only a few hours ago that she might have to go to a very important congress with anyone at all, she would have laughed in disbelief, but to be told that she was to go with Carl Paterson – the dynamic and good-looking business man who made heads turn and waiters come running – nearly gave her mild hysterics. Things like this just don't happen to me, she thought. What would her aunt say when she knew? A smile that belonged to the Bridie from Scotland, and was like the smile inherited from a beloved grandmother, made her lips twitch; then she got down to work again, long after most of the office staff had left.

It was a relief to work alone as she could avoid explaining what was to happen tomorrow. If I was eloping it would cause less fuss, she decided, and imagined the envious glances that she would have to endure once the news broke. The girls in the audio-visual department would be green with envy.

At least I was chosen as the most suitable, she thought to give herself courage. She brightened for a moment. Brian Greene had suggested her. But as suitable for what? She bit her lower lip. Suitable for taking notes, being unobtrusive and smoothing the way for the important man to make his big impact on the trade congress, impressing everyone with his iron efficiency and control? Or to have someone to blame if anything went wrong?

What did it matter? She gave a half-smile again as she recalled his turbulent eyes and the way he ruffled his hair when annoyed, more like a cross and spoiled five-year-old than a smooth executive. I could like the small boy, she decided, even when he scares the wits out of me.

She went into the office early the next day and was told that she could go home again as soon as she collected the briefcase and knew the time that the car would take her to the airport. She sighed with relief as she sank back into the back seat of the company car taking her home again; she was spared making any explanations to the office staff and could finish her packing at leisure.

Rain fell in drenching, relentless stair-rods and the roads were awash, making the wheels throw up mud and garbage from the gutters, and the sky gave no hint of better weather. It would be so good to get away. If only I could really look forward to it, she thought, instead of having to work hard and be careful not to upset the boss, and to do the right thing all the time I'm in Switzerland. On the other hand, I've never flown and never been so far away, she recalled. There must be something good about this trip.

She dashed into her small apartment, gripping the precious briefcase and putting it in the tiny hallway with her raincoat. Her case was on top of the wardrobe and she was glad that she had bought a new one for her last visit home to Scotland. That at least was reasonably smart. Her lighter clothes hung ready to wear and freshly cleaned, awaiting warmer weather, but she knew that they would have to be replaced now that she was earning a good salary, as they were dull and tired and bore no resemblance to the smart clothes worn by other girls in the office. Spring had been late and summer slow in appearing, and the need for pretty summer things to be worn in London had not been pressing until now. She had plenty of fresh underwear though, and a new kimono.

She became absorbed in her packing and tried to imagine
what she might need for such a strange visit. A pair of leather
shoes in case she had a chance to walk, that was if the tyrant
allowed her off the hook for an hour or so! Certainly sandals
and, if they were to stay in a large hotel there might be a pool
. . . Bridget hesitated. She held up her plain regulation-type
swimming one-piece and frowned. It was cut high under the
arms to cover her chest like a swimmer in a school team and
the last time that she had worn it, she had felt overdressed
and very old-fashioned. She ran a bath and hastily cut a
sandwich to eat with coffee afterwards, then stripped in the
small bathroom and touched the birthmark that made it
impossible for her to wear a low-cut dress or a bikini. An
angry red shape spoiled the soft line of her breast where a
deeply cut cleavage would normally show the sweet lines of
her swelling bosom.

Every time she bathed or showered, she touched the mark
as if to will it to go away, but that was impossible. She
wondered if she would ever have the courage to have plastic
surgery, but could almost hear her aunt's disapproving voice.
"Don't be silly and vain, Bridie. It's pure self-indulgence to
meddle with such things. It has been sent to try you, and if
God wanted you to be perfect he would have made you so.
You have your health and strength and you're really quite
pretty in a bad light!"

"It's embarrassing," Bridie had said, but the aunt who
loved her and had cared for her since her mother died, only
pursed her lips.

"There's no need to feel like that. Don't be worrying over
something that nobody will ever see. Or, if they did, then
they'd have no right to see it," she added severely, forgetting
that small plain girls grow up into women with beauty of face
and body and the desire to show their attractions according to
the fashions of the day. "Nobody but your husband should
see it, and then only after you marry," said the unmarried
aunt who had lived all her life in the same narrow village. She

15

had not even approved of her own sister training as a physiotherapist and treating men.

Now she was away from the influence of the manse, Bridget could see her home more objectively. It's as if she's glad I have to hide it. If someone did see the birthmark and she heard about it, she'd say I was 'flaunting my body', as she puts it, and know that I was no longer her good little Bridie.

As she dried and used the sweet-smelling talc that had been a Christmas present, she wondered again about the birthmark. What would her friends do in the same situation? What would someone like Sandra do? She tried to think about it as a problem in an agony column, with a stranger asking the question, and she knew that most girls would have the operation as soon as they saved the cash or could persuade their own doctors that it was necessary to have it done in a state hospital. She sighed. Most families would encourage such an action. Surely it was natural for mothers, and even guardian aunts, to want their young girls to be free of hang-ups and to grow up as pretty as they could possibly be? I do have enough money, she realised. A small legacy could see to all expenses if she wanted anything done privately.

It's time I left home, she decided. I still look over my shoulder to make sure my father or my aunt are not there if I accept a second glass of sherry at a party and I can never wear anything really figure-flattering. Damn! Why do I love them so much that I hate to upset them?"

The telephone rang and she ran to answer it, tucking the receiver under her chin so that her hands were free to continue putting pale varnish on her left hand fingernails. "Roger?" The receiver fell from her shoulder and the last nail was badly smudged. "Damn!" she said.

"Damn because it's me?" The voice was guarded.

"No, of course not." How could she tell him that until he rang she had forgotten that she had a date with him at nine? "It's not you. I just made a mess of my nail varnish."

"I hope you weren't dressing up for me," he said, and gave

16

a nervous laugh. "I, that is, something has come up and I can't
see you tonight, Bridie. I tried to get through to you in the
office but they said you'd gone home early. Are you all right?"

"I'm fine. What happened to make you change your
mind?"

"Well, it's like this. My section-boss is giving a party and he
asked me . . . or rather told me; you know what it's like with
old MK. It really was a royal command, the old army thing – I
want two volunteers, you and you." What is he drivelling on
about? she wondered. "Well, the old man told me to go to this
place at nine to escort someone to his party."

"Now who would that be, I wonder?" asked Bridie. "Not
the pretty blonde daughter with all that lovely money?"

"Don't be like that, Bridie. I have to go. You know how it
is. If I don't do as he asks and toe the line, he'll have a very
long memory when it comes to promotion. Hell! I do want to
take you out. You know how I feel about you."

"It's all right, Roger. Have a good time."

"You don't mind? You really mean that?"

"Of course I mean it. Don't give it another thought. Go to
the party and have a great time. As a matter of fact, I was
about to ring you, but you got in first," she lied. "I had a
change of plan thrust on me, too, so neither of us needs to
worry."

"What change of plan? Who is it?"

"Nothing of importance," she said, airily.

"But you were getting ready as if for a special occasion. I
thought you were dressing up for me." He sounded cross.
"You don't paint your nails for a meeting. Have you another
date?"

"Would it matter? You seem to be doing that so why
shouldn't I?"

"This is strictly business, Bridie. I can't get out of it. You
know how I feel about you. I love you." Bridie inspected her
nails and said nothing. "Bridie? Are you still there? Did you
hear what I said?"

"I heard you, Roger. But my date is business, too. Isn't it a pity that we can't do as we like in this harsh world? I know that you will be just as understanding when I tell you that I am about to be collected by car and taken to the airport and flown to Switzerland with Carl Paterson to spend a working week there."

The gasp of disbelief was both flattering and insulting. Obviously Roger didn't believe that she could land such a plum job, but he obviously didn't want her to go with Carl Paterson. "You have to be joking!" he said.

"Deadly serious," she said. "Have a very good time, Roger. Regards to the little blonde. I have to go now or I'll keep the car waiting. Bye for now. See you sometime." She put the phone back on the rest.

Am I in love with him? she asked herself. She recalled a night when they had danced in a tiny club suggested by her cousin. The party was good and the dancing wild and he had held her close when the music stopped; breathless in a dark corner he had kissed her with a passion she had not suspected. They had dated and taken pleasure in each other's company but never before this evening had he said he loved her. The frisson of desire she had experienced in the dark night-club could have been the beginning of love or, as she suspected, the natural result of two young bodies close together creating a fleeting emotion that made them compatible for a while.

If I was in love with him would I have so completely forgotten that I had a date with him?

She shut her case and picked up her handbag, making sure for the third time that she had her passport, cash, cheque book and plastic bank cards. Her everyday coat looked winter tired and she had no intention of taking a thick raincoat. Both were heavy and cumbersome and quite unsuitable for a smart hotel in Switzerland. She picked up the fake-fur jacket that she had bought in her first flush of independence in the big city.

Her aunt had sniffed audibly and said that only bad girls wore light-coloured fur coats. It had taken a lot of the pleasure away and she had seldom worn it, but now it seemed to be the only garment she possessed suitable to wear with Carl Paterson.

Bridget gave a mischievous smile. I might as well wear it. She'll never believe that I can go away with my dynamic boss on a purely business trip, so what does it matter what I wear? Besides, she said to herself defiantly, I need it to give me courage.

The doorbell rang and she cast an anxious look back into the room. Everything turned off? She thought of Roger. Even Roger was turned off for the present! She picked up her travelling bag, her handbag and briefcase and went down to the car.

"I'll keep the briefcase with me," she told the driver and sat in the back seat. The car seemed under a magic influence. Lights turned green and spaces opened in the traffic to let through the high-powered company vehicle that took her so easily to the airport. Did the use of the car mean that Carl Paterson was thoughtful, or did it mean that he distrusted hired cars when he wanted her to arrive on time? She frowned, unable to believe that he would consider her feelings or comfort, but was simply anxious that his precious briefcase should not be lost.

The airport murmured with a kind of hollow impersonality, and the tap of heels on the polished floors mingled with the relay systems in reception. Bridie was early and went into the shop to buy a paperback. The coat was comfortably warm and felt good. She selected a glossy magazine, her confidence growing, and she wondered how long she must wait until Carl Paterson came along.

The assistant took the money and Bridie put her purse in her bag and bent to pick up the briefcase. Panic seized her. The briefcase was gone! She turned, her eyes dilated with fear. A man stood behind her, the briefcase in his hand. Carl Paterson glowered at her, his blue eyes dark with fury.

"Don't you know anything?" he thundered. "Don't you

19

know that you never, *never* put a case down for a single moment?" She opened her mouth to speak but he cut her short. "Come on, we'll have the bags checked in and I'd better take charge of this."

Bridie followed meekly, praying that she could survive the coming week.

Two

S omewhere in the top of her head, through the faint sounds in the aircraft, Bridie thought of Roger. Roger Franks, the man who at last had admitted that he loved her, and yet this evening would be dancing with a luscious little blonde who was used to having everything that Daddy could buy for her. Would he kiss her? Would his need for personal success make him willing to make love to the girl, if that was what she wanted?

Powerful men could buy most things and Penelope Knightly had a very powerful father who could manipulate a lot of people, so tonight there was every possibility that Roger would hold Penny Knightly in his arms and whisper tender nothings in her ear. Bridget discovered that the idea made no impact on her and she felt no jealousy. Suddenly she just didn't care what he did. I wonder what Carl Paterson buys, if he needs to buy anything, she thought.

But such thoughts faded along with the other images from her exhausted half-sleep. Slowly her eyelids registered light and she opened her eyes to see figures moving along the aisle of the plane. Where am I? What am I doing here? There was a moment of panic, then reorientation. She put a hand down to check that the briefcase was there between her and the seat where Carl Paterson was sitting, but her hand was covered in something soft and warm. Her coat was wrapped firmly over her knees, covering her hands and chest, and she pushed it away. The air smelled stale; the in-flow hissed above her but gave no freshness and she opened her eyes wide as she realised that the seat by her side was empty.

Carl Paterson walked back from the end toilet. He spoke to the stewardess in passing and she laughed in a way that was surely a come-on. The man in the remaining seat by the window asked Bridget to let him pass into the aisle and as soon as he had gone she peered out of the oval window.

"Warm enough?" Carl Paterson asked.

"Yes, thank you," she murmured, trying to push away the folds of fur fabric. Who had tucked her in so carefully? The jacket had been at her feet, and the stewardess could not have known it was there, even if she had bothered to look for a covering for the sleeping girl. As she stood up to look out of the window, she saw that several people were asleep and nobody had put warm coverings over them. Many more were dozing.

She looked out into the darkness. Below the wing were twinkling lights far away, seeming to follow a pattern round a wide area as if surrounding a lake. Cloud lay in thick patches hiding the lights at intervals, and a nearly full moon rose above the cloud bank. Through the clouds, Bridie had her first glimpse of the peaks high on the Swiss Alps.

"Nearly there," said Carl Paterson, but she didn't hear. "Not long now," he said, but she was too absorbed to reply. She stared fascinated at the snowy peaks peeping through the now wispy cloud. "What is it, Bridget," he said softly, as if afraid to intrude into a private dream or to make her gold flecked eyes lose their glow.

"My clouded mountain," she whispered. "It's beautiful."

The pilot cleared his throat, making the intercom crackle. He told them the altitude, the fact that they might meet some turbulence on the way down, and instructed the cabin staff to check that all seat belts were fixed. The aircraft rocked and Bridie closed her eyes. It was worse with her eyes shut but she didn't want to show her fear to the man at her side. She tried taking deep breaths but had to clench her hands on the seat-rests until the white of her knuckles showed.

A warm hand closed over hers. "Soon be down," Carl

Paterson said, and she opened her eyes. He smiled mockingly. "Bridget of the manse doesn't like thunderstorms."

"I'm fine . . . usually," she said. "It seems different up here and I feel more . . ." She swallowed hard to relieve the pressure in her ears.

"More vulnerable?" He still held her hand and she felt a wave of peace and security flow over her. "Any brothers or sisters?" he asked.

"One sister who married last year. She lives in Edinburgh." Bridget found that she could speak more easily.

"And when you marry? Will he be a true Scot?" She looked up, surprised and touched that he should make this effort to take her mind off the landing. She no longer felt the rising panic. He waited for an answer.

"I don't know," she said.

"The man you should have been dating tonight. Is he a Scot or does the manse smile on foreigners from across the border?"

Bridget smiled as she thought of her aunt and her reaction to anything ten miles from home, and her conviction that the English brought nothing but trouble.

"That's the first time you've smiled. You should do it more often." A tremor of something other than fear in his company made her acutely aware of the strong arm touching hers on the padded arm-rest between the seats.

"He isn't Scottish, and yes, my aunt would not approve. To her all Sassenachs are suspect, but my father is a little more liberal."

"So what happens when you tell them that you want to marry him?" Was this idle curiosity that made him question her, a paternal trait inherent in the boss-secretary situation, or a real kindness? He laughed. "I can imagine you having to parade him for family approval."

It was so like the truth that Bridget laughed. "I know I'd never get away with a quiet civil wedding," she said. "They'd never forgive me if I didn't let them have a say in the arrangements, and that means summoning every available member of the family from John o' Groats to the border. When my sister was married she swore that she had never met three-quarters of the guests."

"It would take quite a man to run that gauntlet," he said with a wry smile. "Does your . . . friend know what's in store for him?"

"I've never really thought of that," Bridie said slowly. "I've never thought of marriage with Roger, or anyone so far." The plane seemed to swoop into the ground and Bridie was tense again. The back-rush of air-brakes shattered the night. Then they were down and the plane taxied slowly to the airport terminal. The comforting hand was abruptly taken away and Carl Paterson busied himself with his passport, handgrip and the briefcase.

"Let's get out of here. I'll take the briefcase. You fetch a trolley and wait for the bags as they come off the carousel. I have to make a phone call."

Once more he was a stranger who had done nothing more than made small talk with her as they happened to sit together on a flight. If he disappeared now and she never saw him again he would never give her another thought. Bridie shrugged. At least she had enjoyed a breathing space before he remembered her shortcomings and reverted to the sarcasm and disapproval that she had previously experienced. No doubt there would be a few more cutting remarks as soon as they reached the hotel and she had to work.

It was only then that she recalled she'd been told they would work on the flight, but he had made no mention of anything more vital than the decision to have second cups of coffee!

She found a luggage trolley and consulted her list, ticking off each item of Paterson luggage and her own as they came off the conveyor belt. She added the two flight bags and pushed the unwieldy trolley towards the row of telephones, each with its appendage of human legs under the plastic cowl. She waited far enough away from Carl Paterson to make his call private, but found that she was being forced gradually nearer as more and more trolleys came that way and took up the area near customs control.

To her embarrassment she could now hear his voice clearly. She turned her back but the one-sided conversation came across to her. "Of course, Countess Maria! I can't tell you how much I am looking forward to seeing you again." He listened and laughed. "Yes, of course I remember. How could I ever forget?" His voice was smooth and oozing with masculine charm, and Bridie imagined what effect it must have on the woman on the other end of the line. She wondered a little wistfully what it might be like to have him looking at her with real admiration, and to enjoy the warmth of his smile. How would it be to be loved by such a man?

She heard him say goodbye and saw him leave the canopy, the smile he had worn still lingering as he came towards her, an echo of the humour in his voice during the conversation. He put a hand on the trolley but she darted past him and picked up the briefcase that he had left by the phone; the briefcase that he had completely forgotten!

"Oh, thanks," he said, the smile fading. He thrust the case back into her arms. "Better with you after all," he admitted and took the trolley, pushing it as if he was trying to catch a train.

When they were free of customs he hurried to the exit where a chauffeur in uniform stood holding a card with the name Paterson on it. Carl Paterson raised an imperious hand. "Over here. You are from the Hotel Viceroy?" The man took the luggage and in minutes they were installed in the large black limousine and on the way to the hotel, past brightly lit restaurants and clubs and, in the distance, the glint of lake water and the dark back-drop of the mountain dotted with small lamps.

"The Viceroy Hotel?" Bridie said to break the uneasy silence. "That sounds like colonial India, not modern Switzerland."

"Quite right. It's an old hotel but one that I prefer for day-to-day living. It has a certain old world charm; a kind of peace. I have to use the Astra for most of the congress business, but as that's only a stone's throw away it's no great disadvantage. If I stay in the hotel where I'm working, I find that I talk shop all the evening and never have time alone." He laughed. "I wonder what you'll make of it? I rather gathered from the last visit when Sandra was here with me that she would have prefered to stay at the Astra all the time as they have frenetic music going half the night."

"I like old places," Bridie said.

"Not many retired Indian Army colonels there now, but they still make a very good curry. Do you like curry?"

"Very hot with lots of fruit," said Bridie.

"Full marks. Remind me to share one with you sometime." The car stopped at the entrance to the hotel. A riot of geraniums flounced over a low balcony, making the dignified building look quite coquettish. The wheels stopped crunching the gravel drive and Bridie found herself facing a wrought-iron elevator inside the huge foyer. It was a gem of intricate Victoriana, flanked by statues of bronze tribesmen holding torches aloft. Bridie gazed at them, enchanted, and the man with her eyed her with lazy amusement. She was amazed that Carl Paterson, of all people, should choose this place. It didn't fit in with the suave sophisticated tycoon who she inwardly feared, and yet she found that she was drawn to him with a mixture of emotions to which she couldn't put a name.

"It reminds me of a hotel in Tunbridge Wells," she said. "There were people there who spoke in whispers as if they were in church and the whole place had statues looming up at me from every corner, some carrying spears! There was masses of red plush everywhere just as this one has."

"It sounds terrifying."

"It was a bit intimidating but this is wonderful and not at all terrifying."

"Are you so easily terrified?" He seemed to find her very

amusing. "You might be. Come to think of it, you are a bit of a mouse, but let's hope you have some of the steely resilience of your illustrious ancestors hidden somewhere." He was teasing gently and his eyes held a glow of something almost akin to friendliness, but Bridget knew that this was his way of saying that he expected very little from the girl who had been foisted on to him at such short notice.

It may have been his intention to make her feel that she need not try too hard, but it was depressing to be put down into such a low category. As she followed him into the lift, she felt insignificant and useless. They emerged into the bright light of the second floor. Long curtains at the end of the corridor hung over the windows and no light came from the outside world so that the false brightness of the chandeliers made her want to shut her eyes.

Bridie was tired. She blinked and tried to stifle a yawn. The porter had unlocked a door and was disappearing inside with the cases. Inside, a small foyer led to a sitting room where the porter waited hopefully for a tip and smiled when he saw that this new resident was one of the generous variety. Bridie hesitated, wondering where she would be working and if Carl Paterson would take a lot of time over the cards before she could get some sleep, especially as night would soon be changing into dawn.

He glanced back to see what kept her. "Come in," he said, impatiently. The porter closed the outer door behind him and Bridie stood looking into the sitting room while Carl Paterson raised an enquiring eyebrow. "What is it now?" he asked.

"Could you tell me where to find my room? If you want me to work now, I'd like to freshen up a little." She gave an embarrassed smile. "I haven't a room-key and I have no idea where to go."

"Work? My dear girl, who could work after sitting for hours in that stuffy plane? No, *sleep* is what we need. Sleep is first on the agenda. *Bed*, glorious bed!" he said with satisfaction.

27

He walked across the sitting room and flung open a door, revealing a large ornamented four-poster bed with crimson-velvet hangings. There were baroque carvings of cupids hovering over the bed and lots of gilt and velvet furnishings.

Bridie gasped and took a step backwards. He went to the next door and it opened on to a bathroom with floral wreaths intertwined with hearts in the ceramics of the bath and disappearing into the lavatory basin, the pedestal toilet and the bidet. The carpet in the whole suite was white and deeply-piled, and geraniums and ferns bloomed in white pots, with droplets of moisture on the leaves showing that they had been recently sprayed.

The last and smallest room was bright with a pretty divan bed trimmed with lace to match the curtains and the pastel wallpaper.

"There you are," he said, carelessly. "If that's not big enough I have plenty of room to spare."

Bridie fled into the room and closed the door, hoping that her expression had not given her away, but having a shrewd idea that he knew she believed he intended that they share the huge bed. She recalled her agonised gasp when she first saw the big room, and her cheeks were bright with confusion.

What a fool he must think I am, she thought bitterly. But how was I to know? I saw just that one room, with all the trappings of a honeymoon bed, making a perfect setting for loving partners to enjoy a new relationship; the kind of room a girl could dream about. She put her case on the stand and heard a tap on the door. "Come in," she said in a subdued voice.

Carl Paterson sat on the bed. "It occurred to me that you might not know what I expect from you." She lowered her eyelashes to hide her confusion under the scrutiny of those piercing blue eyes. This was terrible! He thought her such a fool that he must spell out what he wanted in words of one syllable.

"I shall have breakfast trays sent up here at eight," he said.

"That gives us four hours rest. After breakfast we both go to the Astra for a business meeting as a preliminary to the main congress, and to collect the itinerary and the inevitable batch of invitations. I shall lunch with an important contact so you can come back here for a meal and to send out my post; you know the kind of thing. You tie up loose ends generally, then you are free to go out and find an eating place more to your liking than the restaurant here if that's what you want. There is a coffee house here and lots just down the road. You can please yourself."

He paused and she said she understood. "I shall, however, need you back here at five. You will be needed to take notes, deal with matters arising from my lunchtime contact and be general dogsbody." He smiled. "We can discuss events as they arise. I'm for bed." He stretched and yawned and she glimpsed the man who might lurk under his uncompromising shell.

"Thanks for explaining," she said. There were many questions to be asked but she couldn't form the words.

At the door, he turned back and handed a thick wad of Swiss currency to her. "While you are here, you are on liberal expenses. Don't be afraid to spend. It reflects well on the firm if we let the opposition know how well we treat our staff!" He gave a mischievous grin. "Well, that's the impression we like to give and we do try to make it true when we let you off the hook for half an hour."

"Thank you, Mr Paterson," she said. "It's good to know what is expected of me."

What now? she wondered. She heard him go to his room and she listened, waiting for him to emerge and use the bathroom. She heard the shower running and decided to undress. When the taps were turned off, and a door opened and shut firmly, she peeped out into the dimly lit sitting room and crept along to the bathroom.

Bridget locked the door, cleaned her teeth and washed her face and hands. A generous supply of soft towels lay on the heated rails, some red and some blue. One blue towel and one red were folded neatly on a rail and she couldn't tell which had been used. She didn't look up at the upper rack as water was running down her face and she had soap in one eye, but she stared at the two perfectly dry towels.

She opened the bathroom door so that she could find tissues in her room to use instead of towels until the morning. The other bedroom door opened suddenly. "Sorry, I meant to tell you," began Carl Paterson. He stood there in silk pyjamas that made the blue eyes as bright as summer skies.

"The towels," he said and laughed. "I don't have exclusive rights to them, you know, Bridget." He was teasing again but with more warmth. He dived behind her and dragged a blue towel from the rail. "Here," he said calmly, and proceeded to wipe the droplets from her face. He held a hand under her chin and for a moment she was reminded of a man looking at a favourite pet. There was fleeting tenderness somewhere.

"I can manage," she said softly, but she couldn't move. He took no notice and she was powerless to take the towel from him. He finished wiping her brow and put the towel into her hands. He kissed the tip of her nose. "Good-night, Bridget from the manse," he said and was gone, closing his bedroom door softly behind him.

Bridget hugged the damp towel and wondered why her heart beat so fast. She looked round the sitting room and saw that it was far prettier than she'd first thought. And why was the light so soft from the pink shades? The artificial flowers in the wall vase were not vulgar but as fresh as morning dew. She returned the towel to the rail and put out the remaining light. Her bed was soft and the duvet light and warm, and she was very tired, but she couldn't shut out the overwhelming sensation of drowning in a pair of deep blue eyes and the feeling of helplessness engendered by a simple kiss that wasn't even a kiss, only a mocking gesture of affection for anything small and without a lot of intelligence.

She lay on the bed, conscious of her own body as she rested, half-asleep. She ran her fingers down the smooth taut lines of her thighs, then touched the birthmark in an agony of despair. I'll have to do something about it, she decided as she drifted off to sleep, and when she wakened to the sound of china clinking against coffee pots, she was still touching her one blemish.

The chambermaid drew back her curtains and opened the shutters on a day washed free of dirt and sin as only Swiss mornings can be in early summer. Her tray held croissants and cherry preserve, good coffee and cream and fresh peaches. It was a relief to have breakfast alone. When she had finished, she heard sounds in the bathroom and hurriedly looked out a thin dress and linen jacket. One glance at the bright sunlight convinced her that it would be warm enough to wear sandals and she knew that she must also buy some flat shoes as her heavy ones would be out of place if she had to walk far. Her high-heeled sandals were only suitable for evening wear or wearing in the hotel.

Carl Paterson inclined his head in greeting. The crisp summer-weight suit sat well on his broad shoulders and the natural-coloured silk shirt was casual but elegant.

Bridie knew that her simple dress with its faint-line check of black on dark green did nothing to bring a glimmer of pleased surprise to his eyes. It had seemed right for office wear back home, but now she felt all wrong although she was still on duty.

He began to dictate brief notes of places, telephone numbers and names of people who might want to contact him during the congress, then he asked her to look up still more. One name made her take special notice, and she assumed that it was the telephone number of the woman he had called at the airport. Countess Alsfenad. Bridget recalled the affection in his voice when he spoke to her.

The morning passed quickly after the short walk to the Astra, and Bridie became used to the buzz of foreign voices and seeing smartly-dressed women in the foyer. It took little time to adjust and to lose her first awe at the vast and impersonal hotel. It wasn't really very different from working in a busy office, as Herald Enterprises had a huge building, and she soon forgot that her dress was dull.

Carl Paterson glanced at his gold watch. "I have to go to lunch," he said. "I had no idea it was so late. Take these papers back to our suite and then go and get something to eat. I'll see you later, at five, as planned."

Bridie walked back to the Viceroy slowly, past the metal-and-wood modern sculpture in the bare grounds of the Astra, back to the riotous mixture of colour in the older garden of the Viceroy. She tidied papers and made a note of messages left during the morning and was then free to eat. She wanted to find a simple café and she was really hungry. The day sparkled as if waiting to be explored, but the road outside the hotel gave no indication which way to go to find a salad and something light to eat. She sauntered down the road, aware that she had hours to spare before she needed to get back to Carl Paterson and work.

She breathed the scented air and smiled. To her surprise she had enjoyed the morning working with Carl Paterson and he had seemed well pleased with her efforts. For the time at least, he had forgotten his low opinion of her.

"Are you going out to eat?" Bridie spun round to face the tall brown-eyed man who smiled at her. "Anton Gesner," he added. "You were with Carl Paterson this morning and much too busy to notice me when you were taking notes of the speech in the conference room. How fortunate he is to have such a dedicated secretary."

"I'm sorry. It's true I didn't see you. Do you know Mr Paterson?"

"Everyone here knows Carl Paterson," he said easily. "I know him and I have told you my name, but I am at a disadvantage as I haven't the pleasure of knowing yours."

"I'm Bridget Mark." He took her by the elbow and steered

her across the busy road between bursts of traffic. "But where—?" she began.

"I'm starving," said Anton Gesner. "After all that hard work you must be, too. We both need to eat, yes?"

"I don't know," she said, weakly.

"I have to eat, you have to eat, and I am very lonely. I am a shy man and you must take care of me. I ask for so little. Just your company over lunch. I have this obsession that I need a fondue."

Bridie smiled at the idea that this good-looking man could be shy. It was really amusing and she couldn't take offence over the way he had approached her. He *did* know Carl Paterson and obviously was at the congress in some capacity or other, so that was as good as an introduction. It wasn't as if he was trying to make a pick-up. "I've never tasted fondue," she said.

They found a pretty café with blue and white curtains. Flaxen-haired girls in Swiss costume brought the fondue, heating it gently over a spirit lamp, the creamy Gruyère cheese losing its holes as it melted in the hot dish. Anton stirred the cheese and wine mixture and speared a piece of bread on a long fork, turning it in the creamy concoction until it was well-coated. He nibbled at the edges and Bridie copied him.

"You enjoy it?"

"It's delicious, but no, I don't think I should drink more wine with it. I have more work to do today and I need to think clearly."

"Rubbish. You must drink wine with it. it's a rich dish and needs wine." He poured more into her slender glass. "There now, just a little more. I'm sure that you really want it." His eyes were soft and wooing over the table and Bridie saw how intimate a meal this could be, a fondue shared by two people, as both leaned over at night in candlelight. With the right person it would be dynamite, but somehow Roger didn't seem the right person. Life was moving much too fast, and she wasn't at home in the fast lane.

"I must go," she said at last, with reluctance. "I can't tell you how much I've enjoyed this."

He took her hand and raised it to his lips. "I shall see you again?"

"I don't know. I have no idea of the schedule here for the next day or so."

"I shall be in touch. You must have one day off?" He saw that she was surprised, as she had thought that the work would be intensive for the whole time in Switzerland, with no long free time. "It's true. I am right," he insisted. "Every secretary has a day off. It will be the day after tomorrow, when little work will be done."

She laughed. "How can you be so sure?"

"It will be the day after the main banquet."

"The banquet?"

"The biggest function of the week when the women wear everything to make them look even more beautiful and the wealthy hang jewels about themselves like baubles on a Christmas tree. After that, how can anyone think of business for a day? I assure you it will be a very long night."

They walked back to the hotel and she tried to thank him again. To her amazement, she found that with Anton Gesner, she could relax thoroughly, although she was aware that under the casual warmth and easy charm, his intentions were probably anything but honourable. It just didn't bother her a bit! Of course he would know all about the congress as he had been to others and he would know when the secretaries were off duty. He probably tried to date a fresh girl at every conference he attended and made straight for new faces and any who had never been to Switzerland before.

Kept firmly in his place he could be fun she decided, sure that he would cause no problems as she didn't find him sexually attractive.

"I must see you again, Bridget," he said firmly. "I shall meet you on your day off; that is the day after tomorrow, and take you to the top of Pilatus."

"A mountain?" Her eyes glistened. "Oh, I'd really love that."

She stopped. "The day after tomorrow? So the banquet is tomorrow?"

"Tomorrow." He lifted her hand to his lips, smiled and kissed the palm with a graceful and practised gesture that sent tiny shivers up her spine. Perhaps he wasn't as harmless as she had thought.

Bridget went through the doorway into the foyer and stopped by the elevator. The arrow pointed to the second floor, with the lift coming down, so she waited for the doors to open on the ground floor. The lift doors parted and Carl Paterson strode out, nearly knocking her over.

"I saw you arrive. Where the hell have you been?"

"You told me to go to lunch, Mr Paterson. She glanced at her watch and gasped.

"Three hours? Even in Switzerland that seems a little excessive, and with Gesner of all people!"

"Mr Gesner was the perfect companion," she said with more outward composure than she felt. "If you'll excuse me, I'll go upstairs to fetch a notebook." She looked pointedly at her watch. "You said I was to report back at five, so I have fifteen minutes to spare. I am not late, Mr Paterson."

She entered the lift and pressed the button for the second floor. As the elevator ascended, she saw Carl Paterson standing with his legs slightly apart, gazing up at her. His expression held amusement, annoyance and a hint of something that made her want to laugh in triumph. There was a hint of reluctant respect in those blue eyes.

Three

After breakfast, Bridget appeared in the sitting room and waited with as much composure as she could muster. I must keep super cool, she decided. I must be very efficient and try not to read too much into the harsh way he spoke to me yesterday. It was so unfair to hint that, because she had spent three hours with a man during her time off, she was neglecting her duties and responsibilities while she was in Switzerland.

It was puzzling that a man with such an iron will should have given way to that fit of unbridled temper, as if she had really committed a crime instead of just eating lunch in a public place with a man who obviously knew him well. There had been no doubt that Carl Paterson knew Anton Gesner, but the sheer dislike he showed as soon as the name was mentioned – and that was putting it mildly – made her wonder what Anton could have done to deserve such a bad opinion.

Just to think of that meeting when she came back from lunch and met his wrath, made her tremble as if the more relaxed atmosphere the previous night had never been. She gripped her bag and braced herself for more insults, pinning her thoughts to the glimpse of blue sky through the window and the swaying branches of a fine old tree, as if they represented freedom and peace, but she couldn't erase past events from her mind.

She felt that she was being used by someone who didn't care about her but was intent on getting the maximum secretarial service from her even if she was half-asleep on her feet.

Yesterday, at fifteen minutes to five, she had gone to her

room and checked her make-up quickly, grabbed a notebook
and ballpoint and hurried down again at five p.m. precisely.
Her heart sank as she saw the dark eyebrows low over the now
angry blue eyes and knew that he was still in a foul mood.

"I hope your German is good," he said.

She looked at him, blankly. "I wasn't told that I was
expected to need to speak German."

He grunted, as if this was one more proof that she was the
useless woman he had believed her to be from the moment he
knew she was coming with him to Switzerland.

"We have to meet Herr Helmsutter and Monsieur Dubois
at the Astra and we have to communicate," he said slowly. "I
have little German and no French," he added, as if even his
personal educational deficiencies were her fault. "It is also the
main banquet tomorrow when I have to make a short speech,
and I need to be prepared to talk to many very influential
people. Some may not speak English, although most Eur-
opeans do these days, and I have no official interpreter. Bring
phrase books with you wherever we go and please try to find
the right words if that's possible. One more thing," he added
as she turned away to pick up her bag. "Before we meet our
guests this evening you must contact London and this firm."

She glanced at the slip of paper he gave her. "Have you the
telephone numbers, Mr Paterson?" She saw the grim smile
and knew that she had got it wrong again. "Do you need
replies? It's almost out of office hours now."

"What have they sent me? You have heard of *fax*, I
suppose?" The icy tone made her head reel. "In your short
time with Herald, I would have thought that you might have
absorbed the fact that we use fax machines and have given up
communication by carrier pigeon!"

"I didn't know that there was a fax machine here."

"Even here, among the plush and gilt, there are one or two
and the Astra has everything. Use the one here. The Astra will
be humming with activity and you might have to wait your
turn there. Everyone rushes to send messages at this hour. All

good hotels have these facilities now. Find that room and meet me in the bar of the Astra in half an hour." He thrust the papers into her hands and left her to find her own way.

Bridget fled to do as he ordered, inwardly seething. Who does he think he is? God? How much can I take of this? She wondered how she could put up with any more petty jibes and the tiny pinpricks of disapproval.

The business was finished easily once she found the right room, down in a corner on the lower ground floor, and, when Bridget arrived in the bar, feeling inadequate and once again dressed far too much like a girl from the office about to take dictation than a woman at ease in a luxury hotel, Carl Paterson was nodding to two businessmen who appeared to be very solemn and unable to understand a word of the strangled conversation that they were all attempting, in a mixture of languages to try and find a common ground.

She smoothed down the slim black skirt and hoped that the pink and grey striped shirt was neatly tucked in at the back, then forgot her appearance and suppressed a smile as Carl Paterson, with an air of acute discomfort, explained that only one of the men understood English. Herr Helmsutter spoke perfect English but no French, so at least he was no problem as far as Carl Paterson was concerned, but that left the Frenchman out, as he spoke only French. They eyed her with a certain lack of enthusiasm as if she had no power to ease their predicament and, from the pained expression on Carl Paterson's face, it was clear he was convinced they had reached a complete impasse.

"*Bonjour, Monsieur,*" she said, demurely. "*Comment ça va?*"

M Dubois smiled with relief and seized her hand, pouring out a flood of words in a gush of fast French. Bridie's lips twitched as she saw the awed relief on the face of the man who had given her hell such a short time earlier, as she replied easily, and was almost grabbed to sit close to M Dubois and asked to order whatever she wanted to drink.

"Choose anything," Carl Paterson said as soon as M Dubois had finished offering anything from gin and tonic to claret, "So long as it's non-alcoholic. We need you sober!" The talks progressed, with Bridie acting as interpreter and the others answering through her. She also had to take a few notes and tried to write in French, which she found more difficult than the spoken words until M Dubois took some paper from her notebook and wrote his own notes. It was exhausting but stimulating to her wounded ego. Even that precious tyrant must admit that her French was excellent.

"Why didn't you tell me you spoke French?" he asked her accusingly.

"You didn't ask me. It was German you mentioned. I speak no German, no Russian, no Urdu, a smattering of Gaelic and very good French."

It was the first pause in the conversation as M Dubois insisted on bringing a fresh supply of mineral water for her parched throat. "You left one out," Carl Paterson said. He gave a sardonic laugh. "You left out the international language spoken by people like Gesner, as you may find out to your cost."

She smiled her thanks and accepted the cold mineral water in the long, delicate frosted glass and made no reply to the latest remark. Why think of Anton Gesner in the middle of a business discussion? Did he have the man on his mind all the time?

Carl Paterson excused himself as he said he had a previous dinner engagement and the two others insisted on taking Bridget to dinner, where she continued her role as interpreter. Her boss welcomed the arrangement and she wondered why he made no objection to her spending the evening with two men when he was so paranoic over her lunch with Anton.

Later, after a meal of delicately flavoured lemon chicken soup, grilled trout and a cloud of blackcurrant sorbet, and fine white wine with green Chartreuse and coffee to follow, Bridget felt free to leave, and as soon as it was polite to do so, she said that she had been busy all day and needed her rest.

At once the two men were voluble in their thanks and concern in case they had added to her strain, but she smiled and told them that she had enjoyed every minute of their company. Well, it was partly true; there were certainly a few highlights, she thought, smiling at the wonderful memory of Carl Paterson at a disadvantage for once. At last, with a wave and more flattering thanks from her hosts, she was free and able to go back to her room in the Viceroy, feeling that if she uttered another word in French, English or any other language she would find her voice had disappeared completely.

As she passed through the bar of the Astra, she saw Carl Paterson with a very beautiful woman clinging to his arm, her face raised to smile at something he said.

He was laughing, his face relaxed and his dinner-jacket showing off the fine, strong lines of his shoulders. No one seeing him there would have believed it possible that he had a darker side to his nature. To imagine him scowling at an unfortunate employee over a trivial matter was laughable.

As Bridie bathed and put on her dressing gown, she thought sadly of the woman, whose bright hair had the expensive carelessness of a perfect cut and the care of a very good hairdresser. Her clothes were exquisite and worn as if they mattered little as there were more as fine and costly in her apartment, cared for by a skilful maid. Her dress was cut low, revealing a bosom that wasn't her best feature but, in spite of that, the effect of the finely swathed silk bodice and flowing skirt was stunning. The colours were as subtle as the flowers in a Fragonard painting and as enchanting.

Bridie stuffed away the dark green dress she had worn earlier into the back of the wardrobe, silently vowing never to wear it again – even in the office back at Herald Enterprises.

Necklaces of silver and pearl had covered the upper part of the woman's throat but the décolletage was bare. Bridie touched her angry birthmark and envied the woman who could reveal so much of the curves of her breasts without embarrassment. Slow tears of misery fell on to the silky kimono that firmly covered her from ankle to neck, and even half an hour with an interesting book did nothing to dismiss her miserable thoughts.

But that next morning, when Carl Paterson walked out of his bedroom, Bridie thrust aside all thoughts of the previous evening. He was smiling and seemed to be in a very good mood. "You were up early," he said.

"I had a good night's sleep. I was in bed by eleven."

He raised his eyebrows. "So early? I thought you had two very grateful and attentive men looking after you."

"They were extremely kind to me, but after working non-stop for hours, I decided that even Herald Enterprises would consider that I'd done a good day's work." It slipped out before she could think.

"Working you too hard, am I? Well, we'll have to see that you have a day off." He said it as if it was his own spontaneous idea and not the usual routine company policy, or her right as an employee. "As you know, there is a banquet tonight, so you can be spared all day tomorrow." Bridie smiled. It was exactly as Anton said it would be. "Will that suit you?" he asked.

"Perfectly," said Bridie. "I shall go up a mountain." Her eyes sparkled and he looked puzzled, as if resenting the fact that she might have a secret.

"What are you wearing tonight?"

"Me? At least I don't have to worry about that. I don't go to the banquet, do I?" She smiled. "Secretaries stay at home like Cinderella, trying to change ribbons on ancient and not terribly good typewriters," she said with feeling.

"I'm sorry about that but the work was very confidential and I couldn't trust it to a hired typist here. If you really can't manage on that portable, I'll buy another, but if you need to use electronic equipment or a word processor, you'll have to go to the centre where it's noisy and very time consuming, what with every delegate wanting his work done soonest.

Besides, there are eyes and ears everywhere at these functions, and my work is very private at this stage. I don't ask you to chew and swallow all rough drafts but be very careful where you put papers for disposal."

"I tear them into tiny pieces and flush them down the loo," she assured him.

He produced a diary and made a note. "By the way, what makes you think that Cinderella doesn't go to the ball?"

"I can't! Until yesterday I had no idea there was to be a banquet. I have nothing to wear that would be suitable for such a function. I haven't even a dress I could wear to an ordinary cocktail party now that I've seen some of the clothes that the women here wear all the time."

"That was a bit stupid," he said, frowning.

"You really can't blame me for than, Mr Paterson." Her dismay was real and she spoke with unusual firmness. "I came here in a rush and *nobody* told me anything. I certainly didn't think I'd be having dinner late at night with foreign guests as part of my duties. I've worked solidly for hours and done all the work you told me to do, but I can't be blamed for not bringing the right clothes to wear to a function of which I knew nothing. If I'm not told, how I am expected to know?"

Her eyes were over-bright with emotion. It was all very well for him, looking as he did, relaxed and carefree after being out half the night with that countess woman! While I, thought Bridie, spent boring hours looking at photographs of French and German children, while my throat got drier and drier and my head ached.

"A note of mutiny? Well done," he said softly, with a wicked glint in his eyes. "And last night when you made an effort to put those two men at their ease, you glowed. May I dare hope that there is more under that gently heaving bosom than one might suspect?" He laughed. "Calm down, Bridget. I apologise for my lack of whatever it is that seems to annoy you so much. Tell me what clothes you have with you. A skimpy sundress might do, dressed up a little. No?" She shook

43

her head. "A pity. Sandra comes prepared for anything and any contingency. Quite a girl, is Sandra."

"Yes, I see that it's a great pity that she isn't here and that you're stuck with me."

"And you had to miss a date and bear all my bad temper and uninteresting company. Bad luck," he said with a return to brusqueness. "We'll have to make the best of it. The dress *is* important, though. I can't appear without a presentable female on my arm – I'll be the butt of every joker in town and in the industry. I should also have to face an even worse danger." Bridie looked at him and wondered at his wry smile. "If I went alone, I'd be at the mercy of every fond mother here who would fling pale pink *fräuleins* at my head, and the American mothers would have a ball chasing me to meet their preppy daughters. You, Miss Bridget Mark from the manse, are my bulwark against a fate worse than death!" He grinned and was immediately boyish. "You may not have noticed but I am a very eligible man, in fear of being hooked by predatory females."

"I can't believe that it would worry you," she said. The dimples in her cheeks appeared. It was impossible to be angry when he was in this mood.

"It still leaves the problem of what you must wear. Now, what to do?" He took out a small black notebook that held addresses and telephone numbers and ran a finger down a list. "I have an idea." He took up the handset and pressed the numbers. "Madame Rocher? This is Carl. Yes, Carl Paterson. Yes it has been a long time, but now I need your help. Yes, Monique, at once if you can manage it." He explained that his secretary had come out from England in a hurry and had nothing suitable to wear to the banquet. He asked Bridget her size and told Madame. "A handbag, shoes and everything you think she'll need. All the usual odds and ends," he added vaguely.

He returned the handset to its rest and eyed Bridget with speculation. "Now what's bothering you?"

"What if it isn't right when I get to the shop? I may choose something quite unsuitable."

"You don't go to a shop. Monique would have a fit if you referred to her salon as a shop! She is a very bright lady with salons here, in Paris and on Fifth Avenue. She will bring the clothes here at lunchtime. That's the easy part. She will bring a selection for you to try on and I shall choose one," he said, firmly. "You shall wear whatever I choose, even if you are convinced that it is hideous or not right for a small Scottish mouse." His eyes were fierce but only to make his point clear and his mouth smiled as if enjoying her discomfort, but in a friendly way. "First, we have a lot of work to do. Let's not waste time."

The morning passed quickly and when they returned to the Viceroy where they were to have lunch in the suite while waiting for Monique Rocher, Bridie was surprised to find some lovely flowers in the sitting room. Carl Paterson reached the bouquet before she could get there and looked at the small card attached to the ribbon. His frown faded. "That's nice. You obviously made a great impression yesterday."

"Mr Gesner?"

"No," he said with satisfaction and tossed the card to her. "Of course not. Gesner would never waste his time and money on flowers. These are from the two men we entertained last night."

Bridget read the formal card thanking her for all her help and company. It was very sweet of them to bother, she thought, but it would have been more thrilling to have flowers from a man who had looked at her as Anton had done.

Carl Paterson handed her the plate of smoked salmon sandwiches. "Here, eat up or you'll collapse from hunger." He eyed the lunch trolley without pleasure. "Every hotel is under the impression that businessmen are on a diet of smoked salmon, quails eggs in pastry nests and blinis with caviar, whenever they order a working lunch with sandwiches."

He bit into a pastry nest. "At least they make good pastry here."

"It all looks delicious," Bridget said, her eyes wide with amazement that he could say such insulting things about food that to her was sheer luxury. He watched her eat two sandwiches.

"It's refreshing to see you enjoy that. I suppose I did once, but salmon gets monotonous after a while."

"Anything does if served too often. Variety in food is essential," Bridie said, and took a tiny round blini, covered it with sour cream and added a very small spoonful of caviar before savouring the unexpected treat. He did the same as if he might share her enjoyment, but he went back to the sandwiches after one blini.

"Did you know," he said, adding lemon juice to the smoked salmon, "in the middle ages, or some time in the past, servants in stately homes went on strike because they were made to eat salmon too frequently and had to be given the promise that salmon would be served no more than twice a week? I know the feeling."

"You're spoiled," Bridget said with a hint of her aunt's disapproval. "I think this is wonderful."

A page boy brought in several boxes. He was followed by a small, slim woman with twinkling grey eyes and a very brisk manner. She also carried boxes and put them on every available surface in the room, pausing only to take a sandwich as she passed the trolley. The rest of the boxes she put on the huge bed in the larger bedroom, as if that was where they belonged, then ran to Carl Paterson and put her arms round his neck while he kissed her on both cheeks. "It has been far too long, mon cher," she said, then dropped her French accent and laughed at Bridget's surprise when she lapsed into New York American.

"What have you brought. The whole of the salon?" Carl Paterson was amused.

"Sure. Otherwise you'll think I'm on the skids and you

won't want to buy. I expect to sell you some real honeys Carl, so I came myself, but no one more than you knows that time is money!"

She regarded Bridget with interested disbelief.

"Wash all that cream off your hands, Bridget, and we'll see what Monique has brought along," Carl Paterson said hastily.

While she was in the bathroom, she heard their voices; Monique frankly amused and the deep voice explaining that Sandra had been unable to accompany him, but when she went back into the room they were discussing the clothes as the gowns emerged from a flurry of pastel tissue-paper.

"Stand in the light," Monique ordered, as if Bridget was one of her models. She held up one dress in front of the girl and clucked with disappointment, then smiled. "I was forgetting, Carl. I must try not to think of the clothes you bought from my salon on Fifth Avenue back home." She spoke softly. "I was really sorry. What about this one?"

"No, even I can see that she couldn't ever wear that," Carl Paterson said with a trace of irritation, as if Monique had touched a raw nerve. Had he bought beautiful clothes for an American woman at some time in the past? Bridget wondered. "I did tell you on the phone that I hadn't brought Sandra and that this one was darker and pale."

Monique shrugged. "Some brunettes wear dark clothes very well and she is not really dark. She has a good skin and she has glints in her hair that could be brightened."

"What about this one?" Bridget held up a high-necked dress in soft rose red.

"Not festive enough. Good for afternoon tea at the manse, or to a wake," he said impatiently, and Monique raised her eyebrows.

"Hell, Monique. The girl is supposed to at least look as if she's going to a very smart party and must appear to enjoy it. I thought I could depend on you."

"When did I ever fail you, Carl?" she answered calmly. She

held up two more confections and one of pink tulle. "This is festive? Yes?" she said hopefully.

"Good grief! Who made that? It looks like something off a chain store Christmas tree."

"I sold one to a star in Dallas," she said sharply.

"I can believe it," was the laconic reply and Bridie giggled when Monique tried not to smile.

"What about this?" He held up a slip of gold silk covered with tiny stars. It was gossamer fine and pleated to follow the line of the figure under it, almost like the priceless Fortuny dresses that now fetched incredible prices at auction and were too fragile to wear. He shook out the folds on the bedcover and Bridie saw that it had a very low neckline.

"Oh, *no*! I couldn't wear that." The other two exchanged glances. "I rather like the red one. Nice and bright," Bridie said, without much hope.

Monique relapsed into being the French couturière. "*Mais* it is perfect for Mamselle. It will show the lights in her hair and the gold in her eyes. It is good."

Carl Paterson nodded and stared with a sense of shock as if he could imagine Bridie wearing it, then turned away. "I'll be in the foyer, telephoning, while you finish here. After the fitting I want you to send three faxes and then go shopping for the other things you'll need. Tell her where the best shops are and give her your card to show them so that they can invoice you, Monique, and thank you. You've saved my life."

He kissed her again and left without another glance at the panicking girl who stared at the dress as if it was a snake about to strike. It may have saved his life but what about mine when Monique sees that I can never wear the dress? she thought desperately.

Bridie stepped out of her skirt and removed her shirt. "The slip also," Monique said. "It is too high. You cannot wear much under that; anything at all will show." Monique walked across to another box. "A cleavage bra with no seams, I think."

She held up a dull-ivory silk bra that would not show under the dress and Bridie bit her lip and waited for the storm. This was much worse than she had feared. It was much more trying than changing in one of the communal changing rooms in big stores, but there was no escape.

She took off her own bra and put on the other. It was as light as a moonbeam and very comfortable, hugging her breasts snugly and making them slightly uptilted and sepa-rated, but as she looked down, the angry red birthmark glowed like an ugly blossom on the inner curve of her breast.

"It's no use, I can't wear this," she said indistinctly as the fragile-looking garment was lowered over her head. A quick shake and a tug and it was in place and arranged. Monique gave a gasp of delight and pushed Bridie over to the long cheval mirror in the main bedroom.

It was a revelation, but Bridie was almost weeping. "It's the most beautiful dress I ever saw," she said, "But I can't wear it."

Monique looked at the birthmark as if used to seeing one on every client. "That? It is nothing. A little make-up, perhaps?" She looked more closely. No, it would take too thick a layer. Make-up would not last a night in a hot room and it might ruin the dress." She frowned. "You must wear it. Mr Paterson was sure that it was the one he wants and he's been a very good customer in the past when he lived in New York with his wife. I hope that this is the beginning of a lot more business from him."

"What if there is no way I can hide it?"

"Perhaps by tonight it will be better."

"What do you mean?" Had the stupid woman never seen a birthmark before? They didn't just come and go!

Monique looked coy. "If it was Mr Paterson then it does not matter. A little make-up will meet the need and he will not mind it showing a little, but if it was your lover, then I agree that it must be hidden when you are with another man. It would be . . . diplomatic to hide it." She saw Bridie's growing

49

rage and confusion. "Calm down, honey. It's nothing. I've seen a lot that needed more covering than that! This isn't so bad and it's never bad to know that he loves you enough to give you that token of love. Kinda sets a seal on a relationship."

"You think this is a *love bite*? How dare you! This is a birthmark I've had all my life. Since the day I was born," she added as Monique looked sceptical and completely disinterested.

"Then why have it now after all this time? It's simple enough. Not even as much hassle as a nose job. A good surgeon could remove it and leave no scar."

"I don't wear low-cut dresses," Bridie said weakly, and even to her it sounded ridiculous.

"With that figure? You are mad. I dress women who look like cows. No 'vaches' is better sounding. The French are not so coarse about these things, or it never sounds so," she said with a smile. "I dress them and they look terrific but they'd give anything for a body like that. I could use you as a model, with a little training. But first, the knife. It is simple."

"Well, I can't have it done today. I'll take the red dress," Bridie said firmly.

"Mr Paterson would be very angry if you wore that, and he'd never use my salon again. We must hide the place." She dived for a small case and spilled junk jewellery over the bed. There were beads and silver and gold chains and seashells set in silver. She held something in her hand and Bridie saw an exquisite butterfly of silk and gold with a pin attachment.

"Now it is a brooch," Monique said, and unscrewed the pin. "*Voilà*, now it can be attached to a hair comb and have two for the price of one, but without either we can have it flat and I can stick it on your skin." She moistened the back of her hand with spirit glue and stuck the butterfly on it. She waved her hand in the air and the butterfly remained poised for flight. "You see, it will be quite safe." She peeled the butterfly off her hand and held it to hide the birthmark. The effect was wonderful and looked as if it was an essential accessory to the dress.

"It's beautiful," Bridie said slowly. "But are you quite sure it will be safe?"

"Of course! Now for the rest." Monique took out two pairs of tights with tiny stars on the ankles that looked very expensive, especially as they might not be seen if Bridie sat at a table for most of the evening. "Two pairs in case of accidents," Monique purred, and Bridie could almost see a calculator working behind her eyes. She said nothing since they were perfect with the dress.

"It seems so . . . naked," Bridie ventured.

"A light shawl," Monique suggested happily, "Wear it at first until you are used to the men eyeing you, and if you go out on to a balcony later." She winked as if that was more than a possibility. "This small clutch bag of dull gold matches well and here is my card for the shoe salon." She put the junk jewellery back in the box. "Nothing more or the effect will be ruined and you have nothing to hide now."

"What do I do with the dress after the banquet." Bridie asked.

Monique stopped in the middle of parcelling up the other clothes. "You keep it as a reward for being a good efficient secretary, or so Carl said. A small token of approval for all the work you have done at the congress. It is all very expensive," she said in a delighted tone. "The shoes also will cost plenty and I want you to use that salon as we have an understanding." She laughed. "Right, call it a rake-off but it works both ways and he makes superb shoes, and Carl has bought many shoes there so he knows their quality and they match his very good taste."

Bridie wondered how many women Carl had sent to that shop for expensive shoes, as he came to Switzerland on many business trips and may have had other needs to satisfy, for which presents were expected. Monique seemed to read her thoughts. "He has his own shoes made there and says they fit better than any he buys elsewhere."

51

The two women carried the boxes to the elevator and the page helped take them down and load them carefully into the back of a large estate car that had dress rails down one side in the back. Bridie went back to the suite and took away every trace of having used the double room with the four-poster bed; it looked far too intimate what with the clutch bag and butterfly on the bed-cover, and the lovely dress draped across the pillows, as if discarded by someone who slept in that bed.

The faxes sent and the rest of her typing finished without too much stain from the ribbon on her fingers, Bridie was free to do the rest of the shopping. She found the shoe salon without much difficulty and presented the card that Monique had given her, on which she had described the dress and mentioned the colour needed. At once she had the undivided attention of a good-looking assistant who showed her to a pink-velvet seat and took off her plain shoes as if they were treasures to be put aside for a moment. He measured her feet carefully, holding each in such a way as he smiled up at her that Bridie was reminded of Anton. Were all men here as attentive as Anton and as attractive, or was it a tool of the tourist trade used to flatter and make a woman feel feminine?

He went away and a girl brought a cup of delicious hot chocolate with whipped cream floating on the surface. It was all so pampering and leisurely that Bridget forgot her early panic over the dress and began to enjoy herself.

A pattern-book of shades was consulted and she pointed out the ones that would tone with the dress, and the assistant seemed to know what would match when he read the description on the card. He agreed that the muted-gold theme should be carried through to the final creation and produced some pretty shoes that followed that theme.

A pair of high-heeled sandals, which showed off her high insteps and slim ankles to perfection, were a dream. She asked the price and gasped, but no other pair was as good and she had been told to disregard any expense.

"Well, I've made Monique's day," she murmured when the

shoes had gone to be wrapped. "I hope it does the same for me! This banquet must mean a lot to Carl Paterson if he is willing to squander all this money and time on a girl who means nothing to him, just for one evening's use." It seemed such a waste of his money and her time, when he would never look at her with anything better than amused contempt.

She was unsure if her boss would want her for more work or whether he had forgotten her existence, and she didn't dare to stay away from the suite for too long. There were odds and ends to tie up in her work and messages to answer, so her time was filled. She also wrote a note of thanks to the two men for the flowers – their scent still filled the room.

The telephone made her start. She was scared of taking business calls for her boss in case they dealt with something outside her scope.

"Is Carl there?" a woman's voice said. "You *are* his secretary?" She had the kind of voice that made secretary a dirty word.

"Yes, I am," said Bridie. "He's not here at present. Can I take a message?"

"No, I want to talk to him personally. This is Countess Maria. I haven't seen him all day. I have much to discuss with him and I need to see him soon," she added petulantly. The foreign accent became more pronounced as she showed her displeasure. "You will tell him that I need to see him! I know we shall meet this evening, but I do not want to talk business at the banquet. It would be too boring."

Bridie made a note that the countess had called and then raised the house phone and ordered tea from room service. She smiled as she replaced the phone. Yesterday she wouldn't have dared to ring down to ask for anything, but today she was able to order tea in the suite as if she was used to doing it. I'm only being practical, she told herself. I need something to eat and drink as it might be hours before we eat at the banquet.

The trolley arrived at the same time as Carl Paterson. He

lifted the covering cloth and grinned. "Not enough," he told the boy. "We'll need more sandwiches, gateau and chocolate biscuits." He sat down and poured himself a cup of tea. "You must be psychic. I was dying for a good cup of tea, and this hotel serves real tea, not a cup of hot water with a dunked teabag dangling on a piece of string, like they do at the Astra." He took a sip. "That's better. I've been talking all the afternoon and needed this if I have to talk again this evening."

The boy brought another tray and Bridie found that she could sit and talk with no trace of her former fear. Perhaps he is milder today, she thought. Or maybe my one outburst could have made an impression after all. Carl certainly seemed to be enjoying the tea and the creamy cakes, and asked how her visit to the shoe salon had gone.

"I chose some wonderful shoes," she said, and couldn't keep the excitement from her voice. He regarded her benevolently over the rim of his cup.

"What time do you want me to be ready, Mr Paterson?"

"We should be ready by seven thirty. Drinks at eight and dinner at eight thirty." She nodded. "But let me make one thing crystal clear. Tonight you are not just my secretary. Many of the delegates will be there with their wives, but I am not so fortunate." He gave her a long hard look. "You do know that my wife died three years ago?" She shook her head. It could explain a lot. "You didn't know? I thought that everyone in Herald Enterprises knew that and everything else about me, down to the colour of my socks, but perhaps you aren't the type to gossip and so you miss all the best titbits." He gave a wry smile. "Or it could be that you weren't interested enough to ask questions."

Bridie poured more tea into his proffered cup but said nothing. "My wife went into hospital to have a small operation that didn't appear to be urgent or even risky, but she never came out of that operating theatre alive. She died under the anaesthetic because of a slight malfunction of a gland in her chest that had never been suspected." Bridie looked at his face but there was no way of knowing if he still mourned his loss and if he was grieving in spite of his composure.

"I'm truly sorry," said Bridie. "At times like this, you must be very lonely and miss her a lot."

"There have been times when I have felt very lonely," he admitted. "That's why I'm asking you to remember that, and act as if we are friends." She lowered her eyelids. How could she talk to him as if she knew him well? How could she relax with him and even touch him without him knowing that she was falling in love with him? Roger was no longer of any importance, Anton would be a pleasant diversion, but the man sitting in the deep armchair, showing a boyish delight in cream cakes, was fast taking over every conscious thought that she had.

"I'll try," she said, softly.

"I know that you have a poor opinion of me, Bridget, but it would be nice for both of us if you could forget, at least for a while, that we got off to such a bad start. I must insist that you call me Carl and treat me as you would any other date at a special function." His glance was almost pleading.

She regarded him solemnly. "I can if you will forget that I was the last person you wanted to come with you on this trip." She was trying to convince herself that it was possible, and wondered if she would have the courage to try.

Four

B ridie piled the plates back on the trolley and pushed it outside the door of the suite ready for collection. Carl Paterson was already examining the pile of cards and messages that she had put ready for him to see, and as he sat forward, he winced. "Damn," he muttered. "I'd hoped it was better." He eased his shoulders as if they ached and rotated the left one slowly.

"Is it very painful?" she asked.

"Not yet, but it might be later if I get tired, and I can't afford to let anything spoil this evening," he said, grimly. "I hate taking painkillers. They don't mix at all well with champagne and wine."

"You said that the hotels have everything here. They may have a resident masseur," Bridie suggested. "Is it an injury or just stress?"

He glanced up sharply, "A bit of both, I suppose. It only gives me trouble occasionally and I really thought it was better. I haven't needed treatment for months."

"Then it's almost certainly stress. That finds any weak spot," Bridie said. "Some people get a sore throat and some indigestion, and some get pain in an old injury, or feel as if they have a frozen shoulder."

"Yes, Doctor!" He grinned. "I was forgetting that you have another talent, taught to you in the manse by an earnest physiotherapist aunt."

"She's not the one at the manse," Bridie said, as if to distance herself from her.

"But she taught you the magic of massage, didn't she?"

"I haven't even begun my course yet," Bridie said in alarm as she saw how his mind was working.

"I think you know a lot more than your natural modesty lets you tell me." She shook her head. "I can't expect you to help me as it has nothing to do with your work here for me and for the firm, and I've already made you work for many more hours than is reasonable, but if I asked you, as a friend, would you see what you can do?"

"Why not see if they have a professional on the premises," she said again.

He gave a cynical laugh. "Unfortunately that is a service that has got into such bad repute that businessmen with a need for massage avoid it. Once, it was possible to have a massage in a hotel or even in a massage parlour and everyone knew that the treatment offered was purely therapeutic, but now if I visited a place like that, however innocent it was, or asked for a massage in my room in a hotel, it would be thought that I required other services." She looked blankly at him. He gave a sigh of exasperation. "Surely you know what I mean? Massage in these places is usually a thinly veiled request for sexual contracts with a call-girl or prostitute, and I never avail myself of such luxuries."

Bridie blushed, and her eyes were angry. "Are you suggesting that every masseuse is a prostitute?"

"Of course not! These women aren't physios! They are hookers who use their hands, that's all." He laughed at her startled expression. "Poor Bridget, are you finding the outside world a bit big and strange?"

"I've seen a lot more vice than you may believe possible, Mr Paterson," she said angrily. "I've visited refuges for women and a squat where drugs made perfectly ordinary people take up prostitution to pay for their habit. My father does a lot of good work and he's encouraged me to go with him, so I hear a lot about all kinds of vice." She looked defiant. "I object to people lumping massage and physio together and making

---

what is a valuable service and an honourable profession sound grubby."

"That was not my intention and I apologise if I gave that impression," he said, slowly. "As I mentioned earlier, I have every respect and regard for the nurses and physios who attended me when I was injured." He looked at her with enigmatic eyes. "It still doesn't solve my immediate problem. I'm asking you, Bridget, to rub my shoulder and loosen up the muscle." He grinned. "It might make me easier to live with, even if my new relaxed charm gets me no big contracts."

He undid his tie and took off his shirt. "Where do you want me? On the bed or sitting straight?"

"Sitting," she said faintly. It might not be the best position but she knew that if he was lying on his front on the bed she would have to sit on the bed beside him and bend over him in a very intimate way. She washed her hands in warm water and found a tube of cream in her toilet bag that she knew was useful for strains and pulled muscles. It had none of the smell of so many fierce embrocations that athletes used, and it was a preparation that she took with her on all holidays for use if anyone in the party twisted an ankle or ached after trying to walk too far on their first day in the country.

Gently, she touched his shoulder and found a knot of tension in the muscle. She put cream on her hands and slowly began the treatment, first brushing the skin lightly with effleurage and then moving deeper and deeper until he gasped.

"Am I hurting you too much?" she asked.

"No, it's agony, that's all! Go on, I know it's doing me good. You have magic fingers, Bridget. You are wasted at Herald Enterprises."

"I know. I think that this trip has decided me to leave and take the course that opens in the autumn." She spoke sadly. She was useful to him now, but after she went back to her own desk in the office, he would have no further use for her, and as soon as he was back in London, even this small service would be done in the private clinic near to work.

The contact with the broad, smooth back was almost too much to bear. As the muscles relaxed under her hands she felt the warmth of his body, and the clean male smell of healthy skin came up from her moving palms. The back of his neck was soft and the curling hair at the nape suggested youth and tenderness, but the taut body tapering down to the slim hips held force and a masculine vigour that could enthral any woman not blind to his sexuality.

The cream was absorbed and the knot of pain released. Bridie asked him to move his arm in a wide arc and to rotate the shoulder again. She stepped back, much too aware of him to continue the treatment.

"That feels wonderful." He stood up, flexing the shoulder and sending the supple flow of relaxed muscles down over his spine. "You are an angel," he said and caught her up in a tight hug. "Bridget Mark, I'm beginning to think I can't do without you." He kissed her gently on first one cheek then the other in the French manner. Her breasts under the thin cotton of her shirt pressed against his naked chest and she wanted him to hold her close for ever. "Thank you again," he said.

She drew away, her eyes downcast, and took a long time to screw the top back on the tube of cream, so that he couldn't read her eyes. "I must wash my hands," she said, trying to laugh. "I seem to have as much cream on me as you have on your shoulder."

"Any messages apart from these?" he asked as he put his shirt on and looked in the mirror to adjust his tie.

"The countess rang and said she wanted to see you."

"I'll see her tonight," he said easily. "No need to do anything before then."

"She sounded a bit cross," Bridget said. "Is she alone here and needing company?"

"Yes, she comes here alone but has plenty of friends, so she's never really bored or alone."

"Wouldn't she be a more suitable companion for you tonight?" she asked.

"Decidedly not! Maria would never be just a companion for an evening. If I dated her alone, more than a few times when it was absolutely necessary to do so to talk business, I would be taking on a commitment, and such commitments take a lot of thought." He looked very serious and Bridget blushed, believing that she had pried into his own deep feelings and that he was considering taking the countess for more than a few dates when the time was right.

"Is there anything more you need me to do?" she asked. "I've put your papers in your room and sent all the messages."

"Fine. We're clear for today, and tomorrow you can relax. I have to see one of the German delegation and to get some papers from the Astra, so I advise you to use the shower, get dressed for this evening and leave the bathroom free for me."

"Are you sure I can't collect the papers?"

"Quite sure. I've yet to meet a woman who doesn't take twice as long to dress as I do, and I hate to be kept waiting."

She showered, using some freshly scented gel that smelled of musky roses, and found a heady excitement in dressing up in the new clothes. They were exquisite and she ran the silky fabric of the dress between her fingers.

She shivered with a feeling of sensuality for her own body and it was like a caress as she slipped the gown over her head and felt its coolness mould to her body, clinging and yet free as she walked, when it flowed out in a mist of fine pleats. It was like dressing for her own wedding, in silk from the skin outwards, or even a bit like being dressed for sacrifice as the vestal virgins had once been dressed before being anointed and sometimes offered to the gods.

She brushed her newly-washed hair until the golden glints showed, then sprayed it with light conditioner. Cool make-up and softly-coloured lipstick gave her a dewy natural look and she was satisfied with her appearance except for the birthmark. She touched the back of the butterfly with adhesive and placed it to hide the blemish, then stood back from the mirror to see the whole effect.

The butterfly appeared as a perfect accessory to the dress as if planned to be there, and it hid every trace of redness. She stood tall and felt confident, knowing that she looked wonderful, chic, and nothing like the girl in the dark green dress and flat sandals. Her breasts rose proudly in gentle mounds, her skin was flawless and her eyes sparkled. Nothing could mar the knowledge that Bridget Mark was tonight to be taken to a very exclusive banquet by the handsomest man from Lake Como to Maggiore, and she was dressed and ready to do him justice.

Cars began to arrive to take guests to the banquet which was to be held in the large hotel further along the road, on the banks of Lake Lucerne. She looked out of her window and saw several women, all richly dressed, leaving with elegant escorts. She turned away and hid in her own room as she heard steps approaching her door, not wishing to be seen by Carl Paterson until the last minute and feeling suddenly shy.

He had gone into his room so she slipped into the bathroom for one last inspection of her make-up as the mirror there was a better one than in her room. If only he would look at her with the open admiration he showed for the countess or even with the fleeting approval he had for the stewardess on the plane, it would be enough to make her lose her shyness.

She turned from the mirror, the glow from the Victorian wall-lights making a halo of her hair. Carl Paterson stood watching her from the open door and she blushed, wondering if he had been there for more than a few seconds.

"May I see?" he asked. She walked slowly towards him, her heart beating fast. "Very nice," he said, cryptically.

"So you think I'll do?" she asked, disappointed that he

showed no more enthusiasm, but she knew she had no right to expect more than scant approval.

"Yes, indeed you'll do," he said. "If I'm to match you I'd better get my skates on." He went into the bathroom and shut the door and Bridie went into her bedroom and sat on the bed, trying to keep the spindly heels from digging into the carpet.

There was activity in the drive below the window, with muted laughter and an air of anticipation; there were sounds from the water pipes, and distant doors slammed. Bridget draped the light shawl over her shoulders and felt more secure. Each time she looked down and saw the butterfly but no disfigurement on the clear pale skin she could hardly believe it. What a fool! What a fool I've been! I must have the operation, she told herself over and over again. Without this I can be free.

Ten minutes later, the other bedroom door closed and Carl Paterson called to her as if she was the one who had been late in dressing. "Ready?"

"Yes, do I need a coat? Are we walking far?"

"No, just the shawl," he said. "And you can't walk in the dark in those shoes. The car will take us up to the terrace of the hotel." He seemed far away, his eyes were dark and they seared through her like lasers, to she knew not what beyond. She stared at him, too. He wore well-tailored light-weight trousers and the almost-black, damson-coloured jacket matched the cummerband over his taut waist. The silk shirt, understated but faultless, gleamed, and he had taken almost too much care with his hair. She wanted to ruffle it a little. His shoes, which Bridget recalled came from the same salon as her own, shone with much burnishing.

For a full minute they remained in a state of limbo, then he laughed. "Will I do?" he asked.

"I think we are both suitably dressed for this evening," she replied demurely. "I promise to protect you from pale pink *fraüleins* and predatory mothers!" She smoothed the silk of her dress. "This is really beautiful," she said.

"Yes, really beautiful," he agreed, but his glance took in the butterfly and not the dress. He smiled. "Any reservations about the dress now? Not the kind of garment I can imagine you wearing at home in the manse, but you carry it off with style, Bridget, so forget it and enjoy the evening. The car should be here now. Shall we go?" he asked more formally.

Bridget glided rather than walked. She was on the crest of a dream, well-dressed and very much aware of the silent man at her side as Carl Paterson handed her into the car with care and impeccable courtesy. His hand was warm and firm on her arm as he steadied her on the very high heels before she eased herself into the back seat and sat in her own corner with no further physical contact. I really am Cinderella, she thought, but this Cinderella must never let the prince know that she loves him and is awakened by every accidental touch.

The car sped past the Astra and the side road that linked the hotels. They passed banks of flowers and green lawns and along the side of a terrace bordering the lake. The lights of Lucerne flashed by and she saw the rim of the lake through the trees, then more lights, half-hidden by a leafy avenue, and a wide driveway of gravel edged with flowering shrubs that took them to the steps of a softly-lit terrace hovering over the lakeside and a small but immaculate beach.

Bridget gazed up at the imposing façade of the hotel. "What a fantastic place," she said, half awed and half amused.

"The Hotel Rigi," he said. "It was built at a time when labour was cheap and money no object. The rich of every affluent country in Europe came here to breathe the pure air of Lucerne and to promenade by the blue lake. Everything is very clean and manicured in the best Swiss tradition." He glanced down at the beach. "Even the stones look as if they have been scrubbed! Some of my American friends go mad about this hotel and say they have never seen anything to match it."

Lights circled the lake as dusk fell and Bridie recalled seeing

64

just such a circle of light from the plane. Which lake had she seen? Como, Maggiore, Lucerne? She had no way of knowing, but this lake, with music coming softly from the brightly lit hotel, assuaged a longing for beauty that had lain dormant in her heart ever since she left Scotland. She stared out at the lake and beyond to a dark mass that loomed blue-black in the distance, ringed with cloud at the summit. "Is that Pilatus?" she asked.

"Yes," he said. "How did you know?"

"I'm going up there tomorrow," she said.

He looked at her strangely and seemed about to question her but changed his mind and said nothing. He waved a hand to someone on the other side of the terrace and a man waved back.

"Should I know any of these people? Do I let them know if I recognise them from photographs in magazines or on television? There must be many famous people here who know you."

"If I want to draw your attention to anyone important, it will be enough if you just smile," he said.

Bridie glanced at him sharply. He isn't confident of me, she thought. He's afraid I'll let him down if I talk to people. Her newly found confidence sagged, but the admiring glances from men waiting by the powder-room door for their women to emerge, restored her poise. She checked her lipstick and joined Carl, who was leaning against the balustrade with an unlit, long thin cigar in his hand. The water glinted beneath the stone work and her heart missed a beat when he turned to her and smiled warmly.

"Come and meet some of my friends, Bridie," he said. He was the perfect, attentive companion, with charm switched on for the one evening as far as she was concerned. She knew this to be true and it was all part of her job to respond, but she also knew that this night would live in her memory for ever.

She looked up, a hint of mischief making the golden light reflect in her eyes. "How nice, I'd like that, Carl." I'll play it well, she decided. It may break my heart but it will be satisfying to know that I pleased him for a while.

They joined a group of Americans who eyed her with visible curiosity but drew her into their circle as if any friend of Carl's was OK by them, and Carl only exchanged first names as if that was enough. "I just love the dress," Jo Ann said, and laughed. "You do know that every man in this place will want to touch that darling little butterfly? I wish I'd thought of that." She laughed again and slapped her husband's hand gently. "Down, Rover!" He grinned and turned away, more interested in the day's stock market than in butterflies.

"It was Monique's idea," Bridie said and knew that Carl was listening, although he was nodding his head at what his two male companions were saying.

"I just knew that it was her dress," Jo Ann said. She wore a pretty blue number that showed off her blue eyes and sun-tanned skin and, to Bridie, it seemed right for her, but Jo Ann eyed her dress with envy. "The cow didn't show me that one," she said in an aggrieved voice.

"Maybe she didn't have it in Fifth Avenue or wherever you bought your outfit," Bridie suggested.

"That's right, I did go there." Her face cleared. "I was forgetting that Carl is now based in England and seldom comes our way any more since . . . well, you know." She spoke softly and glanced at Carl's back to make sure that he had moved away. "We miss him. You must make him come over soon and catch up with all his old friends."

"You'll have to invite him," Bridie said, gently. "I have no influence over his social life. I am just part of the firm and came as Carl's secretary because Sandra is ill and they had to find someone to take her place at the last minute."

"I don't believe it!" The blue eyes looked amused and slightly shocked."

"I assure you it's true. Sandra fell sick the day before the congress and Carl had a hasty decision to make," Bridie explained earnestly.

"Oh, Hell! I so wanted you to be Carl's new lady." She laughed and her husband raised a curious eyebrow. "Sorry Wain, we were both wrong, so you pay Hubert and Mary. That is if I can't make her swear we are right! We ought a be right!" She turned back to Bridie who was looking distinctly puzzled. "If you want to know, we took bets on it as soon as you came into the room with him. I saw you yesterday with him and the Sandra story seemed right enough then as you looked kinda homely. He did tell us that she was sick, and you didn't look as you do now, honey! But now, knowing that he must have bought you that dress, and hearing that you share a suite, I changed my mind."

Bridie set her lips firmly. "Carl needs space for his work and he doesn't want to spread it all over the offices downstairs in the Astra or the Viceroy," she explained. "He warned me about industrial espionage and we work in the sitting room of the suite together at times. We *do* have separate rooms, if that's what you are hinting! And I have a perfectly good boyfriend who I had to leave to come here. I didn't even want to come, I had to pack in a hurry and I wasn't told I needed suitable clothes for this function, so he had to buy me something to wear. It's all part of my work and, until two hours ago, I called him Mr Paterson and shall do so again as soon as we go back to the UK."

"I'm sorry! Don't be like that! How was I to know?" Jo Ann didn't look all that contrite and she smiled with a wicked glint in her eyes. "I guess he did a double-take when he saw you in that for the first time, and that butterfly is *the* most provocative thing I've seen in years!"

Bridie blushed and tried to laugh. "Not half as provocative as some of the clothes that Sandra wears, even to the office," she said. "Carl must be used to having well-dressed women around him so I couldn't refuse to wear what he chose for me."

"Sandra will never get him even if she goes topless and tries to rape him." Jo Ann's eyes were calculating. "There was only one Mrs Paterson and Sandra just isn't the type for him. Each time we meet I wonder who it will be and each time he is alone or nearly so. I wonder if he knows just how many women would be hot for him if he gave them any encouragement?"

"He knows," Bridie said and laughed. "How could he not know that he is very attractive and eligible? One of my jobs is to dress up for this party, to be with him and discourage the panting females and ambitious mothers." She smiled ruefully. "I never saw myself as a kind of female minder but that's what I am."

"In that case you'll see a lot a dirty looks directed at you when they know he is taken."

"Not taken, just on loan for one evening," Bridie said. "Nothing more," she added firmly as Jo Ann smiled again in that infuriating manner that assumed that she knew better.

"You *do* have breakfast with him?"

"Breakfast is delivered to the suite," Bridie said. "I can't see that it is odd, as everyone has to eat!"

"Sandra had hers down in the dining room in the Astra with the rest of the secretaries and she didn't share the suite. We all thought that he liked to stay in the Viceroy away from the main body of congress, to be free to bring in anyone he fancied, and so Sandra slept in a room along the corridor."

"Perhaps he didn't have a date this time, or there wasn't a room to spare," Bridie retorted. "There are other places where he can meet people and we do have a lot of work to do in peace and quiet."

"He didn't have a date last year or the year before that, unless you include the Countess Maria who clings to him like a limpet whenever she sees him. We'd have known." Jo Ann gave a lazy smile. "You have interesting work but we wives get bored and amuse ourselves by checking up on everyone's sex life."

"If you're so bored, then why do you come?"

"Husbands on the loose get into mischief. That's why,

honey. Believe me, plenty goes on here that would make the wives back home curl up and die! So we come and gossip and bitch about people and sometimes have fun."

"I don't believe half of what you say," Bridie said. "You're certainly not one of the insecure wives. Your husband never strays far away, does he? You're here because you want to be with him. It shows."

"I guess so." Jo Ann laughed aloud. "There's more to you than a sweet face and a good body. I tried to wind you up to find out what really makes Carl tick these days because we love the guy and think he should marry again, but I can see I shall have to do some more homework on that one. You don't think he'll let Maria get her talons into him?"

"Jo Ann, I do like you but I can't gossip about my employer! You probably know much more about him than I do. I haven't met him more than three times in the office, before coming on this trip."

"But he chose you in spite of not knowing that you could do the work? Sandra is good and knows a lot about the patents and new processes and spends her working life with him." The twist to her mouth told Bridie that Jo Ann was sceptical and needed to know more if she wasn't to go away and hint at a sexual partnership between Carl Paterson and the girl with him.

"You'll never believe this," Bridie said, weakly. The memory of the scene in the penthouse office remained clear in her mind but now seemed as if it was a film set and nothing to do with her. "He didn't want to bring me here but I was the only one available who Brian Greene, the PR man, said he could trust to be discreet, to work hard and fill the basic requirements that Carl set for him to find."

"Good figure, nice eyes and lovely hair?"

"Wrong. To quote as far as I recall, not under five feet, no crossed eyes, not entirely repulsive, and knowing which fork to use."

"You must be joking!" Jo Ann's face was a study of disbelief and horror.

"No, I'm serious, so you know now that there could be nothing between me and Mr Paterson . . . sorry, with Carl, as I have been told to call him tonight, so please do me a favour and squash any rumours that get started because I'm wearing this and seem to be enjoying myself." Bridie smiled. "And I intend doing just that this evening. It's the most glamorous thing that has ever happened to me and possibly the last."

"Not the last if you dress like that, honey. I can see three men at the bar who are lusting after you this instant!"

"I'm not interested," Bridie said. "I have a boyfriend." She crossed her fingers and hoped that Roger wouldn't mind if she used his name but forgot about him as soon as possible.

"You must have been scared, coming here with Carl under those conditions."

"Terrified," Bridie said with feeling.

Jo Ann smiled as her husband approached, with Carl following him. "So, he had to keep you under his eyes in case you escaped," she murmured. "Very wise and it does clear up one puzzle. That might account for him cancelling the room along the corridor that his secretary always uses. He did it as soon as he arrived and checked in at the Viceroy. I know the girl in reception at the Viceroy, and she was very intrigued. So were we, honey."

"Dishing the dirt?" Jo Ann's husband said, grinning. "I bet she's asked you all those things best forgotten. I should have warned you. My wife is a witch, but often spelled with a 'b' and sorely needed in the CIA as she gets information that no other agent could get in years."

"I think she's satisfied with what I told her, but I kept all the best bits to myself," Bridie said, laughing. "At least she isn't an industrial spy. She asked me nothing about Herald Enterprises."

"I'm glad to hear it," Carl said. "Wain and I go back a long way and I'd hate to split with them now. He gave Jo Ann a

searching look and she turned away and lowered her gaze, and
Bridie had the impression that Carl had made it plain that
nothing she said must be repeated to her friends.

"Champagne, Bridie?" Carl said and handed her a glass of
the dry sparkling wine.

Five

"Will you be all right if I leave you for just ten minutes? I've seen a man who promised to buy from us last year but didn't follow it up." Carl looked concerned. "I honestly didn't intend mixing business with this evening but I suppose that's why we are in Switzerland." His smile was disarming and warm and Bridie felt relaxed and happy.

"I'm quite happy to stay here," she said. "Jo Ann has gone to the powder room but said she'd be back, and the other Americans are fun too, so I'll wait here."

"Do that. I'll be back in time to take you to dinner and face the line-up of VIPs that we have to meet on the way in."

She watched the tall figure weave his way between the groups of laughing guests. He seemed to dominate the room as he made progress towards the door. Bridie looked about her at the scene that she had thought existed only in films. The skill of haute couture put many women in elegant clothes that smoothed out a lot of deficiencies due to bad figures and over-indulgence in food and wine, and it was fascinating to watch the various faces and to try to guess from which countries they came.

Bridie was aware of someone watching her, not just giving an admiring glance in passing, but really staring. A hand waved in salute and she saw Anton Gesner perched on a bar stool talking to two other men. One of them was M Dubois.

Bridie raised a hand in greeting and Anton excused himself from his companions to come over to her, but first he checked and looked towards the door, as if to make sure that Carl had

73

really left. I wonder why he doesn't want to see Carl? she thought. It was an instinctive response to his obvious caution.

"Deserted?" he said, lazily.

"Only for ten minutes," she replied. "Business rears its ugly head even at parties."

"Me too. I wont stay now as I have business of my own to follow up with M Dubois who I believe you met last night."

"Yes he was very charming. "Do you speak German?"

Anton looked surprised. "Yes, I do, why?"

Bridie laughed. "We could have used you last night. I had to act as interpreter to M Dubois, Herr Helmsutter and Carl Paterson, and they went on for hours talking business. Some of the technical terms were a bit too much for me, but we managed."

"Is that so?" Anton looked thoughtful. "I shall see you tomorrow? Can you be at the jetty for the lake steamer in Lucerne town by ten?" He spoke quickly as if he had to get away.

"That sounds fine. You were right, I do have a day off tomorrow. It was clever of you to work it out."

"Until tomorrow then," he said, and went back to his companions.

M Dubois stared at her without a sign of recognition until Carl returned and then he smiled and put up a hand in greeting.

"I really am Cinderella," Bridie said. "M Dubois didn't recognise me until you came back. I must look very different from the girl who nearly ran out of voice last night."

"Very different," said Carl as he looked down at the bright piquant face and let his gaze stray to the butterfly and the slender lines of her body. "I like the butterfly," he said. "Was it your idea?"

"Partly, and partly Monique," Bridie said and drank the rest of her aperitif. She sent up a silent prayer to whichever god looked after spirit glue!

"It's time we went in," he said. He held out a hand and took

hers, tucking it under his arm. "Don't be shy. You have no
need to be or to feel out of place, embarrassed or gauche.
Tonight, you are none of these things."

She saw that he wasn't teasing her and she could hardly
believe what she was hearing. He was praising her, when he
had no need to do so. If it's a ploy to make me appear
confident, then it's succeeding, she thought, and walked
smoothly on the high heels. They passed M Dubois and
Anton and Carl stopped for a moment to speak to the
Frenchman. Anton stared at Bridie, his eyes narrowed.

"I did not recognise you, Miss Mark," said M Dubois.
"*Comme tu es mingonne, ma petite.*" Bridie smiled at the use of
the familiar 'tu' and knew that he was comparing her with his
own very pretty daughter whose picture Bridie had seen
several times in various settings when she had dinner with
him the night before, but Anton looked slightly annoyed as if
the Frenchman was taking a liberty or knew Carl Paterson's
secretary really well. "Oh, this is M Gesner," he said as an
afterthought.

"I have had the pleasure of meeting Miss Mark," Anton
said stiffly, as if the pleasure had been brief and muted. Carl
looked at Bridie and saw her astonishment. He knew that she
had met Anton for lunch on the first day of her visit to
Switzerland. Bridie just nodded. The man had been talking to
her five minutes earlier and they had a date for tomorrow.
What was going on in his mind? He surely couldn't be so
scared of Carl that he hadn't the courage to speak up, instead
becoming all distant and called her Miss Mark!

"It's a pity that we haven't more time during these conferences to renew longer acquaintance with old friends, and
this evening is the only really social event when I can move
around and at least say hello to a few more, but I hope we
meet again soon M Dubois, and thank you for looking after
Bridie so well." Carl gave the Frenchman a charming smile.
"Now we have to move on. I think that the president of the
congress and his lady are receiving guests."

He exchanged curt nods with Anton Gesner and, as he eased her away, Bridie could almost swear she heard the clash of antlers as the two men showed their veiled dislike for each other. I wonder why? she thought.

"Ready Bridie?" Carl asked. He squeezed her hand and drew her away, the picture of a perfect attentive escort, and more. He used her pet name easily, as if for him it was special, and Anton Gesner froze.

"*A bientôt,*" said M Dubois.

Anton kissed Bridie's hand politely and murmured, "To-morrow," so that only she could hear, and once again she was puzzled. Why was he so secretive? True, he had hinted that it was not Carl Paterson's business what his secretary did on her day off and it might be diplomatic to say nothing of their date for tomorrow but it was really a bit silly. Dozens of people from the Astra and the Viceroy might be on the same boat and would recognise them. Maybe he is married with a large wife and six children she told herself. A clutch of small children would certainly cramp his style!

"What's so funny?" Carl asked her. His tone was light but he paused for an answer.

"Anton Gesner. He's half afraid of you."

"Only half? What's funny about that? Lots of people are afraid of me. I thought that you were at least half afraid of me, too."

She saw that he was laughing. "Not tonight. I am Cinder-ella tonight and I shall be happy until midnight, afraid of nobody."

He steered her towards the line-up of guests. "Be happy," he said softly.

The next hour was a blurred cavalcade of introductions to people already familiar on newsreels and in the glossies. Carl led her from one group to another, laughing and encouraging her to talk to everyone, as if he had forgotten his order just to smile if she was addressed, and many of the people they met eyed this new girl with Carl Paterson with some speculation.

Dinner was served, with light and delicious food and the tables ornamented with ice-sculptures that were cunningly refrigerated from below so they didn't melt in the warmth of the evening but kept the surrounding flowers dew-fresh and the food and the air above the table-centres cool.

Bridie gazed out across the wide terrace, past open windows along the whole side of the dining room. Fairy lights and music, she thought. Lake Lucerne and delicious food and the muted symphony of contented voices; that's what I shall remember about this evening. Once, Bridie saw Countess Maria watching her from across the room. She was staring and Bridie thought that her gaze was rivetted to the gauzy butterfly, where it rested on the smooth cool skin of the younger woman.

She touched the butterfly, her talisman for the evening. It held firm. Monique's glue was safe.

"Shall we walk for a while?" said Carl when the music started for serious dancing. They went on to the terrace where lights on the water made tiny holes of brightness from which a magic frog would surely leap? Carl handed her the filmy shawl and told her to put it on.

"I'm not cold," she protested, but obediently draped it across her shoulders.

"You are in enemy territory," he said in a teasing voice. There are mosquitoes and maybe other predators, all ready to suck the blood of pretty virgins." She laughed and covered more of her bare skin. "That's better," he said, and seemed more relaxed. Was he being solicitous for her welfare or could it be that he was feeling the impact of a young body, lightly clad, just as she was aware of him as he leaned on the balustrade of the terrace, his face in profile above the crisp shirt and his hands resting on the cool stone?

She dismissed the idea as moonshine and a part of her own private dream. The dangerous beauty that rode the heavens and shone over the lake, making a silver road and touching the high mountain with cold fire, seemed to laugh at her and dare her to succumb to magic and desire.

"Are you sad?" he asked her.

"No, just in awe of that very mysterious mountain. I caught glimpses of it but I haven't seen it properly and I know I must. When I do, I shall fall in love with it."

"Do you only fall in love with mountains, Bridie?" His low voice made her tremble. If only you knew, she thought. "What about the man at home?" he asked. "That date I so rudely made you abandon? I suppose that all this is wasted on you if he isn't here?" He looked across the water, his eyes sombre and almost black in the dimness. "These places can tear a man's heart to pieces if they are viewed without a soulmate."

Bridie touched his arm. For a moment he had looked so unhappy, his face hard in the moonlight, as if his memories were too painful to bear. "Don't be sad," she murmured. "If you truly loved her, you can never lose her or the places that you shared and loved."

"But what of warmth, and living love and nearness? A man needs them too." His breath was on her cheek and she felt his lips on her hair. His hands gripped her shoulders and he kissed her mouth with a sadness that held memories of pain as old as the moon. As quickly, he put her from him and her mouth quivered; her eyes were full of tears. "I'm sorry, Bridie. Forgive me, I have no right to kiss you. You aren't just a girl I might meet at a dance, to be taken for a moment and then forgotten. You have to go back to the man you love and you must go back . . . intact."

She wanted to cry out that she loved him and she wanted no other man, even when she knew that he wasn't in love with her, but wanted any girl who could fill a cold corner of his heart for an hour. She stepped back from the terrace wall, to follow him as he moved away, but the moment had gone and with it, the magic.

"There you are, you naughty man! I've looked everywhere for you." The countess came out on to the terrace with two

men a step behind her. She waved them away as if they were
servants for whom she no longer had a use.

"Maria!" Carl said, as if he had been waiting for her all
evening. "You look very alluring." She smiled and looked
past him to Bridget. "Let me present Miss Bridget Mark;
Bridget, the Countess Maria." The two women inclined their
heads and smiled slightly. The huge ruby on Maria's hand
gleamed like a sultry beacon and the diamonds at her throat
rippled fire. She glanced at the one ornament that Bridie wore
and dismissed it as worthless.

"Now I have two lovely ladies," Carl said lightly. "Shall we
go back and join the dancers?" He found a small table away
from the band and ordered cool white wine. Maria sat close to
Carl, demanding all his attention as she deliberately talked of
people who meant nothing to Bridie but who Carl obviously
knew well. The wine was soothing and Bridie was glad to have
something to hold in her hand to give her poise. It seemed an
age since Maria had erupted on to the terrace, just when the
last shreds of tension had been swept away.

I had my moment, Bridie thought. One kiss to treasure that
really didn't belong to me, but to a woman now dead.

From time to time the jewelled hands reached across the
table and touched Carl as if wanting to possess him, and he
was smiling. She'll have him if she can. She'll try to shut out
every other female who as much as looks at him, thought
Bridie, a tight knot of misery making her tense again.

A man with short, thick dark hair and a rugged face came
over and clicked his heels in Germanic greeting. Formally, but
in very good English, he asked Carl for permission to dance
with his lady. Bridie was speechless and Maria looked annoyed, as if reminded that Bridie was with Carl and that
people knew that this insignificant girl was staying in his suite.

"Thank you, but no," Bridie began but the man looked
only at Carl.

"Why not?" Carl smiled and raised a quizzical eyebrow at
Bridie's uncertainty. "Good to see you again, Herr Schmit. If

you like dancing, then do so. It's a good idea. Maria and I have business to discuss."

Maria smiled and, as Bridie stood up, she had the impression that she was leaving one very satisfied lady and a man who seemed to have no feelings that she could identify but who could even be glad to see the back of her.

Dance after dance followed and in one way Bridie enjoyed being flattered and admired by the gallant Swiss, German and French who asked her to dance. Maria sat close to Carl and they smiled at each other. The floor was crowded now and at times it was impossible to see the table where Carl was sitting. The music was more and more frenetic and when Anton appeared and cut in on Bridie's partner, she was ready for a break. He led her towards the terrace where she had stood with Carl and offered her a cigarette, from a silver case that she thought belonged to an era long gone, but which fitted into the style of the hotel and the surroundings. Did wealthy women still give such gifts to their amours? The moon must know it all.

"I never smoke," she said.

"No vices? He was completely relaxed, with no trace of the stiff manner she had noticed when Carl was around.

"Very few," said Bridie. It was a relief to stop dancing as the high heels were tiring her feet and not every partner with whom she danced was a Fred Astaire! Some men seemed unable to dance without trampling on her toes and the music had been suitable only for the old dances with close contact of feet and hands.

Several couples now sat on the balustrade and Anton swung her up to sit there too, but he chose a place where they were screened on one side by shrubs and clothed in dim twilight when the moon decided to hide behind a cloud. "Better?" he asked. "Your feet must be tired."

"What a relief," she agreed.

"Stay there while I fetch some fruit juice, unless you prefer wine?"

"Fruit juice would be lovely," she said. "Lots of ice, please, Anton." She folded her shawl more closely round her shoulders and wondered why she had a sudden vision of Anton as a turn of the century gigolo? Was he just a handsome predator, trying to make any attractive girl who came to the congresses? What did he do? Where did he work? Her hand touched the butterfly, almost forgotten when she danced. It was peeling away from her skin and she pressed it back into position, but that seemed to make it worse and it hung away at the top refusing to stick again. In a few minutes it might peel off completely, so she took the butterfly and put it in her purse, then tied the shawl across her chest like an old-fashioned fichu. Concealing the birthmark, she was ready for the fruit juice that Anton now offered to her.

"*Santé*," he said and began to talk about Lucerne, so that she would know what to look for when they were on the lake. He seemed very anxious to make her day off memorable and something to recall when she was back in London.

He was amusing and seemed to care about her in a friendly way, and Bridie felt good. There were none of the emotional overtones with him that Carl's presence conjured up and it was pleasant sitting on the broad stone wall, sipping ice-cold fruit juice with the music filtering out to them and the moon making the lake a sheet of silver.

When she asked what work he did, he seemed pleased to tell her. "We also research software and many other electronics and invent new processes but nothing as big as Paterson's set-up. We have a big staff to cope with the every-day running of the firm and people like me to attend conferences and to exchange ideas with other firms. A great deal of business is transacted here by word of mouth and we firm up on it later when we are back in our offices."

"Sometimes it falls through," Bridie said. "Carl was going to see someone who had gone back on what had been a firm offer."

Anton tossed a half-used cigarette into the water and took another from his case. "Which firm would that be?" he asked.

81

"I don't know." Bridie shrugged. "I know very little about the business as I have been at Herald such a short time, and have never, until now, had anything to do with the more confidential work."

"But last night you had to know quite a lot about private negotiations when you acted as interpreter."

"I suppose so, but I didn't take it in much as I was far too busy trying to make myself understood."

He laughed. "The perfect discreet secretary! I applaud that as I know the dangers of saying too much in public to complete strangers. We all have to be careful here." He spoke of other things and was amusing but gradually, in a casual way, came back to her work at Herald Enterprises.

Bridie became uneasy as his questions became more probing, and she found it difficult to keep silent when he seemed so harmless. The questions must be just because he was in the same line of business and he was naturally interested. After all, Carl had talked freely to the two men the previous day about all kinds of technical matters. She bit her lip. They hadn't asked about the new inventions that she had learned were in the pipeline and very secret. They had talked of trading in well-established stock and recent refinements in some computer-ware that was known through advertising and so were not the slightest bit secret since they had hit the market.

"I ought to get back to the table," she said at last, to break up the trend of the conversation and to avoid saying flatly that she was not willing to talk about the firm in any depth. "I don't know when Carl wants to leave."

"No need to bother him. I'll take you back and we can have coffee in the Viceroy, in the lounge or in your room."

"That's impossible. Although Carl is talking to the countess he will expect me to be ready when he wants to leave."

"I could follow if you give me your room number. It's far too pleasant an occasion to break it up now. I can't tell you when I've enjoyed an evening more." His dark eyes glowed and he touched her hand briefly.

"I'm sorry, Anton. It's just not on. I have a room in the suite so I can't entertain anyone who hasn't been invited by my boss."

"But Sandra always has a separate room," he began, then laughed. "Herald Enterprises having an economy drive? You'll be telling me they're on the skids next!"

"Hardly. Carl has a palatial room and I have a smaller, very pretty one with frills. We do an awful lot of work in the sitting room there and it's convenient to have all the papers in one place. It's quite a good idea," she added.

His face cleared. "I've heard that he works his staff into the ground. Bad luck. At least if you had your own separate room away from him, you could escape at times."

"It's a hard life," Bridie said, amused to think that Anton had believed for a minute that she was sleeping with Carl and now was relieved to know that she was just a twenty-hour a day slave! "We shall have tomorrow, Anton. I long to see what's at the top of that mountain. Do you think it will be free of cloud?"

"We shall see. It changes from day to day. Sometimes it is so clear that you can see several other peaks from the top of Pilatus. At other times, it is shrouded all day and there is no view." He sat close to her on the wall and the proximity was pleasant. His aftershave smelled of flowers, which on many men would have been effeminate but Bridie was aware of a very virile man under the smooth, good-looking exterior.

"If you will not let me take you home, then I shall go," he said suddenly, and helped her down from the wall. He strode away without looking back and when Bridie glanced across to the entrance to the dance floor, Carl and Maria were walking slowly towards her.

"I wondered where you were," Carl said.

"I didn't think you'd miss me so I stayed out here in the cool."

"Was that Anton who went off in such a hurry?" Countess Maria asked.

"Yes, Countess. He was very kind." She held up the long glass in which the remains of the delicious fruit punch sat in the bottom. "I was very thirsty after all that dancing."

"Fruit juice? He didn't ply you with strong drink and force his attentions on you?" Carl laughed, but his eyes held a hint of anxiety. "You surprise me."

"Anton isn't like that," Bridie said. "We talked about Lucerne and I made the mistake of trotting out the old joke about the Swiss being able only to produce cuckoo clocks and chocolate and he put me firmly in my place and lectured me about the heroic acts of Swiss soldiers and how they defended themselves over the centuries before the country became a neutral zone. It's all recorded in old paintings on the underside of the roof covering the wooden bridge in Lucerne town." She smiled. "Another illusion gone that started with the book and the film *The Third Man*, when he made the cuckoo clock joke. They were invented by an Austrian, not the Swiss!"

Maria looked pleased. "It all sounds very boring. Poor girl to have to listen to that. With me, Anton never talks of such uninteresting topics. Maybe it's hard for you to believe, but he is so charming when he isn't on duty entertaining foreign guests of his beloved Switzerland."

Carl raised one eyebrow and smiled. He seemed to be enjoying himself. He looked at Bridie as if to say, the ball's in your court, but she refused to rise to Maria's bait. It would have been easy to boast that she was going with him for a whole day on the lake and up to the top of Pilatus. "He offered to take me back to the Viceroy, Carl, but I thought you might want me for something."

"And having done his duty, he left without argument? How dull for you." Maria smiled. "I hope you aren't going to make your poor secretary work all night, Carl. I've heard that you are a very severe taskmaster." She fluttered her eyelashes at him. "At one time, I thought that Sandra was more than an employee. She is so attractive and vital, isn't she? But after hearing how hard she works on these trips, I am convinced that she had no other . . . perquisites offered to her." She made it clear that if Sandra, with her air of glamour, had no success with Carl, then a little nondescript like Bridget Mark was no threat to any woman in a position to attract such a man. She regarded the immense ruby on her finger with complaisance.

"Sandra is a very good secretary, Maria, but on this trip Bridget has shown that she can be just as efficient when she knows what is required of her," Carl said.

"And she will have the document ready for me tomorrow?" Maria spoke as if Bridget wasn't there.

"You shall have it, Maria. It's good to think that after so many discussions we have at last come to this agreement." He looked at Bridie apologetically. "It does mean an hour's work. Can you do it tomorrow morning or would you rather go back to the Viceroy now and leave tomorrow completely free for your day off?"

"If it's all that important, I'd rather do it now. If I can have transport and you will tell me what you want, I'll go now."

Maria laughed. "What a good girl, and how well you train your staff, Carl." She eyed the front of Bridie's dress with interest and Bridie pulled the shawl closer in case the birthmark showed. Maria smiled, knowingly. "I was talking to Monique. Tonight we share a couturière, my dear. She has some very amusing accessories in her bag, *n'est pas*? Did she show them to you? She is a worker of miracles and has something suitable for every occasion, even trinkets like butterflies."

For a moment, Carl looked annoyed as Bridie blushed and was embarrassed. "I'll give you the papers and tell you what I need," he said.

"I'll wait in the bar," Maria said. "Don't be long, will you?" It was a royal command.

"In here." Carl led her into a small alcove and switched on a light. "She signed a lot of very important papers today which add up to an agreement with Herald that we have wanted for over a year. It will make a great difference to our export figures."

"The countess works for a living?"

He grinned "It doesn't show, but Maria has a first-class brain for business when it isn't blurred by social activities. She is very difficult to nail down to an agreement as she tries to insert more and more clauses, but once she has signed, she and her company are very good and have a high reputation for integrity. I've wanted this for a long time and now I've got it!" He handed her a folder and laughed. "That's not to say that she doesn't try to find out more than we are willing to tell her about new products, but that's life in business."

"You want the usual copies?" Bridie made a few notes on a pad as she skimmed through the document and asked relevant questions about initialled alterations. If she could forget the magical surroundings, it was like being back in the office and she almost called him 'sir'.

"Is all that clear?" he asked.

"Fine. Shall I ring for a car?"

"It's waiting. I'm very sorry about this but I thought you'd want to get this out of the way tonight," he said. His voice was edgy with embarrassment.

"Don't be sorry. This has been a wonderful evening for me."

"I'm glad. Now, I know that I have no real need to say this, but you are away from the office for the first time on a stint for Herald and I did warn you that there are industrial predators about." She nodded. "This document is highly confidential. Some of the details spell out deals with new processes. You will be the first to see these particular ones, apart from the board of directors and the research team, and now of course, Maria, who will tell nobody as it is in her interests as much as ours to keep it a secret for while. I do trust you, Bridie, but be very careful if anyone tries to talk to you about Herald Enterprises."

"You can trust me, Carl. Shall I ring the Rigi or the Astra when I've finished, or will you be coming back to the Viceroy?"

"Ring Astra. I'll take Maria back to her suite there and wait. As soon as you ring, I'll come to fetch the papers for her. After that, I can escape to the peace and quiet of the Viceroy! He saw that she got into the right car then left without another word, hurrying back inside the hotel.

"Back to work." She murmured with a weary sigh. "It's midnight and, for Cinderella, the ball is over – and the handsome prince couldn't care less!"

The Viceroy was quiet to the point of gloom. Bridie rang down for coffee and opened the portable typewriter that had replaced the first terrible specimen but which was not much better in speed and performance. She examined the document in more detail and knew that an hour's work was a gross under-estimation. Ah, well, I have to do it sooner or later, she thought, so I'll get on with it, before I even change out of these clothes. She worked steadily and the well set-out result of her efforts was pleasing and soothed her tired spirit. The monotonous click of the machine was soporific but she drank cup after cup of black coffee and kept her concentration going until, at last, she tore out the final sheet and stacked it with the others.

She dialled the Astra but no, Mr Paterson was not in the bar. "Try the suite of Countess Maria," the receptionist suggested. There was a long pause and then Carl's voice, sounding elated and rather strange. "I have the papers all completed," Bridie said.

"Oh, yes, the papers! Yes, I'll nip over for them now. Thank you, Bridget." He sounded as if he was talking to room service, an anonymous voice on the telephone, as if the papers were quite unimportant compared to the company he shared in the luxurious private suite where the countess was staying.

A short time later Bridie heard the whine of the elevator and Carl walked in looking weary. Gone was the elation of the evening and he no longer smiled.

"Could you check through them before you go?" she suggested. "As you said, this is the first time I've done anything as confidential. I'm sure it is all there but please make sure."

She handed over the papers and he sank into a chair. She angled the light to give him better vision and asked if he'd like coffee. He nodded, already immersed in the papers and Bridie rang down for more coffee. When the boy brought it she poured out a cup just as he liked it and set it ready to drink. Bridget sat in a high-backed chair and watched him sip it absentmindedly while he worked. She tried to analyse his face.

In repose, it was strong but sad. His was the kind of face that was illuminated when he smiled and the harsh lines softened: the blue eyes glowed and his body relaxed. He must have loved his wife very much, thought Bridie. Could any woman replace that loss? Could even Maria, who must be about the same age as Carl, fill the gap with her vivacity and wealth and the even more dangerous fact that she was his business equal?

She'll have him if she can, and she wants him, Bridie decided. He was fascinated and enthralled, bemused by her experience, so what could an ordinary woman expect if she tried to give him love? How could anyone fight such opposition?

And yet . . . for those few precious moments out on the terrace, Bridie had wondered if he could respond to what she was willing to give him; a lifetime of love and caring.

He looked up, running his fingers through his hair and making it spiky. "Fine," he said and gave a crooked smile. "You've no idea how hard I've had to work for this, Bridie." He yawned. "God, I'm tired, but I have a few more things I must do tonight. Clip this one to that and put the lot in a separate folder while I wash my face and comb my hair." He looked at the cold coffee-pot and then at her, and sounded reproachful. "I could have done with some coffee," he said.

"You've been drinking it for the past three-quarters of an hour," she said.

"Have I?" He saw the empty cup by his elbow. "You shouldn't let me do that. I'll never get to sleep!"

She shook her head and smiled. He was impossible. Even Maria might find him a handful.

He came back from the bathroom with his hair damp and once again slicked into a disciplined smoothness. He looked alert once more. "Get to bed, Bridie," he said and smiled. "I'd like to talk to you in the morning, so could we have breakfast here together at eight thirty?" She recalled that her date wasn't until later and nodded. "I shan't ask you to work," he said hastily. "But there are things to discuss."

"I'll ring down and order breakfast in case I oversleep," she said.

He came over to where she was putting the cover over the typewriter. "Thanks again," he said. "I have to go and be pleasant all over again. I shall be back very late." He kissed her cheek and then his face changed from weary affection to disbelief. She knew that for some reason he now hated her or despised her so much that he backed away, unable to touch her." He grabbed the briefcase and made for the door.

He looked back once and she saw that he was trying to control a deep emotion. "I can't believe it! I could never have believed that it was possible," he said, and his voice was deep and uneven as if under great stress. "With Gesner of all people! When she told me, I almost said she was lying," he added in a stony voice. "And yet it's true."

The door slammed and he was gone. Bridie looked down at the smooth tender lines of her breasts and at the exposed redness of the birthmark.

Monique had at first refused to believe that it was not a love bite, as in her world any girl with sense would have had it removed years ago if it was a birthmark. She had been amused and must have treated Maria to that snippet of gossip to explain the butterfly. Even if Maria believed that Bridie was not lying, there was no reason for her to accept it, if it meant that Carl Paterson would never again think of little Bridget Mark as anything but a rather soiled employee.

How many others had Maria told? How she and Monique would laugh about her when others tried to guess who had made the demure little girl after only a day or two at the congress.

Bridie sobbed as she got into bed. Whatever they believed they had made Carl sure that she had a love bite, and that there was only one man who could have been responsible; Anton Gesner.

Six

B ridie smiled at the waiter and he grinned as he pocketed his tip. He glanced at the closed bedroom door behind which Carl Paterson still lingered, although Bridie had heard him move about long before his early morning tea arrived, as if he was up and dressed. He could have had no more than two hours sleep.

"Breakfast is served," she called, as lightly as she was able, and braced herself to meet him, dreading the expression in his eyes when she recalled the look of pure loathing he had given her last night, or rather, in the early hours of the morning.

The door opened and he came out, freshly bathed, wearing a short-sleeved shirt of grey silk and smartly-cut jeans. "My day off too," he said casually. "Is the coffee really hot?"

"Very good. The croissants are fresh and there are two different preserves. I also asked for a selection of cereals but I wasn't sure if you'd want eggs or any other cooked dish."

"No eggs." He gave an exaggerated shudder and picked out a fat croissant. Bridie relaxed. He was talking of every-day matters and it was easy to fill the silence that threatened to hang over her like a dark cloud. From his polite manner Carl made it clear that last night was not the subject of discussion. He might even consider it was none of his business who his secretary allowed to make love to her.

The forced politeness eased and Bridie found that she was hungry. "Last night I thought I'd never want anything to eat today," she said, buttering a second croissant.

"Does nothing affect your appetite? You've gobbled up everything offered you here. I'd no idea that we starved our staff at Herald. Remind me to look into the pay structure!"

Bridie appeared composed but she wanted to weep. She longed to beg him to listen to her, and to the explanation of the birthmark, but his cool, bland politeness forbade any such approach and put up a barrier that she could not tear away. They talked of the document she had typed. He praised her work and said that Maria had found nothing new to add or with which she disagreed. Perhaps he praised me too much to Maria, and it was then that she told him that I had a lover, she thought.

He spoke of the agenda of a meeting to which he must go on the following day and asked her to check the times of return flights to UK after the congress. "There will be another dinner on the last night, but it will be very poorly attended as delegates from a long distance will want to get away early. Most of the important work has been done and all the serious deals completed that came through social contacts here. The chat between speeches and presentations is more useful than anything and M Dubois has been very cooperative, partly I think, due to your help."

"That's nice to know," she said.

"Of course, there are those who will stay on, making the congress an excuse for visiting friends or having romantic attachments of which their families know nothing. This place is seething with such undercurrents." He sipped his coffee and Bridie couldn't look at him. "Apart from that it is an opportunity to see more of the area and to take a break. I'm tempted to do just that."

"I can see that it might be a good idea if anyone had the time to spare," she said. Was this his way of telling her that he wanted to stay with Maria? "On the other hand, I can imagine that this place is a bit over the top and the atmosphere of the Astra is too much for some people," she went on calmly as if the subject was of only academic interest for her.

"Don't tell me that the lake had no affect on you, Bridie?" He used her pet name for the first time since they had parted last night.

"It's very beautiful," she admitted. "It was the perfect setting for Cinderella, and now Cinderella has put away her dancing shoes and gown and is ready to finish any jobs you have for me before I go out for my day off."

"Of course." He glanced at his watch. "I hope I'm not delaying you?"

"No, I'm not due at the jetty until ten."

"You're still determind to see your clouded mountain?"

She gasped. "How did you know I called it that?"

"You murmured something about it on the plane, and last night I saw your very expressive eyes when you gazed up at Pilatus in the moonlight."

She laughed to hide her sudden shyness. "It was a childhood dream. I longed to see what lived beyond the clouds." She sighed. "But have you noticed? As you climb, it seems that you are in the clear and that all the rest of the world is in cloud while you walk above it."

"We all have our own clouded mountain, Bridie. I hope that you find gold beyond the mist. Enjoy your mountain but be careful and keep your balance. Have you a good head for heights? Are you going with Gesner?"

The question was abrupt after the whimsical speech. "Yes. He asked me to go there when we met on the first day here. He seems to know a lot about the mountain and about Lucerne."

"Does he know that you have told me where you are going with him?"

"No, he said that what I did in my own time was nothing to do with Herald. What does it matter who I tell? Anyone can see me on the lake steamer or on the jetty. It's ridiculous to suppose that I wouldn't mention it to you. We have meals together, we work together, so it's natural to talk about this place and the people we meet, isn't it?"

I have to rabbit on, she thought. I have to talk to break the ice and keep it broken. I can survive only if I keep it light and as if I have no feelings of my own.

I respect what he says, up to a point," Carl said. "I also recognise that it is natural to chat about people that we meet here and to find out as much as we can about the area. But it cuts both ways. He might want you to tell him about your work and the work we do at Herald, and if you don't, then you'll feel less than forthcoming and as though you are snubbing him."

"You can't be serious! Anton is just a very nice and generous man who wants to show me a mountain. I like him very much."

His glance lingered on the delicate fullness under her cotton dress. "I rather gathered that," he said, dryly. "There is one other matter. I'd rather that Maria didn't hear of your date. You may not realise it but Gesner has been very attentive to her over the past few months and she regards him as her property."

"She seems to regard all men as her property," Bridie said coldly.

"Maria is a very busy and able business woman. She is a very demanding female and a fascinating woman who enjoys her just homage."

"And by some divine right she is allowed to take any man she fancies?"

"Most men fall for her sooner or later," Carl said.

"Last night I noticed that she preferred you and had little time for Anton."

"Last night I could have sworn that you were forgetting your friend in London." The tension between them was palpable and Bridie looked away from the accusing blue eyes.

"I have boyfriends at home but I'm not bound to any of them," said Bridie, then wished that she'd remained silent. Roger Franks, the up and coming computer programmer who loved her, had been a refuge when she found her own feelings too much to handle. A safe romance to which she could refer, hid the fact that she was under the spell of one man, even if that man was overbearing, cynical, dismissive and thought the worst of her.

"Don't be too sure, Bridie. Just because you have come to this place with all its glamour and false values, don't deceive yourself into thinking that one brief romance, however passionate, can take the place of a lasting and deep relationship."

"I don't think that," she protested, and got up to leave.

"Before you go, listen to me, Bridie. Last night, you were full of good food and wine, just as you were that first time you met Gesner for lunch. No, don't interrupt. I have no moral judgements to make. I am only saying that in this place, we all act out of character and may be less discreet than we are at home. Last night, for instance, you were quite a different person. You were dressed beautifully, you looked like a golden moth or a lovely butterfly."

She blushed. "Clothes don't change people."

"Oh, but they do. Even if you feel the same inside, they change the reaction of other people to you and that changes you. I read once about a famous theatrical impresario who staged lavish musical productions that cost the earth to dress. He gave all his chorus girls genuine Brussels lace to edge their petticoats, and when asked why he bothered, as from the audience's point of view, imitation lace would look the same, he said, 'My girls know what they are wearing and they hold their heads that much higher and wear my lace with pride. It shows in every movement they make and they look taller and more refined, knowing that I think they are worth the expense,' and he had the most famous chorus line in the world."

"I'm not likely to dance in a chorus," she said, weakly, but she knew that he was right. She had felt like a princess in that lovely golden dress and had acted accordingly.

"Seeing you last night, dressed as you were, was enough to make someone, even as avaricious as Gesner, think that all might well be lost for love; or at least to assuage the desire of the moment. You made a great impression on many people, Bridie. You even amazed me."

He laughed as if he was now rid of any responsibility towards her so long as she was careful what she said. The sermon was over and he'd said his piece. "At least he'll have no illusions about you today, Bridget of the manse! That dress speaks of Calvinism and the sandals are definitely Holy Disciple!" He sounded as if the idea pleased him.

"You are very rude," she said, trying to smile and dismiss his words as a joke. "I can't think why you have such weird ideas about me. If Anton is dangerous, how can you say he is pursuing the countess when he is spending an entire day with me? If he was afraid that she would be annoyed if she found out, and yet doesn't care what she thinks, then she can't be as important to him as you say." She looked at him steadily. "Anton has no designs on me and he acts very correctly at all times. He hasn't made a single pass at me."

"I wish that were true," Carl said. "It depends what you mean by a pass! I want to believe you for your own sake, Bridie, but please remember that he is dangerous. Come on, I'll walk you to the jetty. I need the exercise."

"Not if it's taking you out of your way," Bridie said, stiffly.

"No trouble. I shall have to be by the lake and I want to look at the timetables for the steamers. Could you be back here by five? I hate to ask this but there will be a few faxes to send this evening. If you can be back I'll meet you at the terminus in Lucerne town, then we can finish the business and you can be free for dinner."

"Fine. That should give me plenty of time to see everything I want to see on the mountain." She glanced up at the cloudless sky. It was already hot and the breeze hardly lifted a leaf. "I think I'll buy a hat," she said. "Sun on water is often very strong."

Carl studied the timetable while she went over to a stall and inspected the various hats for sale. He came back and lounged against a wall. "Not exactly high fashion and enough to give Monique a nasty shock, but they do have a certain rustic charm," he said lazily. He gave her a boyish grin. "I am completely reassured. Gesner will find the English Cinderella a bit on the homely side today and you may even retain your virtue!"

She gave him a dirty look and tried on another hat. "This one?"

"Try that one. At least it doesn't look as if it needs holes cut in the sides to fit the ears of a donkey and protect him from the sun. Yes, that suits you better and will keep the sun from the back of your neck. By the way, you did know that the steamer takes you only one way and you come back to a different landing by means of cable car? There are lots of cable cars that move down continuously as they do in the skiing season, with no irritating waiting about for transport down to the terminus."

"What a shame. I thought I'd have two steamer rides."

"No, you'll find that the steamer takes you to the foot of Pilatus and then you go up by rack railway. You then spend as much time as you like on the mountain and come down by cable car straight to the terminus in Lucerne. I shall meet you there." He squinted up at the sun. "It's the perfect weather for it and a good way to spend a free day. I wish I was coming with you."

"Why don't you? You said you had a day off, too."

He smiled at her naively. "I doubt if Gesner would add to my pleasure and I'm quite sure he would resent my intrusion." He shrugged. "In any case, I am committed to doing other things. As Gesner has deserted the lovely Maria, someone has to keep her happy."

Bridie lowered her gaze. "Of course." He would be with Maria, making her laugh and being dragged into the coils of her charm. "Are you meeting her at any set time? I'm sure that the lady doesn't like to be kept waiting."

He sighed. "The things I do for business."

Bridie looked sceptical. "I hadn't noticed that you hate your job or the social trials that go with it!"

"You've no idea! I can hide my feelings most of the time but it gets to be a strain sometimes." He pointed to the painted clock face on the ornate tower. "There is probably someone who might get a bit peeved if he's kept waiting. You'll have to hurry down to the boats." She turned to go and he called after her. "Bridie? You will be there by five? There will be some very important information to send off. If you don't appear from the cable car before that time, I shall ring the terminus on Pilatus, and if you stay up there even after that, I shall scale the mountain and carry you down over my shoulder!"

"I'd better watch the time," she said and laughed, but something in his voice made her take notice. He was deadly serious and the urgency in his voice was real. "I promise to be there unless I fall into a ravine," she said.

"It's not ravines that you have to avoid," she thought she heard him say softly as she went away quickly, clutching her new straw hat on to her head with one hand.

"I thought I'd lost you," said Anton. He smiled, relieving the set expression that Bridie had noticed before he saw that she had arrived. He was once again the laughing, lighthearted man who had entertained her so well over the fondue lunch: was it only days ago? He kissed her hand and squeezed it. "I'm not late," Bridie said.

The steamer waited by a wooden pier, bright streamers fluttering and soft music coming from the cabin. There was an air of carnival as families jostled and squabbled happily while they took their places on the boat. The usual collection of lone walkers, with heavy packs and bedrolls, sank down on to the deck in grubby jeans and clinging T-shirts, ignoring the dust of passing feet. Students hitching through Europe and middle-aged couples from the tourist hotels filled the top deck and Anton found seats where the smuts from the chimney would not blow down on them once the boat was under way.

It was wonderful to view Lucerne from the lake. "You look like a little girl on a school outing," Anton said. "I do believe that you are really excited." She nodded, her eyes shining. "You are so sweet that you make me feel old and blasé," he said. "With you I may perhaps again enjoy the first memory I had of the lake when I was a small boy. I shall enjoy this trip as never before and try to remember how it was all those years ago when I was young and innocent."

"You poor old man," said Bridie, teasing him. "You sound as if life has passed you by and been very hard on you." She looked at the sunny promenade, the blue of the sky and the deeper blue of the placid lake. "I can't imagine anyone being sad or unhappy here for very long." A corner of the ice that had formed and frozen her heart last night was thawing. It was difficult to think of anything but the day ahead and the man at her side in his present mood, while he bent over her, talking and laughing, with every sign of being deeply attracted to her. In spite of my Calvinistic dress and the Holy Disciple sandals, she thought.

It was wonderful. Anton didn't seem to notice what she wore. Why did Carl consider him to be some kind of lecherous beast? He was certainly very masculine under that slightly over-the-top manner and very good-looking, and his care of her on the boat was above reproach. She felt a trace of her sadness returning. Of course she knew why Carl thought badly of him. The birthmark that looked like a love bite was enough to convince a man like Carl Paterson, who jumped to all the wrong conclusions, that she and Anton must be lovers or at least on the way there.

"We're away!" she said in wonder as the giant paddles of the ancient steamer cut the water and sent cascades of white water through the blue, leaving a massive wake of turbulent foam. "It's like a picture book for children," she exclaimed. "I haven't seen a paddle steamer for years. I thought they were all gone."

"We keep them for the amusement of wide-eyed tourists like you." He smiled. "We Swiss study your needs and, being good shopkeepers and businessmen, we do as any efficient company would do, we supply what is needed, even if we have no time for out-of-date inefficiency. I have no doubt that the owners of these old warriors would gladly substitute modern motor boats for these if they thought they would attract custom and pay better."

"Who would want to flash across the lake in a fast motor boat when the lake is so blue and the sun is shining?"

"Exactly. Holidays are for leisure and to be taken slowly. You see, we know how to pander to your every whim whether it be a lake steamer or a disco, a peaceful lido or a beach club, all in the name of money."

"That sounds so cold-blooded, Anton. Ever since I came here, I've been impressed by the friendliness and the eager way that everyone wants to be helpful." He shrugged. "People are naturally friendly here," she went on. "They work hard and they couldn't keep it up all the time even to make money out of people." She laughed. "I shall have to believe that you are only being charming to me for an ulterior motive, if you talk about the Swiss in this way."

"Why do you say that?" he asked sharply.

"What did I say? I said that I was charmed by everyone here and I can't believe that they do it all just for money." He relaxed. "Look," she said. "Even the lake looks friendly. I've never seen such blue water. Not even on a summers day on the Scottish sea lochs. And look! Pilatus has a tiny crown of cloud, just enough to make him look mysterious."

"How easy you are to entertain, Bridie." He took her hand. "You do like me a little?" He had emphasised her pet name and it was the first time he had used it. Carl had used her name when the two men had stared at each other with such animosity, and Carl had given the impression that he had a claim on her with the right to use her pet name. Now she wondered if Anton was challenging that imagined claim. She smiled faintly. If only he knew how little claim Carl Paterson would want to make over her he wouldn't try so hard to be better than him.

It was all very strange. The attentions that Anton thought were necessary were amusing. He rushed to buy ice-creams, a map of the islands dotting the lake, and then a cool drink as soon as she mentioned that she was hot. Anything that he could obtain on the boat that he thought she might need, he brought to her and she found his efforts a little trying.

"Anton," she said at last. "Stop doing all this for me, please. I'm a big girl now and I can throw away my own ice-cream wrapper." She smiled to take away the slight reproof. "You are being very kind but I'd rather that you didn't bob about like a flea in a fit." She laughed at his complete lack of comprehension. "I'm sorry. I forget that you aren't British. Your English is so good, but I suppose some of the idiom is a bit confusing. It only means that I want you to stop rushing about for me as it makes me tired to watch you. I know you want me to enjoy my day off, but I like to be treated as a human being and not as a piece of fragile china!"

He sighed. "I do not understand."

"I didn't think you would. People like the Countess love all this hand-kissing and running to pick up anything she drops. On me, it's wasted. I want you to enjoy today as much as I am and we can't do that unless we are relaxed with each other."

"You have no heart! How else can a man show his devotion?"

"You are doing very nicely, thank you." She smiled and asked the name of the dark blob on the lake that was rapidly becoming an island. She moved to the side of the boat to see the island more clearly and watched it become a place of beauty, hovering above the blue water. The dark shape

101

softened as the boat approached, giving way to details of high terraces, fine trees and glowing flowers tumbling over grey stone walls.

"Does anyone live there?" she asked, and as they came level with the island, she saw that there were villas and a hotel on it. "What a wonderful place to stay," she said.

"At one time whole islands were owned by wealthy families and there are still a few left in private hands; smaller than this one but as beautiful, and of course very private, with no landing for tourists or people wanting to picnic."

"That must be real style," Bridie said.

"They are small kingdoms," Anton said with a kind of reverent envy. "Very special places of which most men can only dream."

"And that's what you would really like to possess?"

"That is my dream," he admitted.

"Everyone has a dream," she said. "But who has enough money these days to own an island in a very popular area like this where prices must be very high?"

"I know people who do," he said.

Bridie laughed. "My uncle owns an island in Scotland but it's nothing like this."

"A whole island? He must be very wealthy."

"Oh, no, he thinks he's very hard up," she said, recalling the windswept island in one of the lochs which no one wanted to buy because it had no natural water supply apart from a brackish stream. The sheep that he kept on it barely paid for themselves and as he grew older he wanted to be rid of it.

Anton smiled contentedly. "You are too modest, Bridie. Anyone who owns an island must be rich." It was obvious that he had never been to Scotland in a force eight gale, alone except for the sheep and gulls and the sparse gorse, on a windswept beach!

"Stop dreaming and tell me who lives on that one over there."

"On this one, a member of the old Italian royal family. On the next, a Swiss industrialist."

"Is he married? If not I ought to get off at the next stop, and meet him," said Bridie and laughed. "Do you think he'd like a nice Scottish girl, in flat sandals?" She was amused at the ridiculous idea and thought that Anton would laugh, too.

Anton didn't laugh but regarded her thoughtfully. "If your family own an island, you might indeed have entry to his world and his ménage," he said, seriously. He is divorced." He smiled cynically. "His wife is as good or even better at business than he is. You have met her. She is the Countess Maria." He pointed to a gem of green away to the right. "That is her private island."

He was lost to Bridie, to anything but the view of the tiny island mass that was coming more clearly into sight. She saw the hunger in his eyes and knew that he wanted that island more than anything he was ever likely to possess. He could never afford it on his own and the only path to it was through Maria's influence. Such a dream had turned into an obsession.

"Is it very lovely?" she asked.

"It is perfection." He came to life. "I have been there often with the countess alone, and with friends. She is very hospitable and likes to have a lot of company of her own choosing. Many people try to be invited but she ignores all such intrusions," he added proudly.

A small boy shouted and pointed back the way they had come. A fast motor launch with powerful engines shot through the water, near enough for people who lined the sides of the paddle steamer to see the pilot. Bridie stared at the man with the grey silk shirt and the ruffled hair. Carl Paterson was holding the wheel in the cockpit and the woman who sat in the bow was laughing. She was well covered against the spray in a bright scarlet, well-cut waterproof coat and her scarf was from a famous boutique, but tendrils of fair hair escaped round Maria's face, making her look enchanting.

"The launch is going to the island," Bridie said with a catch in her voice. "That makes Carl a very special guest."

"They are going to my island. It must be my island one day," Anton whispered. Only Bridie heard what he said and he turned away and passed a hand over his eyes as if to erase the picture he had seen. When he looked at her again, his smile was sweet and there was no sign of tension.

"You are more prettier than islands," he said, his English slipping for the first time. "I want, but so do many. You want what? Clothes, furs, jewels?"

"I want very little," she said. "We all have dreams but I learned long ago that I can't have everything I want." She sighed. "I'm not really pretty enough. I was brought up never to waste time gazing into mirrors and so I have never thought of myself as pretty."

"You were beautiful last night. You are lovely but you do not show it. Last night I saw you as you should be all the time and you were the most pretty woman there, with the best body. You say you want little, but you know that such lovely clothes cost money and so money can bring happiness, everything to make you happy,"

"Not everything." Bridie looked up at the snowy top of a distant mountain. "Happiness is now, this minute, sitting in the sun and looking up at the snows."

"It is well for you to speak like that. You have a family who own an island."

"For Pete's sake! He keeps *sheep* on it."

"Sheep are good. They fetch good prices?"

"Sometimes," she said and admitted defeat. She knew that nothing she said would convince Anton that her uncle wasn't a wealthy sheep-farmer with money to spare, and who knows? That money might rub off on to this lucky girl and any friends she made on the way! "His island is a long way off and often very, very cold," she said, and hoped that Anton would forget about it.

The steamer stopped at three islands to pick up more

passengers and now they stopped at a tiny harbour from which another boat was leaving, packed to the gunwhales with people eager to visit Lucerne for the day. "We get off here," Anton said, "but there's no need to hurry. Most people rush to the gangway and over to the kiosk to buy tickets for the rack railway, but we can take the next one after buying our tickets at leisure so that we go up the mountain in less crowded conditions. I don't see another steamer that is likely to be here before the next carriages arrive."

They strolled over to the kiosk and bought tickets, watching the crowd who had bought red tickets, jostling for places in the overcrowded carriages. Anton put the green tickets that reserved places on the next train in his pocket. "We have half an hour," he said. "There is an inn round the corner where we can have an aperitif before ascending to our lunch at the top."

"It's so warm," Bridie said, closing her eyes for a moment against the sun.

"It is very warm here but I hope you have something to put on when we get further up the mountain. It can get very cold."

"That seems impossible when I sit here and watch the swans," Bridie said, as the graceful birds came closer to see if they had any bread or cake. "But I know you're right. At home the weather in the mountains can change in a very short time. I was once on the Cairngorms when we had a blizzard half an hour after the sun had been so hot that it made me want to take off my sweater. I have brought something to wear." She wished that she had a smart, tailored jacket with her instead of the button-up cardigan that went easily into her holdall, and once again knew that Bridget Mark must change her image now that she could afford to buy some more exciting new clothes.

"I'll order cool drinks," he said and when he came back he sat gazing out at the lake with expressionless eyes.

"You seem very quiet. Are you still dreaming of your island?" she asked in a teasing voice.

"No. I was thinking that there must be other ways of

getting what I want from life without selling myself to a rich woman." He said it so casually that Bridie smiled.

"At least you are frank about it," she said.

He seemed not to hear. "If you take away Carl Paterson, I know that I can still interest Maria and maybe even marry her, but now that I have met you, *chérie*, I know who I prefer. I would like to give you . . . everything, once I find my fortune."

"Don't be silly. I don't come into your scheme of things at all, Anton. You know that in your heart. I am here for a few days and back at home I have a job that I like and a future that could be interesting. I have enough boyfriends to fill my leisure time if I want male company."

"But I thought that all women wanted expensive clothes and jewels. We must write to each other and I shall come to London to stay with you, and when I make money I shall bring you back here."

Bridie laughed. To earn that money, Anton would have to marry Maria or another woman bowled over by his looks and charm, and it didn't seem a very good proposition to be asked back as his mistress! "Come on, the train will be waiting and they will call for holders of green tickets," she said.

The rack was creaking as the train descended and she stared up at the tall pines lining the track, half amused and half annoyed that Anton could envisage her as his lover. He wasn't exactly subtle, with his idea of dangling furs and jewels in front of her at some future time, in order to get her into bed now! What would they say at the manse? Poor Anton; if he only knew about her strict upbringing, he would never have such illusions.

The train stopped and Bridie climbed inside and sat by a window. From the train, the lake shrank to toy-town proportions. Tiny swans lay on a glass mirror and little people sailed in toy boats as the carriage took its load to the top of the mountain. Bridie looked down again. From here, everything was unreal, as unreal as the view of her clouded mountain seen from the plane. But, far out, a speck on the water was a reality that she wished she could forget; Maria in a fast boat with a handsome man at her side. With a determined smile she put him from her mind. Carl was enjoying his day off, so why shouldn't she?

"This was a wonderful idea, Anton," she said.

Seven

"There's no cloud! From below there was a faint haze but now it's all gone and I don't know if I'm disappointed or not," Bridie said.

"You can see the view more clearly," Anton suggested. "After all, that's what most people want to see! Or do you want to walk on cloud as the angels do?" He laughed. "Let's go up on the observation platform while it's still warm enough to do so."

The air was fresh and cool, but the sun warmed Bridie's bare arms and she hoped that she wouldn't have to put on the boring cardigan with its tiny buttons up to the neck. She knew it was a better option than the fur-fabric coat which would have been bulky and made her look overdressed, but it was hardly glamorous. It had seemed quite OK in the office but now it reminded her of her aunt and endless hand-knitting.

"Are you happy to be here?" Anton sounded anxious.

"Very. It was good of you to bring me and I shall treasure it as a very pleasant memory. I had no idea that the colours would be so vivid from this viewpoint." She gazed down at the lake, now a mere patch of deep blue, and at the slowly moving alpine cattle on the slopes, chewing the sweet grass and swaying their sonorous cowbells from thick necks. It was all so theatrical, as if set up for a scene from *The Sound of Music*. "We have cattle on the hills at home," Bridie said, "but our Highland cattle are quite different. They have shaggy coats of thick hair to protect them from the intense cold and give them warmth when it snows."

"It couldn't be colder than it is here in winter, surely? We have snow but it attracts thousands of tourists," said Anton.

"From the pictures I've seen of Switzerland, the sun shines and people sit back and get a good tan and never look cold," Bridie said.

"I suppose it's a dry cold with powdery snow," said Anton. "Very good for the ski; and the après-ski," he added with a laugh. "I was a ski instructor for a year or so. That's where I met Maria. Perhaps I shall do that again in my spare time. I met many rich people, and some who put business my way. Do you ski? It is like being a bird as you float down the mountain slopes."

"No, it's all my worst nightmares," Bridie said, firmly. "In any case I hate being cold and we have a lot of wet slushy snow at home, between good falls when the skiing is good, and even when the conditions are ideal for winter sports the wind can be terrible when it springs up and the sun goes in. It howls and freezes the hands and the blood! I think I'd rather have your winters if I have to endure snow at all."

"Ah, so there is something you want that money could buy! Tell me where you would really like to live if you had the chance to choose."

Bridie sat on a rock and gazed down at the sleepy valley. "I would like a castle in Scotland, a villa here for the summer and, if I had to do it, for the skiing; and, let's see, a very small Greek island! No, cancel the winter here. I'll be in the Greek Islands."

She looked up at him, expecting him to laugh at her ridiculous fantasy, but his eyes glowed with triumph. "I was joking! You can't believe that I was serious, Anton!"

"Everyone wants more than he has," he said, and reached across to put his arms round her. "Bridie, my darling, we could do such wonderful things together. We could work towards our dreams and then we could have all the beautiful things we need, and have wonderful places to live – fine houses, fast cars, everything." He kissed her astonished lips with a passion that she could hardly believe came from this smooth and calculating Swiss businessman. This was not the charm of the conventional flatterer, with studied ardour to make a woman think he was in love with her; it was real and almost harsh in its urgency.

"No, Anton," she said feebly. "You don't understand."

He kissed her again. "If you were mine and we worked together, I could move mountains and make money enough to give you everything." She resigned herself to sitting with his arm round her waist, but was relieved that other people now approached the high viewpoint. It had been a very pleasant experience to which her own body had begun to respond, but she recalled other lips on hers, without this intense passion; a kiss of sadness, loneliness and desperation, from a heart seeking consolation for a lost love. All the passion that Anton could give her wouldn't equal the effect that Carl's kiss had produced. This onslaught lit no flames but did add a tingle of sweet awareness to the perfect day.

"Does the mountain have this effect on you each time you come here?" she asked dryly. "The air must certainly have something special."

"No. I am used to mountains. I live here. The mountains do not make me love you. I just do love you, Bridie. I want you very badly, and together we could be so happy." He sounded less confident before her calmness and took away his arm. "I thought you liked me," he said sulkily.

"I do like you, Anton. I'll never forget that you were the first one to make me welcome in a strange land and to show me something of Switzerland. I've become very fond of you." She kissed his cheek gently, but drew away as he showed signs of seizing her again.

"I could make you love me. I could make you mad for me," he said. "Other women have loved me and followed me even when I was not in love with them. They have given me presents and been very willing to make love. I am not unhandsome? Unmanly?"

111

"You are not . . . unhandsome, or unmanly," she agreed. "Anton, I do like you very much, but today I have another love. I love this mountain and I shall see it for such a short time that I must take my fill of it. You talk of dreams and this is one of mine. Not jewels or furs or fine houses, but this clear air and the distant peaks and the lake down there more bright than any sapphire."

They walked beyond the look-out to a dip in the rocks where thousands of harebells hung blue heads and wild orchis showed pink among scrubby bushes. "Is there no edelweiss here?" she asked.

"Not here." Anton shook his head. "It is now forbidden to pick the flowers but, as there are many walkers on the slopes, the flowers do disappear. On the tourist slopes it is rare to see a gentian now." He pointed to a rock face that couldn't be reached by walkers, and Bridie saw the deep blue of gentians. "It is dangerous to climb there to pick them and so there are patches of flowers clinging to the rocks that are left to grow," he said.

"We have plants like that, growing in rocky places. There is one called Lad's Death, as young men used to climb to pick it for their sweethearts, and boasted of the dangers they suffered in the name of love, but I know of no case where a man died picking some."

They had a late lunch in the restaurant on the top of a plateau below the peak. The dim and cool room looked out on fine views from three sides and Bridie drank in the beauty until she thought she could take no more and found that once again, she was hungry.

Anton lost his amorous mood as quickly as it had taken over and Bridie wondered just how much of an act it was after all. He turned his attention to the menu and they chose salade niçoise, crusty bread and a light, dry wine. The food seemed to make him act more like the Anton she had first met, and he was once again amusing about places he had visited, and suggested beauty spots that she might like to see when next she came to Lucerne.

Bridie smiled and nodded in all the right places but watched him and wondered if he could ever be sincere. I must ask Sandra about him when I get back, she thought. Does he try it on with every new secretary who comes to the Astra or the Viceroy? One thing puzzled her. Why me? Why did he make a set at me when there were many pretty girls from many countries here, who were obviously open to a brief affair away from the prying eyes of home? Some girls were already having passionate sex with some of the senior delegates, who were high in the pecking order and could give them a very good time.

She looked down at her now dusty leather sandals and smiled. The other girls dressed well and were attractive, often giving a bold come-on that many men found hard to resist; and they had had time to plan their clothes for the smart congress, buying new and more daring numbers than they would ever wear at work, yet Anton hardly glanced at them when Bridie was with him. For him there were only two women, Bridie, and Maria who ignored him if Carl Paterson was there.

On the day when he appeared at her side and insisted on taking her to lunch, he could not have known anything about her except that she worked at Herald Enterprises, and her plain uninteresting dress gave no hint of the young and lovely body beneath it. I wouldn't have raised a whistle passing a building site, she decided ruefully, and nobody but Anton noticed my existence, so he must have been waiting to pick me out for his very special attention. He would have done that even if I had been, as Carl Paterson put it so succinctly, less than five foot nothing, with crossed eyes and too dumb to know which fork to use. She gave a start as his voice brought her back to the present time.

"Have you worked for Herald for a long time?" he asked with an almost too casual air.

"Oh, it's much too pleasant to talk shop," Bridie said. "Just look down in the valley. I can see a man walking up the path.

Do many walk all the way up the mountain? If I had the stamina could I walk it in one day?"

"You could if you wanted to be very tired after it. They walk from one station to the next and see if they want to walk on, and it's possible to pick up a train at any of the levels. I used to come part of the way by train to avoid the heat of the lower slopes and often came to the top and walked down in the cool. The air was cold but wonderful and very invigorating. I walked down when the weather was turning cold, the summer visitors had gone and the snow had not yet fallen to attract people to the ski lodges." He shrugged. "That is our slack time when we don't have to be nice all the time to tourists."

"You don't do that now?"

"I am not a ski instructor now. I am a businessman and I take my holidays as others do in my work, as and when we can, and as now, I mix business with pleasure."

"Did you wear those shorts?"

"The lederhosen? Yes. All Swiss walkers wear them or the knee breeches and socks." He smiled at her amusement. "I also have the socks of red and the suspenders for the lederhosen, in bright colours."

"And the hat?" Bridie giggled, peering down at a man striding up the path wearing lederhosen and a natty trilby-shaped straw hat with a feather in the side.

"Sometimes, but I do not play the long pipe that appears in all the travel brochures, nor do I make strange noises to call the cows!"

"You don't yodel? What a pity. This would be the perfect place to demonstrate it to me. I'd love to see what you can do."

"Come outside again and I'll show you what I can do," he whispered.

"If you don't behave, I'll take the next cable car down," said Bridie. "There's no need to try so hard to impress me. I hope that we are friends but you must never expect me to give you more than that, even if I do admit I find you attractive."

"That is sad. I am falling in love with you, Bridie." He frowned. "I wish it was not so. Only a few days ago I had my future planned and arranged very well. I thought that love could be a luxury to be enjoyed – how do you say it? – on the side, as many French do. I am partly French, partly German, but I was born in Switzerland and so have something of each country in my nature."

"If you knew me better, you would know that I am really very straight-laced and Scottish."

"What is that? Straight-laced sounds as if you are tied in a sack!"

She laughed, "Sometimes I feel as if I am. It has the same effect. For example, we aren't noted for showing our feelings in public."

"But you do have feelings! I know that to be true. You have soft lips, soft arms and a body to send a man wild when you dress as you did last night."

Bridie shook her head. "You don't understand. It's not a lack of feelings. It's just that we give ourselves to only one man and if we can't have the one we want then we do without and devote our lives to good works," she added the last as if it was a joke. She saw that he viewed this with scepticism and she looked at her watch. "How long does it take to get down to the Lucerne terminus by cable car? I have to be there by five."

Immediately, she had his full attention. "Why is that? You have a full day off and should not work."

"I had to type out some very confidential documents last night after dinner, and Carl had to finalise a few points today that must be faxed to London."

"He has asked you to come back just to do that?"

"Yes. It makes sense as he wants as few people to know about the new processes as possible. The work I've done here is the most secret material that I've seen since I joined Herald. I don't usually have access to anything of importance."

115

"If it is so confidential, why doesn't he do it himself instead of spoiling your day? I had made plans for us tonight."

"Carl wants me to finish what I began and I can see why. The portable typewriter I use here is the most awful instrument and if he used it he would get so angry that I'd be scared of him!" She laughed. "I doubt if he can type! Also, he hates using the fax and says that he dislikes answerphones and leaves others to sort out messages – he pays vast salaries to be relieved of such chores. Some bosses never type and when they are left alone with the dreaded instrument in an emergency, it shows!"

"Was the business to do with the countess?

"How did you know? I thought this latest deal was all a big secret. Mr Paterson told me to discuss it with no one. Did the countess tell you about the agreement they reached on the other one?"

"I know a little and I can guess much more. I know a big deal was discussed and I do have sources of information that they know nothing about." His face darkened. "Even when Maria is kind to me, she shuts me out of the one area where I could be of help to her, and of course make money for myself."

"But you hope to marry her and then be her confidant?"

He nodded. "She is a very disturbing woman who keeps me with her and yet not with her. She trusts nobody and yet expects me to find out much about the business discussed at these meetings and in the offices abroad."

"I can tell you nothing, Anton. I gave my word and, although I have been at the talks to help the delegates to understand each other, whatever has been agreed must remain with Mr Paterson until it's made public."

"I hoped that you would be more friendly," he said and his eyes held a caress, as if even now he was sure that she would be so attracted to him that he could ask what he liked.

"You flattered me and arranged this outing in the hope that I would talk about my employer and about Herald Enterprises, didn't you? Isn't there a name for that? Industrial espionage? Who would pay you for advance details of the new processes? Someone who could bring your dreams of riches nearer to reality?" Her voice was as cold as the blue-white snow on the peak.

"It was like that," he said, unhappily. "I thought it would be so until you smiled at me and seemed to like me a little. You looked so beautiful last night that I couldn't think about anything but you and how much I wanted you." He laughed. "I was so happy. I thought that I might be able to do both."

"Kill two birds with one stone?"

"That is very good!" For a moment he paused and forgot what he was saying as he tucked the phrase away in his mind for future use. He tried to take her hand but she drew away. "I didn't know that I was to fall in love with you, Bridie. You must believe me."

"No, I don't believe you. I think you tried to use me, possibly to get me so involved that I would have to do as you asked in the future, knowing that I would be in trouble with my employers if I helped you and was found out." She stood up. "How many women have you made love to in an effort to get trade secrets?"

"You are wrong! I swear that I had no thought of making trouble for you."

"Several times, you have tried to make me talk about my work. It ties in with the rest and I know now that I should never have come here with you. Please take me down to the terminus and then leave me. The sooner you forget about me the better for both of us."

"What will you say to Paterson?"

"Nothing. You surely don't think I have anything to boast about, do you? If he suspected that you tried to get information from me he could make life difficult for you, and in some ways for me, if he thought I was gullible enough to think that you were sincere."

"Why consider his opinion of you? Paterson thinks nothing

of women. He is cold and treats you all as worthless. He comes here and takes no pleasure in girls. Sandra said that—"

"So you *do* know Sandra! You dated her I expect, and told her how lovely she was and asked a lot of questions?"

"She was glad of my company and to be told that she is beautiful! She is angry with Paterson as he is so blind that he doesn't see her as anything but a machine. She works hard for him at these congresses and yet he sends her home as she came."

"As he will send me back," Bridie said. "I am here on business, not pleasure, although this has been a wonderful week that I shall never forget. In no way am I anything to Carl Paterson other than a secretary, just as Sandra is, and she should know that she is only another employee." She looked startled. "Sandra didn't tell you anything, did she?"

Anton looked sly. "Just a little when I gave her too much champagne, but nothing of real value. We have exchanged letters and she was looking forward to coming back to Lucerne. I was hoping for better luck with her this time."

Bridie stared at him in disbelief. He was so sure that what he did in this sickening trade was acceptable, that he had lost his caution and was prepared to boast of what he did. "Does the countess use you to get information?"

"It pays her to know in advance what might happen, and to know what to expect in negotiations with the opposition. She can then set her own price as low as possible if she is buying."

"What if she has already signed a deal with Herald? Your advice would be wasted."

"She knows that Paterson has another new invention under wraps that involves Dubois and others, and he has said nothing of that to her in spite of her generous agreement over the last deal."

"So she let you off the leash to try to make me tell you about it?" Bridie gave a tight smile. "Sorry, Anton. I'm afraid that Maria will not be pleased with you. I must be a great disappointment on every level. Maybe she will have better luck with Carl today, on her island."

"I think we have nothing more to say," Anton said with an air of hurt pride. "You are laughing at me and I do not like that. It is time we left and took the cable car. The cloud is forming and it will be colder soon."

Wisps of pale grey folded gently above the peak, but below it, the sun shone brilliantly on the lower slopes. Anton led the way to the nearly deserted platform from whence the bulbous cable cars commenced their downward swing. Two girls and two young guys filled the next car and Anton hung back to allow a couple to take the next one. "We could have gone with them," Bridie said. "If the mist forms, there will be a rush for the cars and they'll need all the space they can fill. They can take six at a time."

He grabbed her arm and almost pushed her into the next one and the attendant pulled over the safety bar and locked the door. It was like being in a bubble of air or a child's version of a space capsule or time machine. They were sealed in so that no accident could happen through falling from the windows on to the treacherous rocks far below, but Bridie sat down and held on to the seat while the wires above them sang.

First the car went up as if tossed on a cloud, then with a stomach-churning lurch they slipped over the platform edge and down the wires as if a giant hand hurled them towards the valley. They paused, sank lower and came to terms with the cables, flowing softly down through the cloud and out into the sunshine, that was now extra bright through the mainly glass cabin, over the tall pine trees covering the hillside.

They reached the first link and went over it with the same lurch that they had experienced at the beginning, and Bridie held on to the rail and closed her eyes. The wires sighed gently and she could feel nothing as they were propelled through space. The silence was unnerving both outside and inside the capsule, but as soon as the car was stable and moving freely, she opened her eyes.

Anton got up from his seat and advanced towards her. Bridie cringed back, scared at the dark and wild look in his eyes. "If I can't get the information I want, then I can at least have you!" He paused, suddenly pleading. "There is still time to tell me the outline of the talks and time for us to be real friends. Tell me we can be friends, Bridie. I want you more than I've wanted any woman in my life."

She shook her head and his mouth tightened. "Keep away," she cried. "Don't be silly, Anton! We shall be down soon and someone will hear if I scream."

"Listen! You can hear the wind in the wires but nothing more. We are too far above the valley to be seen or heard." She looked frantically back at the next car, and could distinguish nothing but vague figures, not as individuals, and certainly nothing she could do would attract their attention. His smile was hard. "There is time. I have done this before. Yes, in a car like this," he added as she seemed not to believe him.

With one hand he ripped away her cardigan, sending buttons to the floor like spilled driedbeans. Bridie put a hand out to protect herself and to shield her dress but he ripped the front fastening of the dress, too. His grip was overpowering as he forced her to the floor but Bridie fought with all her strength. She found that anger and fear made her strong and she pushed him back and away so that he stumbled.

She stood up, pale and trembling, her breath laboured and her eyes wide. He started towards her again, his face distorted with rage and frustration. He released the now painfully tight zip on his trousers and Bridie felt sick. "Please give me strength," she murmured through clenched teeth, then saw his expression change. He stared at her and stopped as suddenly as he had attacked her.

Bridie put a hand to the front of her dress where the modest snap-fastening of the thin cotton garment had parted but spared the fabric from being torn away. The white line of her bra over the taut mounds of her panting bosom, and the red

120

birthmark showed clearly on the swelling curves of her breasts and she felt very vulnerable. She began to do up the studs, two of which were bent and resisted her trembling fingers, closely watching the man who now crouched before her. She tensed, ready to be on guard against a further assault, but he made no further attempt to rape her. For a moment she thought that she had pushed him hard enough to hurt his back on the edge of the wooden seat but he didn't seem to be in pain.

"You lied!" he said. "You are not a virgin as I thought." He was stammering and fighting to speak clearly in English. "You said you were nothing to him and I believed that he could never notice you as a woman. Sandra cannot make him and she knows about men. You know nothing but he took you! I thought he would never care if I took you, but I see that you are his mistress." She almost shook her head to deny it but remained still and silent. "There is the proof, the mark of love, and what they say is true. You share his suite and you share his bed!"

For a moment, she stared uncomprehendingly, then an involuntary smile touched her lips. It wasn't possible! Not Anton, too? Even her fear and fury subsided as she sensed that he was no longer a threat, but she glanced down at the valley and knew that they had a long way to go before she was free and he might once again attack her. I must feed his suspicions, she decided. I have to pretend that what he says is true and that he has tried to rape the lover of one of the most powerful men in the software business.

"You and Paterson? Even Maria did not suspect that. She gave me orders to stay away from her while he was in Lucerne so that they could do business and I know that she wanted to take him as her lover, but she said nothing of you, except that I was to talk to you, give you too much wine and find out all I could before she signed anything."

"So you went after me on Maria's orders?"

"No, I was to flatter you and try to give you too much wine but she didn't tell me to fall in love with you."

121

"Love? Don't you mean sex? You certainly made it clear that you wanted me, but as for love, I doubt if you know the real meaning of that word. You would sell your soul for that island and for the wealth that goes with it, and you would do that even if Maria wasn't as beautiful as she is."

He put his head in his hands. "I was mad. I wanted you so much and I was angry, but I was mad to try to take you. I do want you and you are wrong to say I don't love you. If you would come away with me I swear that I would make a life for us in other place."

"And what would I be expected to do? Find a position of trust again so that you could steal confidential information? Tell me, what is the drill? I gather the information and have the papers photocopied before handing the copies to you?" She gave him a scathing look and picked up the scattered buttons, putting them carefully in her purse. "What do you take me for, Anton? What sort of a life would that be for someone you profess to love?"

"I'm sorry. I'm confused. I've never met any woman as honest as you and I just don't know what to do." He looked up at her with a kind of panic in his eyes. "If Paterson found out that I had tried to make love to his woman he would ruin me," he said. "Not only with my business but with Maria. Such a man, who does not take a woman lightly for pleasure, would be hard, and he must never know that I touched you with desire."

"I'm sure that you are right," Bridie said, but knew that Carl's anger would not be for her and her safety but a protective anger to make sure that anything connected with Herald Enterprises must be kept safe.

Carl's real love would remain with the one woman he had loved and lost, and he was free to enjoy the company of other women without being deeply involved. Bridie thought of him handing her into the car with strong cool hands and the hard bitter kiss he had forced on her mouth as if in desperation, then she recalled the easy way he smiled at Maria, kissing her in greeting and paying court with all his charm. Was there much difference between these two men? They could both use charm to get what they wanted. Was Carl falling in love with Maria? Could a man like him be snared by those birdlike hands that scratched for money and power?

"Bridie, you said you liked me, and I am very sorry that I was rough with you. Can you forgive me?" His nervous smile was ingratiating. "Do you want to ruin me? Can you? Is it too much to ask you to keep quiet? Would you say that . . ." Anton was in despair. Bridie said nothing but saw to her relief that the car had reached the final platform, with just one more sweep down into Lucerne town and, below them, the blue mirror that had seemed so tiny, now became a huge lake again, with ripples at the edges and swans grooming white feathers. Tiny boats with real sails floated across the calm surface and flowers nodded by the reed margin of the shore.

In the distance, a lake steamer sounded its siren in salute to another passing boat, the umbrellas on a hotel balcony were no longer tiny doll's parasols, and a motor boat made rainbow spray as it plied from the green island that belonged to the Countess Maria.

The cable car came to a halt and the attendant unhitched the bar and unlocked the door. Bridie had combed her hair and managed to make the damaged snap fasteners clip back to close the front of her dress, and, apart from the lack of buttons on her cardigan, she looked normal. There was no sign of the struggle high above the pines.

"Bridie?" He walked beside her and she avoided his outstretched hand, then stopped and turned to face him.

"I have no wish to be embarrassed by anyone knowing what happened today up there," she said. "I can't think what made you act like that or what made you think I'd be willing to cheat on the firm I work for, but at least you've been honest enough to tell me your real motives in getting to know me."

"You will say nothing to Carl Paterson?" he said, eagerly.

"I will say nothing unless you do anything to harm Mr Paterson or Herald Enterprises."

"You love him very much?"

"Carl Paterson is my employer," she said in a flat voice. "You might as well know, whether you believe it or not, that he is not my lover."

He laughed, confident now that he was safe from Paterson and his anger. "*Je crois*," he said, insolently. "I believe you! *Zut alors*, it is not possible. He is the man with whom you share a suite, and you have not been with any other man here except me! A woman does not have a mark like that from a flea!"

Bridie smiled, grimly. "I have no intention of showing you my birthmark more clearly but that is what it is; a red birthmark I have had all my life."

His face showed utter disbelief and amazement. "Do you make that excuse each time it happens? You say this now so that I shall not tell anyone, but what you say is a lie. I know a love bite when I see one. I should know." He grinned. "Some ladies like it rough!"

"You make me sick," she said. "I don't care if you believe it or not. It happens to be true and if I hear one word that shows that you have done anything devious against Carl Paterson I shall tell him everything that you told me and what you tried to do to me."

For a moment, the fear returned in his eyes, then his face cleared. "You tell me this, but how was it that at the banquet you had no redness?"

"Remember? I wore a butterfly to hide it." He looked uncertain. "I stuck it on with spirit glue if you must know. Monique gave me some because make-up didn't hide it."

Anton took out a cigarette from the silver case and lit it from a gold lighter. He seemed amused. "To think that all the evening I wanted to kiss the place where the butterfly rested and make love to you. That was so little time ago and here we are back again in Lucerne as if nothing had happened to make me change my mind."

They walked to the sunlit square by the terminal, where a café area was half-filled with people from the cable cars. "I think that today is better forgotten," she said. "Neither of us wants it made public, do we?"

"No, I have no wish to tell people that I failed to make love to a woman I wanted, and that you have another lover who pleases you better," he said with a sneer.

Bridie sat on a chair under an awning. "There is one more thing that you must do," she said, sweetly.

"Anything," he said, cautiously.

"I have to meet Carl here and I'd like tea while I wait for him."

He went to the café and brought back a tray of tea and biscuits. Bridie gave him a bright smile. "Goodbye, Anton. It's been . . . interesting meeting you."

He put down the tray and regarded her in silence for a moment or two, then said, "You can't win. He will marry Maria and we shall both be left. I am good at waiting, and you will come to me later." He turned away and walked rapidly to the rank of buses.

Eight

"Your shirt is soaking!" was all that she could find to say. Carl Paterson had come very quietly to her table and she had no idea how long he had been in the café, hidden by the many small tables with wide sun-umbrellas.

"Tea? What a good idea," he said and lifted a hand to attract service, although most people were carrying their own trays. "Had a good day?" he asked.

"It's been very warm," she said. He sat at the other side of the table, regarding her pensively. "But you must have kept cool in all that spray," Bridie said to break the silence. "Was it a rough ride? That boat certainly shifts fast."

"I might ask you the same. Did you have a rough ride, Bridie?" he said, quietly. "Everything all right?"

"Fine," she said through dry lips. Had he noticed her tension? Although the experience in the cable car had ceased to make her tremble, she knew that she was pale and might seem strained, and she saw that he didn't quite accept what she said. "I'm a little tired," she admitted. "There was more to the trip than I'd imagined."

"Obviously," he said, cryptically. "Where's your escort?" He touched the teapot that Bridie had used. "Still warm but only one cup? He hasn't been gone for long and he left you all alone?"

"Yes, Mr Sherlock Holmes, he brought me some tea and then left to see to other business."

"Elementary, my dear Watson," he replied gravely. Fresh tea arrived and Bridie poured it from the white china pot.

"You came back early," Carl said. "Was it too much for you up there at the top?"

"No, why should it be? I did find the atmosphere a bit rarified but it's a high mountain."

"I wondered if your clouded mountain came up to your expectations or was it overwhelming?"

"Don't," she said softly. "Pilatus isn't my clouded mountain. That's a private dream, an abstract personal thing." She smiled and said in a more normal voice. "Besides, there was no cloud, just blue skies and fine views and warm sunshine. It was breathtaking; the lake looked so small and the people below were like insects. The islands almost disappeared and looked like mounds of green weed."

"It can be beautiful. I went up there once, long ago," he said.

"I saw you on the boat today. Anton said that the island is very lovely. It must be wonderful to own such a place of your own. He envies the countess very much for her island."

"He may well own it one day if he plays his cards right and is a good boy."

"Is that possible? I gathered that he didn't rate his chances very high with her." She watched him, seeking some indication that he was upset by the thought of Anton taking away what could easily be his own if he reached out a hand to grasp it.

"Who knows? Maria is a very secretive woman at times." He frowned. "I don't know what she is driving at half the time. A man can't pin her down to any agreement until she has a very tight commitment, and then once she has decided, everything goes smoothly and the deal is settled with almost too much haste." He laughed. "When she finally chooses a second husband, it will be the same. She drives some men mad!"

"Men like to be kept guessing, don't they?"

"Sometimes, and only for a while. Beyond that it gets tedious and some men find it wearing and get bored waiting for a woman to reveal her true feelings."

"I thought that her feelings were clear enough," Bridie said, recalling the ruby ring and the slim hands stroking Carl's arm as they walked close together on the terrace, her perfume wafting seductively under his nostrils. "Is she in love with you?" she asked impulsively.

He smiled, enigmatically. "I thought that all women knew when another woman was in love." He sipped his tea and reached over for another piece of torte. "Stop me, or I'll have no appetite for dinner." He looked at the piece of rich pastry with regret and left it on the dish.

"Is there another dinner tonight? I don't have to go to this one, do I?"

"I thought you enjoyed seeing how the other half live." He smiled. "No, you don't need to go to this one." He pushed away his cup. "I'd like to thank you again for the work you've done here and for your help at the banquet. I found you a great social asset, Bridie." She stared. He was serious and her heart beat so fast that she thought he must hear it, but his manner was formal and made a barrier that forbade her to speak as she wished to do.

"You looked lovely, except for the butterfly," he said.

"I thought you admired it," she said weakly. Had he forgotten everything?

"It was pretty and it filled in the neckline well, but it was ruined for me by what it concealed."

"But it isn't what you thought," she began.

"Gesner was right. What you do in your free time is your own business and I have no intention of discussing it now or later. Understood?"

Imperiously he called for the bill and stood up. "Sorry I dragged you back early. There are two messages to send, but I find that there is less than I thought and if you want to resume your day off and your date, I can send them. I expect you have plans for this evening and will want to change, unless Holy Disciple sandals and a cardigan with no buttons turn him on?"

Bridie blushed and set her lips. There was just no way that she could explain when he was in this mocking yet distant mood. "I'll do the faxes," she said. "They don't take long and the pressure on the facilities will be off now that most of the secretaries have left. I can do them quickly as soon as we get back to the Astra."

Slow anger made her revert to being what he wanted; a calm and efficient pair of hands; someone to leap to his bidding and get the necessary work done. I can't just say, 'By the way, the mark isn't a love bite, it's a birthmark. You did know that, I presume?' He'd look at me with those cynical eyes and laugh, she thought, and the imagined scene was too painful to contemplate.

"Why bother to explain now or in the future? His attitude to her would be the same in a million years, once he had made up his mind about her, and he'd still think that she was making flimsy excuses for a sordid little episode. She glanced at his set face and knew that he was deeply shocked even if he said that the matter didn't concern him, and the fact that she had been with Anton Gesner all day had made it worse. Wearily, Bridie picked up her holdall. He must think her a fast worker if he believed Anton had got that far during a lunch break on her first day in Switzerland – there was certainly no way that he could have come to her room in the shared suite.

I thought that I could judge character. Bridie looked back with longing to that first day when she had been carefree, sitting at a table eating fondue with a very handsome Swiss, who entertained her and impressed her with his honesty, friendliness and his lighthearted view on life.

"Where is the dinner tonight? At the Astra?"

"Why do you want to know if you aren't going?"

"I ought to know where to find you if there are any messages for you," she said. "I suppose if you leave a number at reception it would find you."

"No need," he said, firmly. "You are still off duty as soon as we send the faxes."

He drove back and they walked over to the office where the main business had been discussed and found it almost empty. "At what time do you meet your friend?" he asked.

"I've made no arrangements," she said. "I doubt if I shall see Anton again."

"What a brief affair!"

"It wasn't an affair. It didn't develop into one," said Bridie, coldly.

"Oh, Bridie! No . . . it's nothing. So, you are having dinner alone?" He seemed politely interested.

"Yes, I suppose so. I hadn't really given it any thought. I took it for granted that I would have work to do and might snatch a quick supper in the coffee bar, but if you don't need me then I might explore Lucerne. It would be a shame to go back having seen nothing of the old city but the terminus, and the top of a mountain."

"I've been here many times and never made it yet." He sighed. "Business meetings are like being in airports. All in very glamorous places but the unlucky delegates see nothing, or at least they see less than the secretaries on their days off."

"You had time off today," Bridie reminded him, remembering the arrogant stance of the man at the helm of the powerful boat and the breeze whipping Maria's silk scarf across her shoulders.

"Partly business," he said. "I know how air crews must feel. They go across the world and see little more than the hotel where they stay and the airports, and have to try hard to think where they are: if it's Tuesday we must be in Africa and I hope I have the right jabs for any bugs that find me on the tarmac! That sort of thing."

"What a waste. You said that some delegates take extra time off and make it a holiday."

"Do you want to take some leave now and come back later?" he asked, and she was aware of a pulse beating in his temple.

131

"No, when I have my real holiday, I hope I shall know in advance and be able to pack more suitable clothes."

He lingered in the office while she made the necessary contacts. It was over in twenty minutes and she wondered why he had bothered to ask her to come back for so little that seemed of importance – it was certainly nothing secret. One of the staff in the hotel could have done the work easily with no risk to Herald security.

"Well, that's it for today," he said. "I refuse to do any more work this evening."

She raised her eyebrows. "I thought it was me doing the work. You could have left the papers in the suite for me to collect and not bothered to be here. You did nothing but look over my shoulder!"

"Ah, but I've been working today," he said. "I work a lot behind the scenes. You've no idea how hard." She smiled. Was it hard labour to sit in a wonderful boat with a beautiful woman who looked as if she could eat him, and probably would if she was given the chance? They had stopped off to visit several islands and had had lunch on Maria's island. Hard cheese! she thought.

"I think I'll skip the dinner and see something of Lucerne," he announced as if that was all his own very good idea.

"You should," she said as he opened the door of the car that had taken them back to the Viceroy. "With a courier like the countess, you will see more than the average tourist." He glanced at her with suspicion, but her face was smooth and guileless. "What will you do about dinner? Do you want me to reserve a table somewhere for you and send your apologies to the organiser of the dinner at the Astra?"

"No, this is your day off. I shall do what is necessary," he said. He looked down at his still-damp shirt. "If you have no objection I'd like to shower first and get changed. I take it that you are in no great hurry now that you have no date?" He gave a slight shiver.

"Please go ahead. You'll get chilled if you stay in that wet shirt," she said.

"If I ache I know where I can find an excellent masseuse," he replied with a grin. "It would be better to have two bathrooms but the suite is usually for couples or families and not two separate people as we are, and before now I've always found it adequate. I'll try to be quick." He was almost apologetic.

"I'm in no hurry. I have some cards to write and some buttons to sew on."

"By the way," he said casually. "If you eat in the old city it might be an idea if you ask the girl at the desk where a single girl can eat safely alone and where you can get good food."

"Thank you. I'll do that. I'll ask her where she eats if she's alone."

She shut the door of her room and looked for sewing thread, wondering how many girls would sit in a bedroom, sewing on buttons when they were in one of the most exciting resorts in the world? The idea of going out alone took the edge off any anticipation and she sighed. She glanced round at the bedroom. It was solidly built, tastefully furnished and very warm and comfortable. The view of the garden under a blue sky made her wish that she was there, not as a paid secretary but as a woman in love, and beloved. This was the perfect setting for a honeymoon.

She sewed on the rest of the buttons. The evening was a void to be filled alone somehow. Fleetingly she wondered where Anton would be. If Carl was dancing attendance on Maria, Anton would be free to wander where he liked and she dreaded meeting him again in Lucerne. He was such a mixture of apparent sincerity and blatant dishonesty that she knew it was unsafe to be near him. His swift transition from violence to abject pleading love was frightening, and yet she knew if she met him again and he was his old boyish and attractive self, she might wonder if she had dreamed his outrageous behaviour.

It was easy to see how he could charm Maria when she was in the mood for him and he used all his magnetism and sensuality. I wish he'd charm her for ever, she thought resentfully. Even if I know that Carl can never be in love with me, I'd hate to see him tied up to Maria. She could make any man lose his identity and force her own personality on him if he loved her, making him less of a man.

Once again, images of the warmth between Carl and Maria told her that she hated the thought of him being in love with any woman, not just Maria. I'm jealous, she decided. I've never really been jealous of anyone until now, but I'd cheerfully throw her into the lake! It's stupid to think like this but there's nothing I can do about it.

"Bathroom's free." Bridget finished the last of the cards and put stamps on them, thinking how much prettier most foreign stamps were than the ones at home. She slipped the cards into her bag for posting and gathered up her toilet bag.

The bathroom smelled of expensive aftershave, and a very masculine-looking sponge bag lay on a chair. It was disturbingly intimate to be taking a bath in the room where he had showered his lean, hard body behind the semi-opaque glass screen. Bridie ran a bath of warm water and added oil of jasmine which took over the scents in the damp air. She inhaled it with relief as the overpowering masculinity of the room was dulled.

It was as if a lover had paused close to her and then passed by, but there hadn't been any physical contact, just a soft yearning for the impossible. She slipped out of her clothes and stepped into the bath. As she soaped her hands and smoothed them over her body, she discovered that she was using his soap. A ripple of awareness sprang from her fingers to each part of her body touched by the white froth. It was a second-hand caress that sent ripples of desire along her spine.

She touched the birthmark that had made Carl believe that she was having a passionate interlude with Anton, the same mark that had in turn convinced Anton that it was Carl's mistress that he had tried to rape, and not just a woman in whom he had no more than a professional interest. It had protected her from Anton but had put Carl Paterson so far away that the furthest star might be closer and a lot warmer!

Bridie dried herself on the soft blue towels and put on clean underwear. If I was alone or with another girl, I could wash my smalls and hang them over the bath to dry, she thought, then giggled as she imagined the look on Carl's face if he came into the bathroom and found a line of washing. At least I shall be back in London before I run out of clean clothes. What a good thing I pack too much.

She tied the belt of her kimono tightly and peeped out of the bathroom. The sitting room was empty and she could hear no sound from Carl's room, so she hurried back to her bedroom and shut the door. As she sat on the bed and did her nails, she saw the golden evening sun and heard sounds of laughter filtering up through the windows. To be here in Switzerland was wonderful but to be alone was not.

Listlessly, she chose a pale green T-shirt and a soft brown circular skirt covered with muted rust-red flowers that she had bought ready for the summer and never worn until now. It was too hot to wear anything heavy now that she was back on lake level, and thinking that she might walk quite a long way, she put on the low sandals that Carl had openly despised. I can please myself what I wear. I shall see nothing of Carl tonight unless we meet after he comes back from dining with Maria.

She waited for the elevator to reach her floor and entered the slow-moving cage that groaned on the way down to the lobby. She remembered the postcards and looked around for a postbox, then asked the girl in reception if there was one in the hotel.

"It will go quicker if you post it outside, just along the road," the girl said.

"Is it on the way to the town? And how far is it to the old bridge?"

She handed in her key and the girl glanced at the number of the suite and then smiled. "If you take the first turning to the left after the postbox, then go through an old square, you come to a road that cuts through and takes you the pretty way." She handed Bridie a small local map. "This may help," she said. "If you want a good restaurant, I can tell you of a very nice one where I go sometimes. It's in that direction. Here's a card to show you where it is."

"I might eat alone," Bridie said.

"Yes, that's where you must eat tonight," the girl said again. "It takes care of women alone, or with anyone."

Bridie smiled gratefully, knowing what an ordeal it would be to enter a strange place and eat alone when she was feeling really shy. This sounded like a place where she could fade into the walls without fear of being pestered by stray men on the make. Even allowing for the fact that the girl had a supply of cards for various restaurants and would possibly take a rake-off for any new introductions, it was still a good idea, and she took the card and examined the small picture of the many window-boxes and the tubs of flowering trees flanking the doors. It looked delightful and she hoped that it wasn't too expensive, but if the girl used that restaurant then it must be reasonable and just what was needed.

Off the main road, Bridie didn't feel conspicuously alone, and began to enjoy looking at the sleepy hotels under their coverings of trailing vine leaves. Scarlet geraniums tossed flamenco skirts over balconies in a profusion never achieved in Britain, and local people strolled towards the town on evening promenades. Waiters appeared in the doorways of bistros, inviting custom, but Bridie decided to wait until she saw the restaurant that had been suggested. I needn't go there, she thought, but it does looked good on the picture. I can turn back if I'm disappointed, and suddenly she felt free and more confident; but only for a few minutes.

She stopped before a heavy door with black hinges and

studded with ornamental nails. Hanging baskets made a riot of colour and the scent of roses came up from a sunken garden behind the hedge. She caught a glimpse of a broad terrace. Candles glowed through cut-glass bowls on small intimate tables and everything was far more elegant than Bridie had expected.

She looked at the card again. This was the right address but surely a receptionist couldn't afford to come here alone, or want to do so! It looked very expensive and had the leisurely appearance of a trysting place for lovers, where they could meet and hold hands across a small table in the flattering light of the candles.

A bubble of misery rose in her throat. She wanted to sob as she turned away. If only she could be here with Carl as he had been before he saw the damning birthmark. Even in his most abrasive mood she would have found him to be wonderful as a companion, but now that one simple innocent thing had put her far beneath any woman he might want or love.

There were hundreds of eating places, much more suitable, she decided. A pizzeria or a snack bar, or even the cafeteria of a campsite, where people came and went and nobody would notice a girl alone, mingling with the crowd. She could take a place at an almost-full table without rousing comment, and she might find someone to talk to.

"I'm sorry," she said, and then gasped.

"You were far away," Carl said. "Do you always step back without warning and stamp on people's toes?" He rubbed his instep with exaggerated force.

"Is this where you are having dinner?" she asked.

"Yes, it's highly recommended, but what are you doing here?"

"I wanted to walk down to the lake and over the old bridge, and have something to eat on the way, but I think the girl at the desk who suggested this place made a mistake." She shrugged. "They get used to directing the delegates and forget that there are secretaries eating alone. She knows I am with

the congress and must have taken it for granted that I was
going to meet up with others later." She began to walk away.
"*Bon appetit*," she said, then registered that he wasn't dressed
formally. His clothes, although well-cut and good, were not
really suitable for dining with Maria if she dressed as she
usually did in the evenings. Even if he'd changed his plans and
was going to the formal dinner, the clothes were not right for
business either, or for him to sit patiently listening to endless
boring speeches.

"Where do you think you're going?" he sounded patient
and his voice was the one he might have used to stop a child
running too close to a busy road. "It's far too early to walk by
the lake. It's hot and noisy there until the day visitors have
gone back in their coaches to the campsites and hotels away
from the lake. I advise eating here."

"I can't impose on your privacy," she said. "You are
meeting someone."

"Don't you listen? I said that I had done enough work for
today and would be exploring Lucerne. Would it be too much
of a sacrifice to give up your evening and eat with me?" He
regarded her with unsmiling eyes. "I hate eating alone. You
don't have to join me, but I'd take it as a favour. If you met
another colleague in a strange place you'd get together even if
you didn't really like each other, wouldn't you? Soon we'll be
back in the UK and you need never see me except in the office
but, here, I'd like to buy you dinner."

"You don't have to do this," Bridie said.

"I don't have to do a lot of things but I want to do this. I'll
try to make this a pleasant evening. I owe you this for the way
you helped me at the banquet and with Dubois." He smiled
more naturally. "Quite frankly you amazed me. A lot of
people went out of their way to tell me how impressed they
were."

"If you put it like that, how can I refuse?" Bridie forced a
smile. It would be heaven to sit with him by the light of the
flickering candles, and yet pure hell to know that he was only

doing his duty by a good employee for whom he had no feelings other than respect for efficiency.

Carl went ahead and she wondered why he was shown at once to the best table overlooking the lake. The waiter removed the reserved sign from the table and pulled out her chair.

"This table was reserved," Bridie said, nervously. "Are you sure there wasn't a mistake?" The restaurant was filling up fast and she saw two couples trying to persuade a waiter to let them sit at a table with a reserved label on it, but to no avail as he shook his head and they were shown to other seats.

"I rang and reserved a table," Carl admitted. "I wanted to dine here tonight."

"Did the countess stand you up?" she asked, and laughed to make it sound light.

"Something like that," he said with a wry grin. "But if you intend talking about Maria all evening, then I'll take you back to the Viceroy with no supper." He handed her the large menu and the waiter hovered deferentially. "Hurry up and choose what you like. I'm hungry and I hope you are too. That's another thing in your favour, Bridie, You aren't afraid to eat."

"Are you calling me greedy?"

"You said it, I didn't." Bridie began to enjoy herself. Now that they kept to trivia as their source of conversation, the atmosphere lifted and she saw that the menu was full of delicious items that had no resemblance to the starvation helpings of nouvelle cuisine. She watched Carl taste the wine and approve it.

'Ah, fill the cup,' she thought. How did the poem go? 'What boots it to repeat how time is slipping underneath our feet? Unborn tomorrow and dead yesterday; why fret about them if today be sweet?'

"That's better; you're smiling," Carl said. "I'm scared of Scottish girls when they scowl at me."

"I never scowl. I would hate to copy you," she replied.

"*Touché*. Now to the serious business of food." He took the first segment of cool melon and Parma ham that preceded the grilled trout and salad, and they discussed the people they'd met at the congress and the schedule for returning to London.

"We've finished here, so we can leave tomorrow," he said, as if sure that she would welcome the news. "When we get back, I want you to carry on with the work we did here. Sandra hasn't been involved with this deal and we might as well keep it to as few people as possible."

He refilled the glasses. "I also want you to set out the documents for another deal with Dubois. This is highly confidential, you understand. It must be kept secret until it has been finalised." He laughed. "Don't look so serious. It isn't really a cloak-and-dagger business, but we do have to take precautions or lose out. I promise that this is all the shop talk I intend for tonight, but this was too good an opportunity to miss as we are here alone. When we get back I may be tied up with other matters so I want you to be quite clear of my wishes for your work on your return. You take instructions from me and from no other person at Herald, and certainly not from anyone working in your office who thinks she might be above you in rank."

He went into more detail and Bridie realised that this was just the kind of deal that Anton and others would like to know about in advance.

"Thank you for making it clear," Bridie said. "I like to know what is expected of me. Just one thing bothers me. Sandra is my senior. What if she asks about the deal? This is really her department and I am only filling in for her while she is sick. It could be awkward. What do I say to her?"

"Just say that I want to put her in the picture myself and that the part you are doing is a small piece that doesn't give any indication of what is happening."

"That's a relief. I'd hate her to think I was after her job."

"Did Gesner try to find out anything about Herald?" Carl rapped it out and Bridie nearly spilled her wine.

"He *was* interested, but I discouraged him very firmly."

He looked at her as if trying to read her mind, then smiled. "I'd pity any industrial spy who tried to get anything out of a girl from a Scottish manse if she didn't want to talk. Thank you, Bridie; I believe you."

"You really think that he's an industrial spy?" She tried to sound surprised.

"As if you didn't know! But I do believe you would keep secrets even during pillow-talk." He flushed with annoyed embarrassment. "I apologise. That was unforgivable. That is no business of mine. Now shall we forget work and all the grubby little people with whom honest folk like us have to deal?"

Her lip quivered but she controlled herself. He's a brute, she told herself. Was there much difference between him and Anton? Anton used charm to get secrets and Carl used charm and condemnation to get what he wanted and to mould her to do as he wished.

Music stole into the candle glow. The faces of the diners softened and took on the beauty of youth and the dusky evening. Bridie glanced across at Carl and found him staring at her. "Your eyes are darker tonight," he said. She lowered her gaze and examined the pattern on her plate. His own eyes had been tender and she wondered if she could ever hate him! He was a devil who put a knife in her heart to wound her, then twisted it so that she bled frustation and misery. When he relented and said sweet things that he couldn't mean or know how they affected her, she suffered even more.

"It's the dim light," she said. " 'Every cat in the twilight's grey, even a tortoiseshell cat,' " she quoted.

"But candle-light is golden, not grey." he said. "Like the specks of gold in your eyes. Did your mother or a good fairy scatter gold dust when you were born? Oh, you are laughing now and that makes the gold appear."

Bridie lost track of time. She knew that she was being

entertained by a man who knew about women. She knew that he would forget her as soon as she was out of sight but she wanted to treasure the evening as she did the memory of the banquet. She wiped the last of the cream from her lips and wondered if she would ever have such delicious food again. Carl gave a sigh of repletion. "We need to walk," he said. "Coffee later?"

Her pulse quickened. So, the evening wasn't over. They walked through the dusk and silently crossed the road. Streams of cars and coaches laden with passengers were going away from the town to other lakes, other towns, other campsites, leaving the waters of Lucerne to lap the pillars of the empty pier, and the doves to settle on the roof of the ancient bridge for another night.

The bridge creaked as the warmth of the day receded, allowing the timbers to contract. The water was still, a dim mirror on which a row of white doves lay, replicas of the ones drowsily cooing on the roof. Bridie paused to look through one of the glassless windows along the sides of the bridge and saw well patronised cafés on the shore and children still playing by the water. Carl stood close to her and she was conscious of his hand resting near her arm as he leaned on the window ledge.

"It's so beautiful," Bridie said. "It's like an old oil painting of ancient Lucerne. From here, it's not easy to see the detail of clothes, only the muted colours. It could be any period in history."

"Of course. I suppose they had old Swiss soft drinks advertisements on the sun umbrellas way back in the seventeenth century," he said with a teasing smile.

"You have no soul!" she said. "I expect that you haven't even noticed the paintings under the roof?"

"On the contrary; after you mentioned them I was determined to see them. I bought a guidebook and read about them. Come and be educated!"

They walked slowly along the length of the bridge and he

pointed up at one picture after another. Age had dimmed several to pastel tones, but most were clear enough for them to make out what was represented. Carl told her the story of early invaders and the way that the Swiss defended their land. Heroic tales were depicted in immortal paintings, under which thousands of visitors passed each year, some completely unaware of the treasures spread out on the ceilings overhead.

Bridie listened, her lips parted and her eyes shining. He paused at the point halfway over the bridge and they looked out again. The shore was a mass of small lights from the flickering candles of the cafés. Laughter, softened by distance came over, and in the sound Bridie could imagine the hidden ghosts of ancient Switzerland, unseen in the darkness that now hid the doves. Night fell with soft murmurings on the water and the lazy stroke of a swan's wing.

From time to time, Carl glanced at the vivid face beside him and his eyes were full of pain. So innocent to look at and surely it was impossible that she and that little tyke Gesner could . . . Bridie drifted along on a cloud of content. What of tomorrow, if today be sweet?

They crossed the rest of the bridge and found an empty table on the other side, by the water. The air was still soft and warm and Carl ordered coffee and biscuits in spite of Bridie protesting that she had already eaten far too much. He smiled when she absentmindedly reached for a second biscuit and began to nibble it.

People in holiday clothes walked by and a distant clock struck a half-hour to remind her that time was passing. Tomorrow I have to leave all this, she thought with a flood of sadness and Carl saw her change of expression.

"Tomorrow, we leave," he said, echoing her thoughts. "Are you glad to be going home to pick up the threads of your own life?

"Not glad, not sorry. It's a curious mixture. I've had a wonderful change as if I have been on holiday and yet I know

I've worked hard and done my best, so I am ready to leave."
She shivered slightly.

"Are you cold?" He stood up and asked for the bill. "If you
are, we can go back, but I'd hoped to walk along the shore for
a while."

"I'm not cold. Just a goose walking over my grave, as they
say, but what bad thing could happen here?" They started to
walk back across the bridge and once more it was fairyland. A
stall, with a boy in charge hoping to get the very last
customers willing to buy, had sandals, Swiss cheeses, hand-
bags and shawls. Bridie found herself alone and looked back
to see what was delaying Carl. He was buying something at
the stall.

Carelessly, as if he had bought a stick of seaside rock or a
bar of chocolate of no particular value, he flung a heavy pure-
silk shawl round her shoulders.

"I can't accept this!"

"Well, I'd look very silly if I wore it," he said. "I assure you
that this is a very selfish gesture. I don't want to go back yet
and I can't have you dying of pneumonia!" Bridie arranged
the folds of silk over her arms and in the headlights of a car
swinging into a hotel car park, she saw just how pretty it was.

The lakeshore was made up of pebbles and shingle. The
moon hid behind light cloud and Carl put out a hand to
steady her as Bridie slipped on the shifting path, and her hand
remained in his warm clasp. She felt cherished and warm, the
sensual touch of silk and his nearness making her want to turn
to him to give him her lips, her body and her life. Why can't
you know instinctively that I am not Anton's woman? she
wanted to say, but there were no words.

The silent lake glittered, and above the rim, lit dimly in the
fitful light, the mountains rose into a wreath of cloud. "It's
just as well you went to the top of the mountain today," Carl
said. "Tomorrow you would see nothing but cloud. The
pressure of his hand increased. "Why were you so upset
today, Bridie?" It wasn't an accusation but a need to know,

and only sadness and not anger came over to her in his voice.

"Upset? I wasn't upset."

"You were sitting at the table in the café, tied into knots of tension. I watched you for a few minutes before I came over to you. What happened on the mountain that had that affect on you?"

"It was nothing."

"Don't lie to me, Bridie. It made me angry to watch you. What did Gesner do to make you look so fraught? Did he try to get information about Herald or was it more than that?" He smiled, grimly. "Mountains can make people lightheaded and careless, and the ride down in the cable car can be romantic or dangerous." His insistence made her reply.

"You decided before I went up to Pilatus with him that he would try to get information, and as I told you, I handled that quite easily. I told you I would never tell him anything and I kept to that promise. Can't you believe me?"

"I wasn't worried about your integrity as far as our business is concerned, but I was worried about the manner in which he would ask you. Why do you think I insisted that you meet me at five? A bit early to finish a wonderful day out, wasn't it? I didn't want to ruin your pleasure but I couldn't trust Gesner with you up there on the mountain after dark."

She gasped and began to struggle for words.

"Now don't bother to tell me that you can look after yourself," he said, sternly. "Listen to me! I trust you implicitly to keep the secrets of the firm, but you are a very vulnerable and inexperienced woman and I know that man! I have observed Gesner over a period of time and I know of his notorious reputation with women. He can be a very awkward cuss if he is frustrated. I've heard that if he can't get his own way he sometimes resorts to violence."

"There is nothing to tell you," she said in a low voice. "You said that anything I did, away from my work, was my own business and nothing to do with you. I am here, unhurt and with nothing on my conscience, and I go home tomorrow." I can't say anything, she thought. I gave my word to Anton that I wouldn't betray him as it would cause more trouble than it was worth, and even to you, Carl, the man I love, I couldn't say anything of the attack in the cable car.

Carl stopped and took her in his arms. "You little fool! Can't you see? You must never play around with a man like Gesner. You and he aren't in the same league! He is completely unscrupulous and you must never feel loyalty to someone like that!" He kissed her fiercely, as if to impress his words on her as forcefully as he could, but the kiss was in anger and not desire. Bridie couldn't break away. Her knees felt limp and she knew that if he had taken her then, by the dark lakeshore, she would have been lost in the helplessness of her own longing.

He kissed her again more gently, as if to say, It means nothing. This is a kiss between friends because I was angry and we are both lonely and the moon plays hell with my feelings.

She clung to him but the sudden sound of a high-powered boat shattered the night. The muffled voice through a loud hailer was difficult to understand and a searchlight from the bows of the boat, made a lane through the sullen water.

Carl listened intently as the boat came closer. The man on the boat was calling, first in French and then in English for everyone to look out for a missing woman. Carl walked to the water's edge and peered across towards the boat which they now saw was a police launch. It swept on with smaller lights scanning the water, and on the far side of the lake, lights appeared on moored boats as the owners cast off to join the search, and, on jetties, emergency searchlights were rigged. The police launch circled and a man shouted and turned the searchlight back into the darkness.

"My God!" Carl shouted. "Look!" Out of the water away from the shore, a motor launch floundered like a wounded whale, but kept going erratically through the water, listing at a dangerous angle. "It's Maria's boat," he said. "Come on!"

Nine

B ridie put a hand on the cold coffee-pot. It was full and in exactly the same place as it had been when she ordered it last night, thinking that when Carl came back he might be cold and needing hot coffee, but at two a.m., when she climbed into bed half dressed, he had not returned. Unable to keep her eyes open she must have slept for a few hours because the sounds of early morning traffic came to her from the outside world along the lake road.

She tapped on the door of the other bedroom but there was no reply. She opened the door slightly and saw that the silk pyjamas were folded on the pillow and the bed turned back ready for use but Carl had not slept there. Bridie rang down for breakfast and asked if there had been any messages for her or Mr Paterson, but there were none. She waited for the breakfast trolley and turned on the local news in French.

As she poured hot coffee, she listened to the usual tales of holiday traffic hold-ups at the airport, a strike of cross channel ferries and the expected visit of a high-ranking American politician. The local news came next and she listened carefully, putting down her cup so that she could concentrate on the fast French words. A high-powered motor launch had gone out of control and crashed into a yacht mooring, then careered away in an uncontrolled arc, half submerged. A search had been set up to find two people who were believed to have been on board and the latest newsflash said that two people had been picked out of the water.

She left the channel open but no further bulletin was issued and it wasn't clear if the people brought ashore were alive, dead or injured. The announcer switched to an account of a cycle race and on to other sports, and Bridie turned the sound down as soon as the the programme ended.

She felt helpless. Carl had been sure that it was Maria's boat but had seemed puzzled to think that she could be on board as late as that after a day out in it with him. It was possible that she had ordered the boat to be transferred to another mooring, but in that case there would have been an inflatable dinghy with an outboard in tow, to take the man on board back to his base afterwards. More likely, she decided, it might have been stolen by joyriders with no knowledge of fast boats and they had lost control of the powerful engines.

The doors of the ancient elevator clanged and she sprang to her feet and opened the door of the suite. "Carl? Are you all right?"

"Me?" He shrugged, "I'm fine. Any coffee?" He sank into a chair and she handed him a full cup. "Thanks. Is that toast fresh? I'm famished." She pulled the breakfast trolley close to her chair and buttered some toast, piled marmalade on it as he liked it and put it on a plate by his elbow.

"You look very tired," she said. "What happened after you bundled me off in the taxi?" She couldn't hide her disappointment and the resentment she had felt when she sensed his sudden change of manner. He had brusquely ordered her to go back to the hotel and wait there, ignoring her protests and offers of help. He was once again remote and wanted to be rid of her. He had one thought and that was for Maria, which made it clear to Bridie that Maria was the one woman who meant anything to him.

"I'm dog-tired," he said. "They found the boat. There was a newspaper reporter searching, hoping as usual for something to blow that would make good pictures and a fairly lurid story, so we went together and scoured the whole lake, but it was the police who scooped them out of the water."

"Was it Maria? Is she safe?"

"Yes, it was Maria. She had a very nasty fright. She also has a broken arm, is suffering from exhaustion, shock and exposure."

"On the news they mentioned two people."

"The other was your friend Gesner. I know that you will be mightily relieved to know that he is safe."

"Anton was there with Maria?"

"Of course. Who else? He had to report back to her, didn't he?" He looked at her without expression and his eyes were tired.

"Report back?" she said.

"Don't repeat everything I say, there's a good girl. I really am not in the mood." He added mildly, "Gesner must be a very relieved man this morning. In spite of a broken wrist and various cuts and bruises, he must be very happy. When he left you he would have been in Maria's black books for failing to find out anything about the new venture and about the future plans for research with Dubois, but now, all is forgiven!"

"Why do they bother to do this? Surely the countess knows what's going on and can guess your moves?"

"Yes, up to a point, and it's a joke between us. It's a bit like playing chess. Maria believes the old saying that all's fair in love and war and she extends that to business to get the best prices for her software. She isn't devious in the usual way, as she freely admits that she does everything she can to find out about her competitors and about those with whom she has agreements. She has no moral code where business is concerned. In a lopsided way it is a part of her charm! I admire a go-getter."

"How does an accident make Anton happy? A broken wrist wouldn't make *my* day!"

"Ah, well, Gesner was with Maria on the boat when the steering went haywire. He fought to control it and Maria radioed for help but he couldn't stop the boat and it hit a mooring. That didn't stop the launch, which went off in a wide arc, sinking slowly, and a huge log came up and glanced off the boat, nearly knocking the life out of Gesner. He knew that a big crash or an explosion was inevitable and black smoke was pouring out of the engines so he grabbed Maria and threw her into the water. As the boat twisted away under her, Maria's arm was broken and Gesner had to swim with her to a swimming-raft anchored off shore. He clung to her but couldn't lift her on to the raft as his own wrist was broken, but he saved her life. She was in deep shock and would have drowned."

"And you have seen her since then?

"The police took her to the island and we followed. I felt that the reporter had earned a close exclusive look at her private island. Maria forbids the media to put a foot on it, but he did try to help, as I did so I took him along. Maria was hysterical by now and swore that Gesner had tried to kill her, so we stayed until her arm was in plaster and she had calmed down, then we put her in the picture." He gave a weak smile. "I never thought I'd be the one to tell her that Gesner was a hero!"

"How did you know, if you weren't there?"

"The reporter took a lot of polaroids of the wrecked yacht and mooring and of the flames in the distance when the boat blew up a minute after Gesner had flung her into the water. She was horrified when she saw the pictures." Carl yawned. "It took ages to explain and we thought we'd never get away."

"But why did you leave? If she needed you, surely you should have stayed?" Bridie tried to be reasonable.

"I said I needed to rest and she had been given a shot to calm her down. She wanted me to stay as a house guest, but I explained that all my luggage was here and I had a few loose ends to tie up. More toast," he ordered and she plastered another piece with butter and marmalade, aware that he needed calories and not a lecture on cholesterol. He drank more coffee and seemed to relax.

"You need to sleep," Bridie said firmly. "Nobody can think straight after a night like this one."

"You're so right. I'll go over to the island later. Maria can reach me here if she needs to be in touch before then." He stared at her. "I think that I underestimated Gesner. He really did act fast and in a very brave manner. Now of course, Maria admits that she was wrong to accuse him of trying to drown her and he is lording it in her boudoir with a bed in her dressing room, the picture of the perfect wounded hero!" Carl's laugh was free of mirth. "He has a very white bandage round his head and his wrist is in a silk scarf as a sling while Maria wears a plaster that ruins the line of her négligé. I'll go over later and check," he said.

Listening to him, Bridie wondered if Carl was jealous of the man who had now gained many plus-points with Maria. He'd have to go back to make sure that Anton didn't take over completely if he ever wanted Maria for his own wife. It would be the right time to press his own claim to her as soon as she was fit, making sure that he was there all the time.

Carl frowned and looked apologetic and it was no surprise to Bridie to hear him say, "I'll rest for a few hours and then go over to sleep on the island tonight. You'll have to go back to London alone. Will you cancel my ticket and tell Brian what happened. Say I'll be back when I can get away?"

"Of course. Leave that to me. Can I help in any other way?"

"I think not. I gave you the outline of what I want doing when you are back at the office. Explain to Brian what happened here, tell him that the new scheme is well under way and he needn't do anything fresh, but ask him to manage without me on the work not under wraps, using a bit of initiative for a change, if he has to do so!" Bridie smiled. As if she would dare to say that to a senior executive! "He can meet the people in my diary and put off any I have to see personally. I'll phone him tomorrow when the situation here is more certain."

"Does this accident do anything to change the agreements?"

"No, the most important papers have been signed. Maria

knows very little about the new one with Dubois. For that I have several other clients interested and Maria will have to join the queue." He grinned. "She's aching to know more about prices and suppliers and you haven't helped her one little bit. That is now quite obvious. If Anton had been able to tell her a fraction of what we worked on out here, he'd be home and dry in her good opinion."

"I can't understand. You fight and yet you come to some agreement in the end," Bridie said.

"I get a better deal if I keep a few secrets," Carl said. "It's like having sealed tenders for a transaction and it adds a lot of interest to Maria's life," he added laconically, as if Maria had to have a toy to keep her entertained.

"When I've finished the documentation, do I sent it to you here or over at the island?" she asked.

"How long do you think I'm staying here? Good grief, Bridie, I've other work to do that doesn't involve temperamental foreign countesses!" He looked cross, half resenting the time he had to spend on the island, and Bridie knew that with Gesner there in residence, it wouldn't be easy for him.

"You'll stay for a while?" she asked.

"I shall leave as soon as I tactfully can. Maria isn't really ill, just shaken, and she's beginning to enjoy the drama of escaping from a shattered boat that blew up. Not strictly true as she was clear before it broke up and burst into flame but it makes a good headline! The Paris papers and glossies will love it and her enemies will be envious. Gesner will appear, looking suitably romantic and caring and he will have enough newspaper cuttings to fill a folder! He might even get discovered for films after the television interview he's giving this morning!"

"Does a woman like that really justify all the fuss made about her? People fall in the water all the time, and they break arms and legs and have their lives ruined, but it never hits the headlines. Frankly, I'd never heard of the lady until I came here."

Carl grinned. "That's because you don't move in the right circles. Poor Bridie, you look a little bit miffed. Can it be that you think the space given to this accident as headlines in the popular press will be wasted? Isn't a lovely woman worthy of notice?"

"I have no idea of her worthiness or otherwise. I just can't think how she can go through life getting everything she wants without effort. I admire people who work."

"You are mistaken, Bridie. At least in this event you are quite wrong. Maria fills her life with matters that you with your level-headed Scottish intolerance would condemn as completely frivolous, but it's people like Maria who can organise a ball for funds for refugees, sick children or other vital charities, and make more in a night than others could raise in a year from flag days and coffee mornings and tombolas. She's a very clever woman under that froth and all those sparkling jewels." He stretched and winced. "I'm going to bed or when I next meet the lady, I might be as intolerant as you are."

She flushed with indignation. How dare he accuse her of intolerance when, in the office back in England, he could reduce an employee to jelly for a quite minor offence. He was making excuses for Maria to justify his own interest. "I'll get packed," she said. "I'll see to the tickets and if you are asleep I'll slip away. I hope that everything goes as you want it. Please remember me to the countess, if you think of it, and say that I was shocked to hear about the accident."

"I'll do that." He walked towards his bedroom then turned wearing an odd smile that was a mixture of amusement and tenderness. "Do you like children?"

"That's a funny question! What's that got to do with going back to work in London?" She had to sound faintly annoyed to stop the violence of her own emotions. *Children?* And he asked her if she liked them! She could imagine his children, with deep blue eyes and that same semi-defiant expression when he was out of temper. "Yes, I love children," she said.

153

"And when you marry what's-his-name, you'll want some?"

"*If* I ever get married I would like children," she said, correcting his assumption that her future husband had to be Roger.

"Well, remember this when you have your first bouncing baby with all its toes and fingers complete: you will have something priceless that nothing can replace. Maria can have no children so she fills her life with candyfloss and business." He closed his bedroom door quietly and Bridie wiped away tears of humiliation. Miserably she packed, cancelled Carl's airline ticket and checked the time of her own flight. One half of her was numb with loss, while her brain made her do everything that had to be done with calm efficiency.

She had glimpsed a life that she thought existed only in dreams or in American soap operas, she had been kissed by a man who could make all her dreams come true, but all he thought about was a woman with money, power and a good line in pathos when it suited her. Bridie knew that she was being unfair but had to console herself with uncharitable thoughts to justify her own sense of inadequacy. It was hard to leave now, with the memory of his face haunting her, looking reproachful and knowing that he inwardly despised her. It would have been easier to bear if he shouted at her as he had done when they first met, but his gentle reproach was agony.

"Bridie?" She left her luggage on the rack and went out into the sitting room. A tousled head looked round the door of Carl's room. "I'm bloody tired and yet I can't sleep. My shoulder is playing hell and I need help." He went back and slumped down on the bed, confident that she was following him into the room. He lay on his stomach, naked from the waist up and tugged at the pillow under his shoulders with angry fingers.

"I'll get the cream," Bridie said faintly. "It's in my toilet bag. I left that until last." That's all I need, she thought. I've braced myself to say goodbye for ever and now I have to sit close to him and smooth cream into his skin. This was much worse than when she had massaged his shoulders while he sat in a chair, and she flexed her hands and willed herself to think of him as just a patient who needed the ache eased away. She traced the line of his shoulder blade and found the knots of tension, then kneaded the muscles steadily and more firmly.

"Does it take a lot of effort?" he asked in a muffled voice as his face was half buried in the pillow. "You sound breathless."

"Is that better?" she asked, loving the sensuous rythmn of the treatment as her hands moved over the supple back, but distrusting her own reaction to his nearness.

"More," he said, softly. "You are magic, Bridie."

She gulped and resumed the treatment, longing for him to turn and take her in his arms, but his breathing grew deeper and slower and when she asked if that was enough, as she couldn't take any more, she knew that he was sound asleep. Gently, she took the discarded duvet and covered him, then bent and kissed his cheek before leaving him to dream.

With her new-found confidence, as far as work and travel were concerned, she arrived at the airport with time to spare, her bag neatly packed and her passport ready. She watched the bustling holiday crowds, most of them bronzed from sun and swimming and with no thought beyond that of making the most of the duty-free shops, and she envied their laughter. She saw a tiny girl sitting on a black plastic-covered seat in the departure lounge. Carl's child would look like that, a tiny figure of complete composure from her shining hair to her small red shoes, her eyes as bright as cornflowers. Bridie looked away and when she looked back again the child had gone.

The book-stall held no interest for her but she bought a glossy magazine to look at on the plane – if she could drag her mind away from the Viceroy hotel in Lucerne. She tried to think of all the activities she had abandoned when she came to Switzerland in such a rush, but she couldn't recall what they were. When she had shut Carl's bedroom door, she had experienced a sensation of finality. The next time I see him, he will look over my head or at best say, 'Oh, it's you. Had a good trip, did you?' then walk away and forget me completely.

Bridie had a window seat and looked down at the grey runway. The engines roared, the ground receded and the mountains came into view below the plane, but today they were obscured by cloud and there was snow on the highest ones that peeped through the mist. It all seemed unreal. So many clouded mountains but none with a golden secret for her. She sat back and closed her eyes, hoping that the woman beside her would be quiet as she desperately wanted to be alone.

"Excuse me, but are you being met at the airport?" the woman said.

"No," Bridie replied shortly. "I've been away on business, not on holiday." As if to prove it, she took some papers from her bag and pretended to examine them.

"I hope my son is there," the woman went on. "I hate airports, don't you? I get lost so easily."

"I wish you would," Bridie murmured.

"What did you say?"

"I said that's never good," Bridie lied and put away her papers, resigning herself to hearing all about the woman's family, their shortcomings and how the hotel had charged too much for coffee. The endless flow of words went over Bridie's head and only the meal break made a slight relief.

"It will be too early to stay in London for a show and too late for the shops," the woman said. "I hate travelling at this time. I hope my neighbour remembered to order my milk."

It will be just an hour before they come out of the office, Bridie thought. She gave a wry smile. I shall have a few domestic problems too. I shall really come down to earth with a bump after being waited on in a luxury hotel. She couldn't recall if she had anything in the freezer suitable for a quick meal. It had been so easy to lift a phone to order what she wanted and it now seemed light years ago that she had lined up in the corner shop for groceries. I could get used to easy living, she decided ruefully.

The sun shone on England as if to tell her that it wasn't so bad to be back. The trees were green and the sky a gentler blue with wisps of white cloud, and there was no harsh challenge from the huge mountains that might overpower her in time. I'll settle for a gentler peace, she thought; gentler people. Carl Paterson was a force with which to reckon: a rugged, beautiful and often cruel mountain; her clouded mountain. She realised that she had not given a thought to Roger in ages. He was more like the predictable, undemanding landscape over which they passed. Less complicated and perhaps more comfortable for every day living.

She was through customs quickly and as she stepped out into the lounge, she gasped. "Roger! What are you doing here?"

Roger Franks laughed. "I heard on the grapevine that you might be coming back this afternoon, so as I was going nowhere in particular, I thought you might like a friendly face to welcome you after all that hard work. I rang the airport to see when your flight would be in and just made it."

He kissed her and she felt a sudden rush of affection for the nice-looking man who was so obviously pleased to see her.

"What a lovely surprise," she said and the day brightened. "What shall we do? Have you time for a meal?"

"I thought we'd stay in town and eat and then find a club or something." He eyed her case and then the briefcase with all the important papers in it. "That looks important. You ought to put it somewhere safe," he said. "If that belongs to Mr Paterson you can't leave it around in a cloakroom."

"We could call in at the office and I'll leave it with Security. I can leave my case too and just bring my passport and my purse. There's nothing I need from my bag until tomorrow." It was good to walk and talk of the trivial incidents that had happened at Herald while she was away for a week. Only a week? It seemed like a lifetime.

"Keep the coat. I like it," Roger said, so the fake fur that had been in the way in Switzerland came into its own in the cool of an English evening.

"I've something to tell you," he said later. "I've been promoted."

"So that's why you look so pleased with yourself." Bridie laughed. "You look more confident and at least three inches taller," she teased. He looked vaguely uneasy. "I mean it. I'm not laughing at you, Roger. I think it's wonderful news."

"Yes, it's what I wanted, or a part of what I wanted," he said and looked unhappy for a moment. "But it never follows that any situation can be perfect."

"No, life isn't like that," Bridie agreed.

"I'm glad you think as I do," he said. "Come on, we can eat in the wine bar near the office. There won't be any of our lot there at this time of day. They use it for lunch but it's better in the evening, like now."

"Since when have you been here in the evening?

"I've often worked late and grabbed some food there," he said. She nodded. That was not surprising. Herald had a reputation for expecting rising young executives to put in extra time if it was necessary. The fact that Roger had this promotion pointed to the fact that he had been prepared to work harder than his colleagues and than his job demanded. It also explained why he often had to break dates with her. "How was Switzerland?" he asked.

"Good in parts," she said. "I worked very hard but it was fun to sample the delights of high living."

"Did CP make you earn your bread?"

"I think I earned everything I got," she replied with a wry smile. He regarded her quizzically. "Don't misunderstand me Roger. It was an experience I wouldn't have missed, and if I ever want a spur to make me work to get a better-paid job, that memory would make me aim for something really big."

She looked pensive. "I learned that hard work counts for a lot but personal contacts count too. A lot of influence can come from meeting people. One of the French delegates hinted that he would offer me a job if I got in touch with him and I wanted to leave Herald. Most of the real business was done over dinner or drinks, not in the main conference centres."

"I've come to the same conclusion," he said, quietly. "I work harder than most and I'm quite bright but when it comes to the plum jobs in the higher ranks of the firm, the old boys act comes into play and a favoured few, friends of friends, relatives or contacts made in the way you mention, get the jobs."

Bridie spread pâté on her Melba toast and nodded when Roger offered her more wine. The wine bar was pleasantly full and they could talk in peace. "So you've decided to choose your friends with care?" she asked. It crossed her mind that Roger thought she might have influence with Carl Paterson, now that she knew him better, but she dismissed the idea as unworthy of the man who was being so attentive and caring. Roger wasn't like that. He loved her and would never try to use her in that way.

"It shouldn't matter but it does," Roger said. "It's frightening how a guy can get caught up in something." He took a deep breath. "I've been invited for drinks to the Knightly home tomorrow evening. I think I have Mr Knightly to thank for my promotion."

"Penelope Knightly's father?"

"Yes, you remember I was asked to escort her to the Rotary dinner for a party her father had arranged? It was something of a royal command."

"So you told me. Who can refuse a royal command?" There was irony in her smile.

"I knew you'd understand. You, of all people would know, having been to that congress and seen how it works. How did you get on with the great man? Is CP as hard as they say he is?" He laughed. "Sandra is less than enthusiastic about him. According to her, no girl who goes with him on these visits gets a lot of fun. She said that everyone works like stink and he's such a cold fish that the secretaries who go expecting to have a good time, have to find their own amusement on the side."

"What do you mean by a good time?"

"Well, they tell me that he books a suite of rooms in a cosy old hotel and it could be a nice intimate set-up, but Sandra complains bitterly that he never once made a single pass at her and she had a room down the corridor. She even had to sit alone to have breakfast in the main dining room as he said he liked to be quiet and to look at the necessary papers for the days work, and to catch up on world news in the newspapers before she joined him in the sitting room of the suite to work all morning."

"But he . . ." She was about to say, I don't believe Sandra. I had breakfast with him every morning and slept in the spare room of the suite. He made me listen to the local news in French so that I could tell him the gist of it as he said he hated reading boring and irrelevant news that had nothing to do with the work in hand! She bit her lip and remained silent.

"I know what you think," Roger said, and laughed indulgently. "You take it for granted that he would act like that and keep everything on a business footing, but Sandra once worked for a firm where she was expected to hit the town with her boss everywhere they went together, and he gave her marvellous presents when they came back and he returned to his wife."

He thought for a moment, then said, "I asked her what she did in Lucerne to pass the time and she mentioned a Swiss bloke who was very attentive to her. She said that she'd meant to warn you about him as he's a bit of a lecher. Can't think of his name now, but she seemed to know all about him. She seemed worried in case you met him. Can't think why. Sandra isn't the type to worry about your morals and from what she said about him I wouldn't imagine that you'd be his type!"

"Anton Gesner," Bridie said automatically.

"That's the name. So you did meet him. What was he like? I bet that Sandra exaggerated. She said he was very good-looking and full of charm and he knew how to treat a lady, which was more than Carl Paterson did."

"Good-looking, entertaining and quite dynamic," Bridie agreed. "He is also involved with the Countess Maria, one of our business rivals, and he has hopes of marrying the lady and through her obtaining great wealth."

"Sandra said that Countess Maria had her eye on Carl Paterson. She said that he was in the hotel for only an hour when she called for him and he had rung her from the airport to say that he had arrived in Lucerne. Whenever the phone rang while Sandra was working in the suite, it was usually the countess wanting to speak to him."

"Did Sandra say what she thought of the countess?"

"I believe that they met when Sandra had to go to a stuffy dinner party with CP and another delegate. The two women hated each other on sight." Roger sighed. "It all comes back to influence. If Sandra had hit it off with her, who knows what kind of a job she might have had by now? Everything in business depends on who you know."

"Maybe that's true up to a point, but I can't really believe that your new job could have anything to do with taking Penelope Knightly to a dance! You just made up numbers in the party, didn't you?" Bridie smiled. "Don't underestimate yourself, Roger. You work very hard and everything you've achieved so far has been from your own efforts. I think it was the other way round. Mr Knightly invited you into his circle of friends to show how much he appreciates you. That's rather nice. Obviously you'll go far and Herald wants to encourage your potential."

"Has CP ever mentioned me?"

"Yes, he did, but I didn't say that you were a particular

friend of mine. Perhaps I should do so now that he admits that I am good at my work, in spite of my other failings."

"What other failings? So you didn't actually hit it off well?"

"I wouldn't say that. We were fine where work was concerned."

Roger nodded sympathetically, recalling Sandra's words. "I wish I'd known that you were going away with him workwise. If only I *had* known, and you'd talked about me, he could have done more for me eventually, than Mr Knightly."

"But you never work in his department," Bridie said, laughing as she remembered that Mr Knightly was the director in charge of accounts, where Roger was based, programming the firm's computers for internal use and nothing to do with the innovative side of the firm. "A social contact might be more useful if you happen to meet him at the Knightly house. Not that he's much of a socialiser and I don't know if they are personal friends."

She saw Roger's mouth tighten and he stood up. "Let's go," he said. "Can we have coffee in your place?" Bridie slipped into her coat and they walked to the underground to join the half-empty train that took them close to her flat. The cold fug of the tube made her hungry for fresh air, and the fast-moving escalator at last released them into the quieter street.

They walked in silence, content with each other's company and when they reached the small apartment, Roger put coffee mugs on a tray while she put fresh coffee grounds into the filter. He eyed the package she took from her holdall and put on the kitchen table. "That looks good."

She smiled. "Open them if you like, but you've just finished eating! Now you want to start on my special Swiss biscuits, I suppose. Well, it gives me an excuse to have some too. They go well with coffee. We used to have some every evening."

"You did?" He regarded her with interest. "You and CP had coffee together each evening? How cosy."

"I had work to do, remember. Coffee kept me alert to do it," she said, crossly. She reached over for an almond knob. "These are rather special so I brought some back to remind me that I had been away." It's as well that Roger is here, she thought, or I might have sat here eating them alone and getting really miserable. Impossible dreams are just that; impossible.

Roger seemed to be in no hurry to leave, and talked of his new job as if trying to convince himself that it was worth taking. "It will pay me to stick it for two years and then perhaps I can move on," he said.

"You don't sound as if you are really keen on the move," she said. "Is there a snag?"

"Yes." He took his coffee mug to the sink and rinsed it under the tap. He seemed tense and when he turned back to Bridie, his face was pale. "I told you that I love you, Bridie and you must believe that it is true." He came and sat by her side. "I do love you, and seeing you again tonight made me realise just how much you mean to me." His voice was husky. "I don't know if my job is worth it if it means losing you."

"You mean that you might have to be transferred away from London?"

"No." He looked unhappy. "It isn't that, although some travelling will come into it. There is, as you suggested, a snag." He smiled bitterly. "If you like to put it this way, there's an unwritten clause." He took Bridie into his arms and kissed her as if he was leaving on a long journey. "I love you, Bridie, but I can't ask you to marry me."

"Penelope Knightly?" He took her surprise to mean acute anguish as she drew away.

"I couldn't help it, darling. Right from the start, her old man hinted that Penny liked me and they'd had a few problems with her. She's been a bit on the wild side and he thinks I have a good influence on her. The first time I met her, he had given me a spare theatre ticket and I found I was one of a family party. After that, it seemed only polite to see Penny

163

home to her flat and to ask her out for a date." His voice tailed away.

"And then?"

"Well, one thing led to another. He asked me about my job and what I wanted to do in the future, suggesting ways to improve my position if I applied for the right jobs as they became vacant." Roger shrugged. "Looking back, I just don't know how it happened."

"What did happen, Roger?" She asked calmly, knowing that he was leading up to a parting, a new love and possibly an engagement to Penny.

"To put it bluntly, I had too much to drink and asked her to marry me."

"And she said, 'Yes please', and dragged you off to tell daddy before you changed your mind when you'd sobered up?"

He nodded, unable to meet her scornful eyes. "I'm sorry, Bridie. I'd do anything to put back the clock."

"Anything but risk your nice new job and all those lovely prospects?"

"Oh, what's the use? I feel terrible. I knew you'd be very hurt."

"What makes you think I'm hurt? The fact that before I went to Switzerland, you rather relucantly admitted that you loved me doesn't mean that I love you. I've never said so or even hinted that it was possible." He gasped. "Have I ever said I wanted to be anything but a dear friend? That's what you have been and that's how I think of you, Roger, a very dear friend who I loved in just that way. For ages, I took it for granted that you felt the same, and, as neither of us was serious, that suited me fine."

"You can't say that! I don't like being taken for granted. You must have known how I felt, he said with more dignity. "I thought you loved me."

"In fact, it was you who took *me* for granted," Bridie pointed out. "I don't love you enough to marry you, even if you weren't engaged to Penny. I sincerely wish you all the joy in the world and I think you've made a very good bargain. She's pretty and unless you hate each other in six months, you just can't lose." She tried to smile. Anton was ready to bargain his body and charm and usefulness to get what he wanted, and Carl seemed to be ready to do the same with Maria. Was all romance dead in the world and would she have to put herself up for barter if she wanted something?

"That's it," Roger said, eagerly. "It's a contract, not a love affair. Even Penny knows that I'm not head over heels in love with her but I seem to be what she wants."

"Poor girl. I wouldn't change places with her for anything," Bridie said and wondered how any girl could accept a lukewarm lover.

Roger looked self-righteous. "Of course, even though I'm not deeply in love with her, I shall try to make her happy," he said. He tried to take Bridie by the hand. "But I shall love you for ever," he added.

She snatched her hand away. "Don't say that! Don't even think it! You have no right to say anything like that to me now. The only woman to whom you should speak of love must be the girl you marry and not another woman who could haunt her future!"

He bent over her and tried to kiss her. "I need you, Bridie. I love you and want you. You can't desert me now!"

"Stop! You must be out of your mind." She wriggled to escape. "You are about to get married!"

"I need you and I need your love, Bridie," he pleaded. "Don't you see? I need to know that I can come to you when everything gets too much for me, and you'll be here waiting and giving me love."

Bridie tore herself away and stood facing him at arm's length, her breast taut with emotion and a trace of fear. "You say that you will marry Penelope Knightly and yet you want to have an affair with me on the side?" The ice in her eyes made him look away. "You should be ashamed! I suppose

165

you thought it would be a good idea to celebrate your engagement by hopping into bed with me? Tonight if possible? Dear old Bridie who is always so sweet and quiet and understanding and who would be very discreet?"

Her eyes were blazing and he looked at her with a mixture of admiration and regret. "You've changed, Bridie. What happened to you?"

"I'm angry, Roger, really angry. You'd better get out now before I really lose my cool. I don't love you enough to marry you and I certainly don't want you enough to have a hole-in-a-corner roll in the hay with you. Good try, but *no*! I'm not that hard-up."

"Bridie, listen. I must have been mad. Seeing you again today was too much. I knew only that I wanted you and I need you with me for ever. If I'd known I could feel like this, I would never have asked her, drunk or sober! I'll go back and ring her and tell her it's off. I can't go through with it."

"It will keep until tomorrow, Roger." He was so upset that she kept her voice low and steady. "Before you do anything, think this over carefully. Even if you finish with Penny, it doesn't follow that I shall fall into your arms. We all make mistakes and cling to dreams. For most men, success is more important than any dream, so don't do anything that you'll regret."

"I love you."

"I know it's true now, but you need success more than that. Once Penny is married, she may mature into a very nice person if you love her and give her a chance to prove herself. She will certainly be a great asset to you in a social sense and I've discovered that is very important in business. A lot will depend on her to provide a smooth background to your endeavours." She put out a hand. "I'll try to forget that you tried it on with me a bit crudely. No hard feelings?"

He squeezed her hand in both of his. "I'm sorry. More sorry than you'll ever know. Life is unfair, isn't it?"

"Not always. It has it's moments," she said, and watched him go out of her life.

So, she thought as she nibbled another biscuit. For Bridie Mark there is no man to say he loves her enough to think the world well lost for her, and no man who she could love but one, a man enjoying the favours of a rich divorcée on a sunlit island.

Ten

"Thank you," said Bridget Mark to the man in the security office. He took the ticket she offered and reached down for the briefcase. "I'll leave my own case until I go off tonight," she said, "but that one will be needed."

"Is Mr Paterson due back today, miss? There are a several packages and mail for him which we've kept here as instructed. Did he ask you to handle them?"

Bridie hesitated. She was very conscious of the fact that she wasn't Carl Paterson's regular secretary, and now that she was back at Herald Enterprises, she felt cut down to size and very low in the office rating. She didn't want to upset Sandra but could see that her orders from Carl might make things difficult, so she braced herself. After all, she had her instructions and nobody could countermand them until he came back and took over.

"Send them to his Personal Assistant in the penthouse," she said. "He can sort out which are to go to Sandra Michael and which are confidential." She glanced at the postmarks of some of the letters. "Any with Swiss or French postmarks are specially confidential," she added. "It is safer to send them all to the penthouse for sorting."

"Did you have a nice trip, miss?"

"I'll be glad to get back to normal," she said. "At least I don't have to cope with any of that pile as I have to finish the work we began in Lucerne." She tried to smile. Some things would never be back to what they were before she went away. Work might be the answer now and, if she could lose herself in it and get really tired, it could save a lot of heartache. Never again will I grumble about being overworked and having no time to think, she vowed.

The elevator in the vast white corridor was flanked by well-tended potted plants and more sat on the island by the central stairway. Smaller arrangements made shadows on the narrow window-sills and they all looked disciplined and healthy, as if they would never dare to wilt while employed by Herald Enterprises. Not for the first time, Bridie thought that the whole set-up looked like something from science fiction, with an undercurrent buzz of high-powered electronic miracles. She was taken at high speed to the fifth floor where the huge open plan office, full of even more greenery and well chosen pictures, had clear, bright light and a view of the park.

She tapped on the door of the inner office and Brian looked up from the pile of mail that had been delivered from Security. "Have a good trip?" he asked. "What's all this about an accident?" Bridie told him the details and passed on Carl's messages in a more tactful form than he had given them to her. "Maybe you'd better work up here while you finish your papers about the new deal," he said. "Sandra is in the outer office and can help you if you need anything." He grinned. "That's if she has the time. This lot will take her a week!"

"I'd rather go down to my own desk," Bridie said. "I have some calls to make and my list of telephone numbers is there. Mr Paterson said that the work is for his eyes only and I know what he wants me to do," she said firmly. "I can finish it quickly today and be ready to get back to my own work by tomorrow."

Brian raised an eyebrow. "If that's what the man said, then it's OK by me. Any problems, just give me a bell." He eyed her with interest. "Swiss air suits you, Bridget. You look . . . different."

Sandra was sitting at Bridie's usual desk when she went back to her own floor. "Just thought I'd come down and catch up on the news," she said. "Everything tied up over there?"

"Nearly finished. I have a few papers to get through from notes I made, but it should be done by tonight and then I can tackle the backlog of work here. I saw that you have a lot up in your office too, so it looks as if we shall both be busy. I have loads of routine stuff to wade through once I've finished the work for Mr Paterson. Are you really better?"

"I've been back two days," Sandra said. "I expected to have work to do for Mr Paterson as soon as he came back. Didn't he give you any messages for me about it? I can take over now. I *am* his confidential secretary."

Bridie smiled. "He did say that I was to finish the papers but to tell you that he'd put you in the picture as soon as he came back, as he has the full details and I have only a part of the transaction that means very little when seen away from the whole." She tried to look annoyed. "I'd better get on with it. You were right about having to work hard over there, Sandra, and I have a feeling that he'll blow his top if this isn't finished immediately! He may be coming back today or tomorrow."

"Not much fun, I take it?" Sandra laughed as if very pleased that Bridget Mark had not enjoyed the trip. "Not a bundle of laughs is he? I wondered how you'd get on with him." She seemed curious to know what had happened in Lucerne and asked a few leading questions but Bridie showed no sign of going into details. Sandra looked at the empty desk and then at the briefcase which Bridie had close by her side. Bridie made no attempt to take out the papers but opened her desk and took out a list of telephone numbers that Carl has asked her to ring as soon as she got back. "I ought to do these or he'll be livid if he finds them left," she said apologetically. She raised the phone and made no move to take out any papers.

Sandra looked cross. She stayed while Bridie made the first call that had nothing to do with the work that Carl had set her to finish, then exclaimed with annoyance as the bleeper called her to the penthouse to see Brian, leaving Bridie free to unlock the briefcase and begin her work.

171

By lunchtime, the new clauses in the agreement were set out neatly and had been put through the word processor. Bridie went late for lunch, after locking away the papers and the disk containing the information in a secure drawer. Sandra was obviously too busy to come down again and Bridie breathed a sigh of relief when at last the work was done, and the papers in triplicate, together with the disk, were put together with the rest of the contents of the briefcase.

She locked it at once and hurried down to Security. "I've finished with the briefcase," she said. "Now it must be locked away for Mr Paterson's eyes only, or for whoever he names if he phones, and for no other person."

"Sure you've finished?" the guard said. He grinned. "Once it's in the safe as top security, even you can't get it out without his signature."

"Great!" Bridie said with feeling and went back to her routine work, feeling that a great load of responsibility had been lifted from her shoulders. Sandra had asked for an extra typist to help her with a stack of work and that left Bridie free to get on with hers.

It was with surprise that Bridie saw the first girl pack up her desk and get ready to leave for the day. She checked her own desk and locked the drawers, deciding that she had done well by Herald for one day. Sandra was waiting at the ground-floor door of the elevator as if waiting for someone and when she saw Bridie she smiled and came towards her.

"I meant to ask you. Did Carl Paterson telephone today? Nothing came up to us and he usually hammers away on the phone if he's away for a while. He can't leave us alone. Even Brian gets fed up with him at times. He's the world's worst slave-driver."

"Why do you put up with it? I'm sure that you could get a job anywhere."

"Would you want my job? I'd have thought that a week with him would make you run a mile if you had the chance of being offered it." Her eyes narrowed as if she was suspicious of this quiet girl who had come back from Lucerne with a new air of confidence about her work.

"He wasn't so bad," Bridie said. "He works hard and expects everyone else to do the same. By the way, I met a friend of yours; Anton Gesner."

"Oh yes, he told me. He rang me today personally and said he'd met you," Sandra said, a hint of triumph in her eyes as if she thought that the news would surprise her junior. "He said he was sorry that I wasn't at the congress and he missed me."

"I'm sure he did," Bridie said. "He spoke of you as if he had a lot in common with you. Did he say how the countess was progressing?"

"The countess? Why should he mention her? He hasn't seen her for months."

"Oh, I just wondered. She had an accident escaping from a boat and everyone was talking about it." Bridie said. "Mr Paterson was worried about her and that's one of the reasons why he stayed for an extra day or so." She knew from Sandra's expression that Anton had said nothing about the accident or his part in rescuing Maria, in spite of his love of publicity and the fact that he was now living on the island.

"He couldn't have heard about that. In any case, he doesn't like her and wouldn't be upset about it. He said he might come over to see me. He's quite a dish, isn't he?"

"Quite a dish, but not for me," Bridie said. "Far too sophisticated." Sandra smiled as if she agreed, and alarm bells rang in Bridie's head for no reason that she could justify. "Did Anton mention Mr Paterson?"

"He said he saw him at the congress but nothing more." She giggled. "He was far too busy telling me how much he missed seeing me and that he might be over here next week. I might try to get a couple of days off if he comes to London."

They walked to the main entrance and Bridie stopped. "Aren't you getting the tube?" Sandra asked.

"Yes, but I have to collect my case. I left it in a security locker last night as I wanted to stay in town for a meal after the flight back. I must collect it and do my washing or I'll have no clean clothes to wear. This is definitely a night to stay in and wash my hair and clear up after the week away." She laughed, thinking that Sandra would walk away now, but she continued to walk with her.

"I'm going as far as the tube. We can walk together. You haven't a date for tonight?" Bridie shook her head. She was puzzled. Sandra had never been this friendly, and it was unheard of for her to be so nice to anyone beneath her in the office rating. "I'm at a bit of a loose end and a bit limp after the flu, so I don't want to cook. Come and have a sandwich with me across the way. It saves bothering at home, but I hate sitting in a wine bar alone."

Bridie sought for a good excuse but could think of none. In fact it would fit in with her evening quite well. She could go home and get straight into her odd jobs and clean her flat while the washing churned away in the launderette round the corner. "Fine," she said. "I'd like that."

Sandra watched her bring her case from the locker and hand the key to the security officer. "Is that all you brought back with you?" she asked.

"I didn't bring back Sir's dirty washing too, if that's what you mean," Bridie said and laughed.

"No, I mean the briefcase and anything he sent you back to work on. The briefcase you brought back is quite safe, I hope?" Sandra asked as soon as they sat down to Chicken Kiev and cider.

"Mr Paterson's briefcase, you mean? Oh, yes, that's safely stowed away until he returns."

"Have you finished all the work he sent back with you? Do you need any help?"

"It took longer than I'd imagined but it's all done now. It's a relief to know it's safe. I was very glad to hand it over to Security and be rid of it."

"It's in Security? Not locked in your desk?" Bridie detected a hint of disappointment in Sandra's voice.

"I thought it best to put it there as it was highly confidential work. You'll see that when Mr Paterson puts you in the picture. I can catch up with my own work tomorrow now that I am straight again."

"Very wise to put them in a locker in Security," Sandra said.

"I didn't do that. I put it all in top security," Bridie said.

"What about the disk from your word processor?" Sandra asked quickly.

"That's in there, too," Bridie said.

"My, you have learned fast," Sandra said with a brittle smile. "You took copies?" She tapped the table top in a distracted way.

"Of course. I took the usual three copies. They are all there."

"Did you give one to Brian?"

"No, I was told to keep it all together."

"Ah well, I suppose you weren't to know, but he likes five copies, not three. Three with the notes and two more in a separate folder. Once, a couple of copies got lost and he raised hell, so now I always do five and keep a couple safely tucked away in case of accidents. I really think you should do a couple more before he comes back, or at least do them as soon as he signs for the case, if you are sure that you can't get at it now."

"He was positive that he wanted three copies," Bridie said. "I'm sorry if you need a couple of extra copies, but you can take more photocopies as soon as he puts you in the picture, can't you? He's sure to take them out of Security the minute he returns as he wants to get on with the latest agreement as soon as possible."

"Well, be sure to do them if you see them first. When he gets mad the whole office hums," Sandra warned her. She twisted her wineglass pensively, sipped and found it empty. "Have the talks gone well? Do you know if they got as far as mentioning prices? I wonder who is bidding this time?"

"Several people were interested, but I'm sure that it usually happens like that," Bridie said, as if totally disinterested. "I only set out the first drafts and all we have are provisional figures."

"So you think a sum has been mentioned or even agreed?" Sandra sounded eager. "Can you recall any details?"

Bridie took a mouthful of chicken and seemed to have difficulty in swallowing it, which gave her time to think clearly. "Surely you've had enough of the office for today?" she suggested. "I just want to forget work for the evening. I've had Herald Enterprises up to my eyeballs!" She crumbled her bread and looked down at her plate. She had a sensation of being pushed into a corner and wasn't enjoying it. "I really can't recall the details. I just hurried to get the notes down correctly."

"You still have the notes?" Sandra's mouth was set and her eyes looked hot.

"No, he told me to shred everything that I'd used once the papers were complete and I did that as soon as I finished." Bridie smiled. "I just did as the man said and I never was much good at keeping figures in my mind. Even at school I had to have notes if I was made to talk, as I can't give details of anything off the cuff. Maybe I should go back to my original choice of career and train as a physiotherapist. I begin to think I have no head for remembering figures."

Sandra forced a smile. "You've done very well, but now I must take over. You have your own work to do. If you hear from him first and he gives you permission to get the case out of Security let me know and I'll pick it up for him." She glanced at her watch. "Just remembered. It's later than I thought and I have a call to make."

She flung down the money for her meal and started for the door. Bridie had a strong suspicion that before long, Sandra would be talking to Anton over the line to Switzerland. Maybe I'm misjudging you, she thought, but I don't think so. A call from Anton, piling on the flattery and saying nothing about the countess, when there just *happened* to be another big deal in the pipeline seemed unlikely to be a coincidence. She finished off the wine and gave a sigh of relief, knowing that all the papers were safe in Security.

Back at the apartment, Bridie unpacked and sorted out her clothes for washing. The rigid box in the bottom of the case came last and lay unopened on the bed. She almost dreaded looking again at the beautiful dress that she had worn to the banquet. She left it until she had filled the hungry maw of the washing machine in the launderette with grubby clothes, and she dusted and vacuumed, putting off the moment when she must hang the dress away in the wardrobe.

At last the damp clothes hung on a rack in the utility room and Bridie made coffee and untied the box. The dress was even lovelier now against the more spartan surroundings of her own small sitting room and it glowed like a living thing. Bridie held it to her face and shut her eyes, thinking of the night when she had dressed with such care, like a modern Cinderella.

She put the delicate garment away from her then held it against her body, doing a few sad steps of a dance, a pavane. On impulse, she stripped off her clothes and dressed in the golden silk. She looked in the long mirror, and slowly her hand touched the birthmark that prevented her from wearing the dress as it should be worn, and prevented her from wearing anything as pretty and as revealing. Tonight, the blemish on her skin seemed even uglier and more angry-looking and she hated it as she had never hated anything in her life. In her mind she saw again the horrified look in the eyes of the man she loved when he thought that Anton Gesner had given her a passionate love bite.

She took off the dress and hung it away as if saying goodbye to it, as she never expected to wear it again, then drank far too much coffee and tried to read a book. When at last she sank into bed, she couldn't sleep and, when she did, it was fitful and filled with dreams of the dress, of Anton and Carl and the almost vicious look that Sandra had given her when she knew that the papers were safe from prying eyes.

The birthmark haunted her. It had caused two men to believe that she was a girl with no moral values and had been the source of amused contempt when Monique knew that it was a birthmark that had been left for so long to disfigure a good body. "I must do something about it," she decided.

In the morning, she searched for the letter that her own doctor had written to introduce her to a plastic surgeon if she ever wanted to take advantage of it and go to a clinic. It had been written a long time ago but Bridie knew that if she had the operation privately she could choose the time and the place where it would be done, and have more privacy than if she went to a consultant dealing with NHS cases.

I hope the surgeon is still at this address, she thought, and during a quiet period at work she dialled the number that her doctor had suggested. "I've been recommended to consult a Dr Courtney," she said nervously to the woman on the line.

"Which Dr Courtney do you mean? There are two."

"I don't have an initial or a first name, but he's a plastic surgeon," Bridie said and began to wish she could put down the phone and forget about it.

"Ah yes, you mean Dr Clive Courtney," said the friendly voice. "I'm afraid he's operating this morning but I can make an appointment for you to see him.

Bridie felt deflated after all the time it had taken her to make the decision and raise the phone. The woman sounded warm but businesslike, as if Bridie was making an appointment to see a dressmaker and not a doctor. She stressed that the operation would be a very minor routine one and there would be very little waiting time to have it done after the first consultation. I can't turn back now, Bridie thought with a sense of subsiding panic. No bells rang and when she talked to the other girls in the audio-typing section nobody said that she looked different, but she felt a new and almost fatalistic calm.

Even taking time off wasn't as difficult as she'd imagined as Brian was very pleased with the way she had handled the week in Lucerne. He admitted to himself that she had let him off the hook with Carl Paterson as he had suggested she was the only suitable girl available to accompany him to Switzerland. "I don't know how you did it, but you were a great help, I hear," he told her, as if he still had doubts but now believed in miracles. "We have two temps wasting time in the outer office who can take on some of your routine work. You've earned a bit of a rest, so take an extra half-day today. Got a nice date?"

Bridget smiled. "No, I'm seeing a doctor about a minor surgical proceedure."

"Oh, I am sorry," Brian said. "I hope you aren't scared. I would be. I hate the sight of my own blood."

"It's something that ought to be done soon but I hear that it isn't painful and shouldn't take long to do."

"Well, you look healthy enough to me. The Swiss air definitely suited you."

"It was all that wonderful food. It made me put on a few pounds," Bridie said and laughed. "I must do something about it or my skirts will refuse to zip up."

"Don't try too hard. It suits you. You were far too skinny for my taste." He smiled. "Just let Personnel know when you need time off and make sure you take enough sick-leave if necessary. I'll make it right with them."

Bridie went back to her work and by lunchtime she was half regretting her decision, but she walked to the clinic, which she found was quite close to the huge buildings that made up Herald Enterprises, and she took a deep breath as she entered the smart front-doorway. Inside, it smelled of fresh flowers over a hint of antiseptic, and she was conducted along a pale pink corridor to a small square waiting-room with doors on either side of a teak reception desk. One set of doors was pastel blue and the other a pale green.

She was amused to see that the long teak desk held notepaper, cards and clinical charts in colours to match the doors, then she decided that this made sense if two doctors worked in the same area of the building and needed to have their notes kept separately. The secretary could tell which patient was due to see the right doctor, and it must help her filing system. A smaller pile of plain white stationery sat in the middle of the desk and a typist was busily working on pale-green letters.

After five minutes she was shown into the pale-blue consulting room where the low chairs were covered with dove grey leather and the flower arrangements on the desk were backed by grey leaves. The youngish consultant shook her by the hand and smiled. "May I see the letter from your own doctor?" he said. He took the note and read it, then pursed his lips and eyed her with mock severity. "You took your time in coming to see me. This was written a very long time ago."

Bridie blushed. "It didn't ever seem the right time," she said, lamely.

"Why wasn't it done when you were a child?" he asked. "Does the idea still scare you? I assure you that there is absolutely no need to be frightened."

"I'm not scared," she said. "I didn't dare have it done when I lived with my family in Scotland. They were against it." She smiled sadly. "They said that it didn't show and would be a sign of vanity if I had it removed."

"And now," he said, kindly, "you want to be like your contemporaries and wear the tiny scraps of material that pose as garments, without feeling self-conscious?" He stood up. "Well, let me examine it and we'll decide what to do. Nurse will give you a wrapper."

Bridie took off her skirt and bra behind a Chinese screen with deep blue-and-white figures on it, and was led to a chair under a strong light. "You may agree with my aunt that I am just being vain," Bridie said, and blushed. "It may be vanity but I am finding it increasingly embarrassing."

"Certainly not vanity," he said gently. "I can see what you must have suffered. Now, this is quite straightforward. Can you see? "He took out a slim ballpoint pen and drew a curved line over the birthmark. "I shall make an incision here and carry the skin across here. There will be no stitches to take out as I shall stitch under the skin, underpinning it with very fine catgut that will dissolve with no trouble once the skin has healed. You will be free of this in a very short time and there will be no trace left."

He rang for his secretary. "Miss Boyd will make the appointment for as soon as possible. Have it done at the end of the week so that you can go back to work after the weekend and feel that it was just a minor and private incident."

Bridie went to the supermarket to stock up with food in case she didn't feel like doing anything very strenuous after the operation. The apartment was freshly cleaned, the laundry done and she now had time to spare as she was off for the rest of the day. The appointment had taken very little time and so she had nothing planned to fill the rest of the afternoon. The sun was almost as warm as it was in Lucerne, so she walked in the park. Children played by the swings and a stray dog came up to her and made friends, but Bridie needed someone to share the sunlight, the lightness and the laughter; someone who would make rude remarks about the filthy old dog and to hold her hand as she breathed the sweet scent of the flowering shrubs.

She thought of Roger with a mixture of amusement and disbelief. What a nerve he had! He wanted everything! Penny to bring him advancement through her father, with good social status and eventual wealth, and Bridie on the side as a docile and willing lover.

She wondered if Carl Paterson had slept with many women since his wife died, and if he had been passionately in love with her. For no reason that she could pinpoint, she recalled his voice saying, 'She went into hospital for a minor operation and didn't recover from the anaesthetic.' She shrugged. It was something that happened, sometimes, to other people. She looked at a clump of field daisies without seeing them. To other people, not to her. All she was doing was having a birthmark removed. It wouldn't take very long to do; the doctor had promised her that, but she had a vision of a beautiful woman, and any wife of Carl's would be beautiful, lying on a neat white bed, without a sign of life in her empty eyes.

Bridie shuddered. It couldn't happen to her, could it? And wasn't she guilty of putting herself in the place of another woman, his wife? What right had she to do that, even in her imagination? She knew that she could never compare with the beloved wife who had died. If I died, would he even care or remember me?

The children were now closer and sounded shrill and bad-tempered. They were rough and began to taunt the poor old dog who slunk away between the trees. Suddenly Bridie hated the park and gathered her belongings to go back to the apartment. She wished that she was back at her desk and knew that she was being silly. On any other day she would have welcomed the break from the office at this time of day but she suspected that she wanted to be there in case Carl telephoned or invaded the office with his usual force of character, making everyone jump to his slightest command.

Every day that he was in Switzerland, she could imagine him being with Maria, her tiny, clawlike fingers picking at his jacket, and the heady perfume that she wore lulling his senses into believing that she was the most important woman in his life as well as in their business dealings. Jealousy was a strange and frightening emotion and Bridie was shaken by the intensity of her reaction to it and the harshness with which her dreams were being destroyed.

As she put her key in the lock, she heard the last two rings of the telephone but, when she grabbed it, the line was dead. "Damn!" she said and knew that the call could have been from the office, from a shop where she had left a coat for alterations, or even from Roger apologising for his behaviour the night before. She stacked the groceries and made tea, bringing out the Swiss biscuits again. She smiled grimly.

Roger liked nothing but the very best. He had taken most of the chocolate-coated ones, just as he wanted to skim the cream from life for himself.

The telephone rang again. "Bridget Mark here," she said crisply.

"This is Miss Boyd, Dr Courtney's secretary. Is it convenient for you to come in for your operation on Friday at nine thirty for ten o'clock?"

"That's fine," Bridie said through dry lips. "Who gives the anaesthetic? Is he good?" she asked with a nervous laugh.

"Oh that's all settled. Dr McEllery does that and works with both the doctors as they operate in adjoining rooms. The other Dr Courtney is a very well-known gynaecologist."

"Surely he can't give two anaesthetics at the same time?"

"Oh, no! He gives one while the other theatre is being prepared for the next case and then goes there as soon as the first case is finished."

"So he'll stay with me all the time? I'd hate to wake up and feel the pain," Bridie said.

"Please don't worry about a thing. Dr McEllery is very good and I promise that you won't leap off the table wearing a theatre gown!" She paused, "I did want to mention something. For minor cases, he says he prefers to give a local anaesthetic, and for many like you he often uses acupuncture, but has local ready if you are uneasy and ask for it, so that at no time are you in any discomfort."

"Acupuncture?" Bridie was surprised and immensely relieved. "That sounds wonderful. I've seen films about it and often thought it looks less dangerous than conventional anaesthesia. I hate the thought of being put to sleep by drugs and gases."

"You agree to do that? I'm so glad and I know that Dr Courtney will be delighted. He prefers to have his patients conscious so that they can cooperate, and, of course, there is no period of recovery after anaesthetic with this method."

"What do I bring with me?"

"Not a lot. You will be free to go home by taxi after resting for an hour or so, but you may need fresh make-up and a hairbrush as the theatre cap does rumple your hair; and I advise you to wear a loose shirt and leave your bra at home, or bring a very light and fairly loose one."

"I shall feel quite different without the birthmark," Bridie said."

"I do know about that. Dr Courtney removed a very unsightly mark from my face and it made all the difference to my self-confidence. I never ever notice the suture line now."

But who will see it? Bridie wondered sadly as she put down the phone. Do I have to wait until someone like Anton tears away my clothes? Do I wait to be mugged, secure in the thought that whoever does it will not be repulsed by the sight? She made tea with the water that had been bubbling away while she spoke on the phone, and she dreamed of the man who would never see her smooth breast, never caress the place where the scar had been, and never look on her with love. His deep blue eyes were now filled with love for Maria and he thought of Bridie Mark as a cheap pick-up for men like Anton Gesner, sleeping with the first man who looked at her as she arrived in Lucerne.

She thought about Maria and the accident and the fact that Anton had said nothing to Sandra about it. It made sense for him to keep quiet if he expected any favours from the girl who might give him important information, and if he had suggested a visit to London, then he was desperate for that knowledge. He was playing it cool with everyone.

Bridie rang the Personnel department of Herald to let them know as soon as possible that she needed to take time off. "I only need Friday, I think," she said. "Brian told me he'd clear it with you if I needed more, but I hope that won't be necessary and I'll be well enough to get back to work on Monday."

"Nothing bad, I hope?" the girl said.

"Oh, no. I need to have a very small operation. I shall go home to sleep and be back at work on Monday. They say it isn't painful."

"I don't want to pry and, if you tell me, I promise that it will remain confidential, but we do need the name of the surgeon and what the operation will be."

"That's a relief. I find it a bit embarrassing and I don't want everyone to know, but I'm having a birthmark removed by a Dr Courtney, on Friday morning." She heard a paper rustling. "Would that be the Dr Courtney who lives not far from the office? I thought he was a gynaecologist."

"My doctor is Dr Clive Courtney. There are two brothers who work from the same address."

"I see. Isn't the other Dr Courtney the one who operated on Mr Paterson's wife?"

"I wouldn't know. I didn't even know there were two doctors there until today. I had no idea that Mrs Paterson was a patient at that clinic. It was before my time here."

"Very tragic. She was a bit silly, though. She assured them at the clinic that she had eaten nothing that morning, when in fact she had eaten breakfast, and when they gave her the anaesthetic and it became apparent that something was wrong, the fact that she inhaled vomit made everything more difficult. They thought that the sickness was causing her collapse and missed the fact that she had a malfunctioning gland in her chest. It was a tiny gland I'd never heard about, that should have disappeared at puberty, but is dangerous if a patient has to have an anaesthetic, and she died."

"How terrible," Bridie whispered.

"Yes." The girl seemed to want to talk about it and continued. "She was having a dilatation and curettage to see why she didn't seem to be able to have children. Such a pity. Mr Paterson would make a lovely father. I never did think they were really suited but I couldn't wish that on anyone. He's very sweet under that severe manner. I like

185

him, in spite of what Sandra says about him. You went to Switzerland with him, didn't you?"

Bridie wondered what Carl Paterson would say if he knew that his private life was being discussed, and hoped that the girl would be more quiet about her case. "Is that all?" she asked. "I shall take Friday off and maybe Monday if I feel a reaction or there are any snags." She had no intention of discussing her boss with anyone, even when he was in her thoughts constantly and her heart leapt when she heard his name. "Just one thing. I wondered if there were any messages for me from Mr Paterson. Could you put me through to the office?"

"Hold on." Bridie heard her call someone. "No need. Barbara is bringing round the late internal post and messages and I just caught her. There is a message for you. Mr Paterson is coming back tonight and wants to see you in the office at nine. That's Thursday! What a good job you aren't having the op until Friday morning." She laughed. "If I know him he'll give you enough work to fill your time and put the op out of your mind!"

Eleven

It was stupid to be excited, but the thought of seeing Carl again so soon was a spur, and Bridie couldn't just sit and read a book or do anything that didn't involve moving around, so she cleaned out a cupboard that she had meant to do for weeks and polished her one good piece of silver, a tray on which she put a bowl of fruit, and she grouped some potted plants to better advantage.

She glanced round the small sitting room. It was comfortable but even with her own furniture and personal bits and pieces, like the picture of the loch near the manse in Scotland, and a pair of prints of the Highlands, it lacked any real feeling of home. I don't know why I bother, she thought. It's not as if he'll see any of it. He doesn't really see me as a friend, so if he walked in now he would never register the fact that I have dusted everything in sight twice in two days!

The telephone rang again. "Bridget Mark here," she said.

"Carl here. Sorry if I took you by surprise, or did you have to run up the stairs to answer the phone?"

She nearly dropped the receiver in her surprise and pleasure and her free hand tried to still the pounding of her heart. "I was cleaning out a cupboard in my bedroom and only heard the phone when I emerged. I ran in case it had been ringing for ages," she lied.

"I rang the office and they said that you were at home. Nothing wrong, I hope?"

"No, I'm fine."

There was a pause at the other end of the line, then he said,

187

"I thought you'd have enough work to occupy you for a week after such a long time away, but Brian said that you were ill and had taken time off to see a doctor."

"It's nothing serious," she assured him.

"When a healthy girl takes time off to see a doctor, I get worried," he said. "You aren't the neurotic type and I can't think that you'd do this unless you really needed medical attention." He spoke lightly but Bridie sensed that he really wanted to know what was happening to her and she didn't know if she was pleased or embarrassed. I can't tell him now, she decided. Later, I might be able to laugh about it, but not now. Her lips softened into a secret smile. He cared enough about her to be concerned. Even if that concern was just for an employee, it was still a kind of warmth that she would treasure, and she felt that he was closer.

"I shall be back at work on Monday. Surely I can have a half-day off to have a check?"

His voice deepened. "We don't like our friends and our employees to suffer in silence if there is anything we can do to help. Tell me, what is it? Toothache? Headache after late nights and the flight back? Tummy-ache after all that good food and wine that you managed to push down?" He was teasing her and didn't seem at all cross that she hadn't been in the office when he rang.

"Something quite minor. Did you find the papers and were they all right?"

"Yes, thank you. They are very good. I want to talk about some of it as it may have to be altered, but your basic work is fine. The changes have nothing to do with that but I had to change one clause and a couple of points that cropped up after you took the briefcase and came back here. I didn't call you from Lucerne as this is still confidential."

"Do you want me to do them or will Sandra take over? If they have to be altered there's not much point in her taking extra copies of the old version, is there?"

"What do you mean, extra copies? You gave me three as I asked."

"She said that she usually did five copies in case of accidents."

"She told you that I asked for five?" His voice sounded grim and Bridie wished that she hadn't mentioned the extra copies but it was too late now to cover for his private secretary.

"Yes, she was obviously being extra efficient. She seemed afraid that you would be cross if there weren't five, but it was too late for me to take them out of top security to make further copies, and I did tell her that you'd insisted that they must remain for your eyes only until you put her in the picture when you came back."

"Good girl. Three copies are fine and there will be no need for you to worry about them." He gave a sudden chuckle that sounded really malicious. "I bet she was hopping mad when she couldn't see them, wasn't she?"

"Yes, I think she was convinced that I was trying to take her job away," Bridie said. "It was awkward as she is queen bee in the office and I have been at Herald for such a short time and so the idea was ridiculous."

"You acted with discretion, Bridie, and I have a little sorting out to do in the office. There are some things that have to be investigated but you have done what I asked and there the matter ends as far as you are concerned."

As he talked, she wondered what had happened to the extra copies of transactions that Sandra had kept in the past. Maybe one copy had gone to Anton each time and then on to the countess to put her into a much better bargaining position. If one copy went to Anton then the other might have gone to another firm. The memory of Sandra's tight lips and angry eyes showed how much the extra copies had meant to her. Anton wouldn't be pleased if she didn't manage to get a copy for him when he came to visit her, especially now that he was in such favour with Maria. She felt cold and sorry for the girl. Sandra had never seen the violence that lay under that smooth handsome charm, and how the gentle touch could turn to rough handling and sexual harrassment.

"Do you still want to see me at nine tomorrow?"

"Who told you that?"

"I rang to see if you were back and needed any information," she said. She kept her voice steady, hoping that he would think that she was just super-efficient and not just longing to hear his voice again; anything to bring him closer.

"I'm glad you reminded me of that. I have a meeting tomorrow morning that can't wait. Better make it Friday."

"I shan't be there on Friday."

"But you've had all this afternoon off. Now Friday as well?" He sounded cross. "I take it that you saw the doctor, got some medicine and can get back to work?" He sounded like a spoiled boy. "Or was this afternoon taken up with a private appointment? You don't have to make excuses to justify your absence from the office. You've earned some time off but at least be open about it."

Bridie searched her mind for a way out but could find none. "I had to see a consultant about a small operation," she admitted. "He wants to do it soon and so I have to take time off to fit in with his schedule, but I can be back at my desk soon after."

There was silence and Bridie wondered if they had been cut off. At last he said, "Is it really necessary, Bridie? Be very, very sure that you really need treatment before you undertake anything lightly if, as you say, it is a minor thing." Bridie heard the sadness in his voice and knew that he must be thinking about his wife and the way in which she had died.

"Thank you for being concerned, but it's quite all right. I've considered all the risks and, in my case, I think there are none."

"But is it really necessary?" He persisted.

"If I am to live a normal life, going about as other girls of

190

my age do, it is vital to me," she said. "Dr Courtney assured me that there will be no threat to my health if I do as he says."

"Who did you say?" Carl's voice was hard.

"Dr Courtney. He has a good reputation and I like him."

"You are going to be operated on by him?" The tension in his voice grew worse, and she could almost see the dark blue eyes blazing with anger and disbelief. "Bridie? What have you done? You little fool! You stupid, innocent, gullible, precious little fool! Are you sure you want to go through with this?"

She wondered if the phone might catch fire under the force of his words and couldn't understand his emotion. "Quite sure," she said. "I admit that it took a lot of courage to go to him but now I am very glad I saw him. I go in on Friday morning early and I should be back here by taxi in the evening. No stitches, no lasting discomfort and only a bit of local pain that can be taken care of with just aspirin or codeine."

"You must not be alone. You'll need a nurse with you for at least the first night."

Bridie laughed. "I was told that I can carry on as usual after a brief rest and there will be no surgical shock involved." She tried to sound businesslike but his sincerity nearly overwhelmed her. "Can I help tomorrow after your appointment? I shall be at work all day Thursday. I can be with you in the office at any time and leave the rest of my routine work to the temp that Brian brought in to help out, if that suits you."

"I'll see you at twelve tomorrow and we'll have a working lunch," he said brusquely. His throat seemed to need clearing as if something had got caught up in it and was giving him trouble in speaking. "And Bridie? Please think about it. Give it a lot more thought and consider all the alternative possibilities. There's absolutely no need for you to go through with this if you suddenly find that you hate the idea as much as I do."

He rang off, giving her no time to reply and leaving her confused. What could he mean that made him sound so fraught? She put down the silent receiver. It was no use shouting down the line to ask why he sounded like that. She considered. He must have an almost paranoic hatred of hospitals and clinics after losing his wife in such a senseless way, but it was very unusual for a man to work himself into such a state over a mere employee who just happened to have been in close contact with him for a week, strictly on business.

A warm glow suffused her as she sensed that he cared enough about her to wonder if she would be safe. It was like a loving hand ruffling her hair, a caring hand that she wanted to hold and gently kiss.

I was taken by surprise when he called, she decided. I wish I'd talked about it more instead of trying to make light of it. I must have made it sound much worse than it is. Stupid of me not to take the opportunity of telling him that the birthmark was being removed, probably with no general or local anaesthetic, but just acupuncture. She shrugged. Soon she could tell the world that she no longer had a rather unsightly blemish on her skin. "Yes," she could hear herself saying. "I had it removed and it was nothing."

He obviously knew what I was having done, she thought. I wonder who told him that the mark he had mistaken for a love bite was really a birthmark? Maria knew and so did Monique, and he had been with Maria for hours after her accident; enough time for her to gossip, although the fate of one young secretary was hardly sharp enough gossip for Maria and her like. It was probably the girl in Personnel, who had given the impression that she would not be as discreet as her job required. She might think that Carl Paterson had a right to know every intimate detail about his staff. That was the most likely explanation.

A man like Carl Paterson would consider it to be vanity to have cosmetic surgery of any kind if there was the slightest risk involved, but his anxiety had gone deeper. She knew that he had wanted to say more but had kept his feelings hidden under a gruff pretence that he was angry that she had to take Friday off.

But he did ring me, she thought, and smiled. It was like having him in the room with her for a moment, and she glanced at the flowers on the table to make sure that they had looked fresh. She laughed. How silly can I get? As if he could see me or my apartment.

"You say you're having lunch with him?" Mrs Dean emptied the waste bin and paused long enough to take a good look at the girl who had caused such speculation when she left for Switzerland with Carl Paterson. As office busybody and carrier of news along the grapevine, as she trundled her trolley from one department to the next and put used print-outs through the shredder, she had a duty to find out why the girl looked so much more confident and had a sort of sparkle that could mean only one thing in Mrs Dean's mind; a man! "Well, fancy that! You sit there and say calmly that you are having lunch with God and yet I never thought you could say boo to a goose!"

"I don't have to say boo! I'm having a working lunch to catch up on some of the things left after the Swiss visit, and I shall be busy."

"Rather you than me, dear." Mrs Dean dumped the waste bin back by the desk as if dropping her worst enemy. "Everyone in the office is on edge as he's been that bad-tempered you wouldn't believe. I kept out of his way when he was in the penthouse as you could hear him giving someone a right rollicking. I couldn't catch what it was all about," she said in a disappointed voice, "but I wouldn't want to be in her shoes."

"He seemed fine, even quiet, when he rang me to confirm that we were to have lunch together," Bridie said, and felt a wave of growing uneasiness. Why was he so angry? Was there a crisis in the office while we were away and he'd only now found out what it was? She smiled, weakly. "Has someone done something terrible? If he's been back only a day, he can't have found out all the awful sins committed while he was away."

"For a start, he made that nice Sandra cry, and she's not one of your milk-and-water bimbos who burst into tears whenever someone looks at her. It takes a lot to make her cry. A bit on the hard side but you've got to be if you're a woman in a man's world." She gave her trolley a vicious shove. "Take me, I don't stand no nonsense, be they high or low, and I've found it's as well to be firm with them all, as you may have learned after this trip, mixing with them over there where they don't even speak English.

Mrs Dean eyed the slim girl with the wide, clear eyes as if she might fit in with the milk-and-water image better than Sandra ever would. "Mr Paterson might be the best-looking man in the whole firm, but that doesn't give him the right to be a bully and make his lovely secretary cry. You mind what you say to him," she added, as if Bridie might enrage him even more.

"Maybe Sandra deserved it," Bridie said mildly, as Mrs Dean waited for her reaction. She recalled her conversation with Sandra in the wine bar when she had almost asked to see the confidential papers that Carl had been so insistent must stay in Security until he could collect them. What if he suspected her of industrial espionage and had confronted her with that?

"Thanks for the warning, Mrs Dean," Bridie said. "I shall tread very carefully. I know he's very busy just now and maybe some things weren't on his desk when he came back from Lucerne, but Sandra had been off sick and couldn't do everything," she reminded her. "Some men expect miracles, but I doubt if he'll be mad at me. I got over that in Switzerland and I have nearly finished the work I have to do for him."

"Just be careful," repeated Mrs Dean, as if her warning might protect Bridie from whatever devils theatened her, as in her opinion, she was not able to look after herself.

"Do you know where he has working lunches?" Bridie asked to change the subject. "Do we have sandwiches sent up to the penthouse? He must do this quite often."

Mrs Dean shook her head. "Could be anything. He goes out to lunch sometimes, but then again he has sandwiches sent up if he's very busy. When he goes out he only takes important people," she added as she pushed her trolley away to spread news to the next office.

"That puts me firmly in my place," Bridie murmured with a smile. "A plastic mug of coffee and a sandwich!"

She tried to concentrate on her own work, half dreading the moment when she would see him again and half longing to be near him. It would be agony to sit by his side, knowing that although he had left Maria and the smooth opulence of her world, he would still carry the memory of her clinging charm and charisma. He would never need to spare more than a fleeting glance for the girl in the slim dark skirt and fresh white shirt, who was once again absorbed into the general office staff, even if she was inwardly burning for him and luxuriating in the vibrations of his masculinity.

She longed to hear his voice and, as the time came for the meeting, she made silly mistakes that would never have occured if she was completely sane. Her concentration slipped so badly that she was alarmed and was convinced that she might make a complete fool of herself when she had to work with him again. Each time the phone rang she was startled, and hardly dared to go to the powder room to get tidy before lunch in case she missed his call.

At last she went to tidy her hair and make sure her tights were not laddered. "Phone for you," the junior called as she came back into the office. She took the handset.

"This is Mr Paterson's office," a voice that was not Sandra's, said. "Mr Paterson wants to see you at the main entrance in five minutes, ready to leave."

Bridie raised her eyebrows. No sandwiches? No plastic cups? Where did this command put her on the sliding scale of importance? She collected her jacket and noticed that the sun was very bright and that summer was on its way. She put on the huge and fashionable dark glasses she had bought in

Switzerland on the day when she had gone to the top of Pilatus with Anton Gesner, and when she saw Carl she was glad that he couldn't read her eyes. She held her shoulders straight and gripped her purse so firmly that the buckle hurt her fingers.

He lounged against the doorpost, dressed in a sober business suit that seemed to enhance rather than hide his taut body. His hair was burnished by Swiss sun and his tan was enviable and even. He half smiled, as if unsure that he really wanted to smile at her. "Good," he said and swung away with no other greeting. Bridie followed to the car park breathlessly, as his stride was twice as long as hers and her skirt was narrow. He unlocked the car. "Nice day," he said as he swung his legs under the steering wheel. Not the huge black limousine with the chauffeur that took him to business appointments but a rakish, white sports car that he used for weekends and leisure.

Bridie saw that he had no briefcase with him. "What about the papers?" she asked as he turned the key in the ignition. "You said you wanted a working lunch but you didn't tell me to bring anything." The engine purred. "I can go and get them now if you give me the authority," she said, anxiously.

"I've changed my mind. I want to talk about work but I have no need of those particular papers just now. I've seen them and dealt with them. In fact, I've dealt with all aspects of that deal now." He negotiated the traffic at the first island. "Do you object to meeting me in your lunch hour?" he asked pointedly. "I hope I'm not keeping you from something more interesting?"

"Of course I don't mind," she said. Suddenly she didn't know what to call him. Mr Paterson would sound false away from the office after being with him and learning to call him Carl on the business trip, but she was back to earth now and so was he, dressed for the part he played in high-powered business. There was no luxury hotel, no social adventures to be enjoyed, and she was once more a humble member of his staff.

It was a silent journey but blessedly short. The tension between them lay like a barbed-wire shield. Once, when using the manual gear change, Carl's hand touched her thigh and a thread of yearning reminded her of the dangers of his touch and nearness. She moved slightly to avoid further contact and, when they stopped, she was glad to be out of the confined space of the sports car. She looked about her in wonder.

"Did you know about this place?" he asked.

"No, I would never have suspected that it was here."

The car had wound its way through back streets to a canal, long abandoned, where rotting warehouses and rough cobbled paths had been the haunt of rats and junkies. Bridie stared. It had been transformed into a walking precinct backed by lovingly restored granaries which retained the façades of warm red brick. The high curved windows, originally set to give better light to the people working there and so save expensive gas-light for the owners, rather than ease the lot of the people working there for long hours six days a week, were now elegant highlights of smart eating houses and waterside pubs. The canal water lay like molten lead tinged with gold in the sunlight and swans sailed over the still surface.

"Not quite the lake at Lucerne but not bad," he said. "Come on, I'm hungry, and if you've been doing your work you should be too."

"I ought to diet," she said, "But I do love good food." He glanced at her figure and she blushed. "Please don't say that I have put on weight! I know I have put on six pounds and two people have remarked on it." She laughed. "A few evenings with a salad and no delicious bread or croissants will soon shed it again, especially if I go for long walks in my spare time."

"You look just right," he said, "And when you come back from the clinic, you will be completely back to normal as far as the casual observer can see, just as if nothing had ever changed."

"It shouldn't make any difference. I shall still have to watch my weight. Maybe the physio idea would be best for me. I'd get far more exercise than I have now, sitting at a desk."

He looked at the firm and seductive lines of her body and smiled sadly. "You don't need to change, Bridie. "I wish you'd leave things as they are and live with it. Would it be the end of the world if you didn't go to the clinic and you cancelled your appointment?"

"No, I suppose not, but I want it done soon." Bridie was confused and annoyed. News certainly spread like wildfire in any office, as she knew, and everyone latched on to the latest titbit of new information even if it wasn't of much real interest to anyone but the person concerned, but this bit of news had done the rounds more quickly than she'd imagined possible.

"I just wish that you'd forget the idea and cope with the situation," he said, then shrugged as if he'd done what he could and must now let the matter rest.

I didn't even tell the girl in Personnel where the birthmark is, Bridie remembered, and wondered what sniggerings there had been as one after another tried to guess the most embarrassing place where it could be. To have got to the penthouse so quickly, the news must have flown! Did the higher ranking members of Herald mention it over their morning gin and tonic? Did they discuss all their staff in this way? The information given to Personnel was private and not to be divulged to anyone who wasn't immediately concerned with an employee's welfare.

Bridie pushed her hair back from her face. "Why did you bring me here, Carl?" she asked.

"I had to talk to you about Sandra. Sandra and Gesner to be precise, and I know it may embarrass you. It isn't something that can be discussed in the office but I do need a few more facts that only you can give me." Bridie took a deep breath. His eagerness to get her away from the office was only a ploy to discuss office business and had nothing to do with his concern for her health. In one way she was glad as it took the tension out of their meeting, even if it left her heart empty.

"From what I already knew and from what you have told me, I know that Sandra has been trading our secrets with him for some time. Maria had information that could only have been passed from Sandra to Gesner and from him to Maria. I know now that there have been other firms who have learned a lot through those two and it's time it stopped."

"What can I say? I know nothing and I certainly told Anton nothing that he could use."

"I was annoyed at first when Sandra couldn't come with me to Switzerland, until I realised that with a new secretary I could break the chain without having an internal scandal at Herald and nothing need get into the press." He smiled wryly. "Fate sent me you, Bridget from the manse, with your clear and honest eyes that most people would say could never hide anything wrong and, as far as work goes, I was right to trust you." She opened her mouth to protest at the hint of an insult contained in his words, but he thrust the menu into her hands. "We haven't all day. I'm having whitebait, granary bread and white wine. Will you have the same?"

She nodded, and sank back into the cane chair by the window-table and unfolded her table napkin. "What are you going to do?" she asked.

"It was a very tricky situation," said Carl. "You see, Gesner has done nothing really illegal, and, as I said, Maria makes a game of it that she plays quite openly: getting what information she needs from various sources by bribery, flattery and a few underhand methods that she doesn't make public! It happens all over the world and most of the time we grin and bear it and tighten our security. I manage quite well as I refuse to see it happening under my nose, and take steps to avoid a situation getting worse."

"You've spoken to Sandra?" Bridie recalled Mrs Dean saying that the usually cool secretary had been in tears.

Carl moved impatiently. "Yes and the silly girl had hysterics!"

"Do you wonder?" Bridie smiled. "You can be quite terrifying, you know."

"Me, terrifying?"

"Mrs Dean was full of what was happening when she came to our office. She hinted that you might be beating Sandra and warned me to watch my step with you. I think she might send out a search party for me if I get back late from lunch."

Carl took her hand in his and laughed. He looked out at a slowly moving canal barge that lay low in the water under its load. "I think I'll kidnap you and make her really worried. Where shall we go? Come on, we'll jump that barge and float down to the coast and across the channel! We could sail away for a year and a day and forget so many things."

"Don't," she whispered. "No, please don't drag me away," she added more clearly, and smiled. "I haven't finished my whitebait yet and this bread is too delicious to leave." She longed to do as his joke suggested, and wanted to be rushed away, hidden from the world to be loved and loved with all the passion she knew that he could give her. She laughed to hide the tremor of her mouth and he let her hand drop. She sipped her wine. "This too, is delicious," she said, to fill the sudden fraught silence.

"Quite delicious," he said softly.

"What will happen about Sandra?" she asked. This was safer ground.

"She's a first-rate secretary and I think she's been led by Gesner who has used his slimy charm on her over a long period. We pay her well, so there's no real need to cheat on us from spite, and, before a couple of years ago, I would have trusted her with anything. Make no mistake, Bridie, whatever you think of him now, that man is devoid of all moral values." His voice was bitter. "It's difficult to believe how a man can achieve so much by sexual attraction, but he's a real stud when given the chance, and she must have been blind. If he can't use a woman to help him get what he wants for his own advancement, then he doesn't want to know."

"A lot of women do find him attractive," Bridie said. "Even the countess, who must know all about men," she added bluntly.

"Who am I to tell you anything about him? You know all about him, to your cost." He gazed moodily out of the window at the now smooth water and Bridie wondered if he had heard of the incident in the cable car when Anton tried to rape her. Perhaps Anton had told Sandra a watered-down account of it and laughed about it, pretending that he had tried only to scare the puritanical little girl in the buttoned-up cardigan. She thought quickly. It was possible that when Carl had confronted Sandra with her disloyalty, she might have told him that his nice little stand-in secretary wasn't so pure either.

"Is she leaving Herald?" she asked.

"No, I shall transfer her to another department where she has no access to secret material. Keep it in the family, I think, and, if she's wise, she will keep quiet about it all. He grinned. "That man can certainly mesmerise every female in sight. Poor Maria will lose one of her best contacts and he will have to work even harder if he is ever to have her island now." He regarded Bridie with stony eyes. "Now that he knows that you will not help him, he will keep away, Bridie. You may never see him again unless you meet by accident. Does it worry you that he is such a swine?"

"Of course not." She looked away, knowing that Carl thought she was a fool ever to trust Anton and take his outward charm to be genuine, but he must know by now that she had never been in love with the handsome Swiss; flattered, yes, but nothing more. It annoyed her to think that Carl still regarded her with doubt after she had made it clear that she had refused to cooperate with him in any way.

"Are you going to let him get away with cheating other firms?" she asked bluntly. "If you let this matter go without doing something about it, he can seduce other girls as he did Sandra, in other business concerns, to get what he wants."

"Are you so bitter about him that you want revenge?" he asked.

"Bitter?" Bridie laughed. "No, not that. I find him a bit of a joke now that I know more about him. I'm annoyed to think that you take it all so calmly when you could warn your business associates, nice men like M Dubois and the other man who dined with us, and many more who might have susceptible staff willing to be flattered into betraying secrets." She laughed. "I may be wrong, as it didn't take me long to know what he was really like." She paused. "I did discover that he had a darker side but that was only after I had made him angry. Any woman who took him seriously would be stupid. It takes one glance to know that he thinks he's God's gift to the female race, fun to be with but never to be taken seriously as a lover."

She saw growing bewilderment and doubt in his eyes. He stared at her as if he had never seen her before now. "Either you are a very cool chick indeed, and one I never knew, or I have made one hell of a great and totally unforgivable mistake." He held up a hand to command her to say nothing. "Whichever it is, I have no intention of enquiring into it now! I have a feeling that I could be falling into a very deep pit of very cold water."

"I wish I knew what you were thinking," she said.

"Thank God you don't!" He called the waiter and ordered coffee. "Cream?" he said, "or are you anxious about those lovely new curves?"

"It's not that bad. I'll have cream but no sugar."

They finished the meal and walked along the canal bank. It was warm in the sun and Bridie was reminded of the dusky walk beside Lucerne. As if reading her thoughts, he said, "No wooden bridge today; no paintings, no doves and no place for lovers." Her pulse quickened. How strange if Carl shared her thoughts and had wondered what it would be like to walk there with a lover. It was foolish dreaming. She glanced at the firm profile, the slightly cynical turn of the lips and the dear, beloved lock of hair that tumbled awry after he ran his fingers through it.

It's usual for a girl to dream like that, she thought, but he was a widower, who had suffered and now had no time for romance, unless he could combine business with pleasure and embark on a union with Maria and a more contrived glamour than that of first love.

"I ought to get back to the office, *sir*," she suggested. It was impossible to call him Carl now, so it was better to make a joke of their respective positions at work.

"I suppose so, but I could stay here all day," he said.

"I always thought of you as a man who hated to leave the office. I didn't think you could enjoy leisure such as we mere mortals do," she said.

"That's true at times, but I learned a lot in Switzerland," he said quietly.

They drove back through dusty streets, with the pale leaves turning on the plane trees lining the avenue by the Herald offices, and Bridie felt drained of emotion. Soon, he would tell her that he and Maria were to be married. Everything he did led up to it. He had stayed on the island with her after she had broken her arm and Bridie knew that the island could weave a spell over anyone fortunate enough to stay there. He said he had learned a lot in Switzerland and the spell of indolence and relaxation gave him space to discover the delights of just watching beautiful scenes and inhaling the voluptuous scent of flowers and the sensual perfume of a lovely woman.

Even enforced idleness must have enchanted him and shown that it was wrong to fill his entire life with work, ignoring the beauty around him. Maria would share her island with him, but the picture that Bridie conjured up wasn't right. Maria was as restless as a lovely bird and could make no man feel rested for long. Her vitality would make men restless, passionate and burning, but not tranquil.

"How is the countess," Bridie asked.

"Maria? Oh, very well. She has had time to think now that she is forced to rest a little. It gives her time to work out what she really wants for the future." He smiled. "I think that at last she has made up her mind and has chosen the man with whom she wants to share her life. Since the accident she is much calmer and more positive and even allows others to make a few decisions for her. She has also learned that it isn't good to keep people dangling for too long or they might grow away from her and seek other women."

Bridie felt her heart grow cold. The warmth of the brief contact with Carl diminished and she knew that this might be the last time that they would be as close again, physically. "Did she mind very much when you had to come away and leave her?" she asked, turning the screw tighter in her soul.

"Not really. She said she'll phone and she's coming over here to sign papers so I'll see her very soon."

"I see." Bridie could imagine what lay ahead. "Will she come to the office?"

"No, I shall go to her hotel. It's much easier to talk business to Maria in her own kind of surroundings. She hates formal offices and is much more reasonable if she is comfortable!" Bridie gave a sigh of relief. At least she would be spared the humiliation of being treated like dirt while Maria swept by in a couture gown and fabulous jewels, leaving a wake of expensive perfume behind her to be savoured wistfully by every little office junior who would never aspire to such luxury.

"Back to work," Bridie said.

"Yes, back to normality," Carl said. But Bridie knew that this was never possible for her.

Twelve

Time passed quickly. Bridie found several messages for her as soon as she returned to her desk and a list of telephone numbers to call. She took them one by one, knowing that she had no time to do them all before she went off for the day. She gave a few numbers that she knew were just confirmations of appointments for her immediate boss, to the temp, and concentrated on ones she didn't recognise.

One number on her pad had no name and she rang it to find out who it might be. To her surprise it was the receptionist at the clinic. "Oh, I'm so glad I've caught you," she said in a flustered voice. "I do apologise, Miss Mark. It's entirely my fault. I made a mistake in the bookings. The time I gave you at ten tomorrow morning is for a gynae case for the other Dr Courtney, and Dr Clive Courtney wants you here at six tonight. Can you possibly make it?"

"But I asked for a day off tomorrow so that I could rest after the op. Does this mean I can be back home to sleep tonight?"

"Yes, there will be no need for you to stay in here. You can rest on a very comfortable recliner in the waiting room for an hour or so if that's what you want, or go straight home by taxi. In fact, our beds are pretty full, so even if you were fitted in tomorrow and felt you needed to rest in a bed, there would be no bed for you as the case tomorrow at ten will have the last one. She will have to stay overnight after a termination of pregnancy."

"It doesn't give me much notice," Bridie said, mentally

205

backing away from what was now becoming far too close for comfort.

"Please say you'll be here this evening," the woman pleaded. She was nearly in tears. "I'm new here and I muddled the notes as I thought that the different colours were for times and days and not the two consultants. They didn't make it clear that the blue notes had to be kept separate from the others to keep the two doctor's records in their respective compartments."

Bridie's rising anger made her voice sharp. "Well! I don't know what to say. Suppose you tell me what I'm expected to do and get it right this time! Are you sure that the anaesthetist will give me acupuncture, or will I be put on a table and sent to sleep and who knows what they might do to me?"

This was impossible. It was very unlikely to happen but a few people now knew that she was going into the clinic and if they rang to enquire after her well-being and the notes were muddled, there was a chance that it would be all over Herald Enterprises that the rather nice, quiet girl on Level Five, who went to Switzerland with Carl Paterson, was pregnant and had gone in for an abortion! What if Carl Paterson followed up his concern for her and rang the clinic tomorrow morning? Bridie held her breath for a second to quell rising hysteria. She mustn't over-dramatise the situation. She could ring the office tomorrow to make sure they all knew that the operation had been done and she was nowhere near the clinic at ten a.m. when the other case was being done.

"I'm truly sorry," the woman was saying again. "If you could come here at five thirty, on your way from the office, it will be all over quite soon and you can go home to rest."

"And what do I do tomorrow?"

"I spoke to the theatre nurse and she assures me that you can go back to work if that's what you want to do, but personally I'd advise a day off. Many cases like yours are done in hospital outpatients and although it may be a little sore, they spray the scar with a sealing compound to prevent infection and you can wear ordinary clothes and bathe normally. I shall be glad when the other receptionist comes back and we can deal with one doctor each and avoid this happening again."

"Oh, well, I suppose I can manage it, but if I arrive late I shall blame you and say that you told me the wrong time."

"You won't say that I muddled the days, will you?"

"No, we all make mistakes, some more harmful than others," Bridie said.

"I can't tell you how grateful I am, Miss Mark. I feel such a fool and I was afraid that I might lose my job if the doctors found out what I'd done."

"Ah, well, get it over," Bridie said as she walked away from the telephone and put a folder on the small desk used by the temp.

"Get what over?" the girl asked.

"Today. Just get today over. I have to get away promptly so I'll leave you to clear up." She glanced at her watch. Brian had told her to take what time off she needed and she certainly needed an extra hour now to compose herself.

She hurried home and changed into a summer dress that buttoned up at the front, collected make-up and a light shawl and called a taxi to take her to the clinic.

As she paid off the cab driver, she saw two nurses, dressed in crisp white uniform dresses and white shoes going into the foyer of the clinic. They looked professional and impersonal, and the sight of them made everything seem more imminent and scary. She experienced her first real twinge of fear. Was her aunt right after all? Was she taking a risk just to feed her own vanity? She could imagine the pursed-up lips and the shocked expression over such self-indulgence, and the suspicion that Bridie, who had been brought up with Victorian modesty, might want to expose that part of her body to . . . a man!

She nodded to the girl in reception who was obviously very relieved to see her, and the nurse touched her on the arm as if she thought the patient might take fright and run away from her. "Come with me," she said and led her to a pretty cubicle with a dull-green velvet chair and matching chaise longue. The floor was bare and tiled but the matt-painted walls were a pleasant dusky pink. Through the half-open door she saw the theatre with spotless white floor and tiled walls but the table was hidden from her by a screen. A covered instrument trolley was ready and another that held a selection of apparatus that meant nothing to Bridie, was also ready. She wondered how deeply they would insert acupuncture needles and if it would hurt.

The nurse smiled in a friendly way. She couldn't have been any older than Bridie. "Would you take off your dress and bra and tights and just wear your panties under this gown? For the operation it's best if you wear the gown with the tapes at the front so that it can be undone to the waist."

Bridie took the white gown in cold fingers, although the room was warm. The nurse stayed while she undressed and, as she removed her bra, the girl eyed the birthmark with detached interest and a critical look, assessing what would be done. "I'm a bit scared," Bridie admitted.

"No need. That's nothing," the girl said, airily. "He'll do it in no time at all and you shouldn't feel a thing."

"Nothing to you, maybe, but important to me," said Bridie.

"I know." The girl smiled. "I can see that it's very important but, as far as surgery is concerned, this is simple, and with acupuncture there are no after-effects."

Bridie dragged on the shapeless garment and shivered. She felt as if she had been handed this awful gown so that if she escaped she could be spotted and brought back, like a mentally disturbed patient. Perhaps I *am* mentally disturbed to consider having this done. I must be out of my mind!

Dr Courtney came in at once and examined her again as soon as the nurse settled her comfortably on the operating table. The anaesthetist brought in the gold needles he used for acupuncture and, after he found the right median, used them.

Bridie found to her amazement that she had no feeling in her breast or in the tissues surrounding it. The table on which she was lying was comfortable and she no longer felt cold.

"I have a local ready if you need it, but I'm sure that it won't be necessary," the anaesthetist said. "It's just here to make you feel safe."

A face screen was erected so that she couldn't see the actual operation and she was relieved that she need see none of her own blood! She felt pressure but no pain and was almost asleep when Dr Courtney said with a note of pride, "It's all done and, though I say it myself, I've made a good job of it! You can see it in the mirror now." He sprayed the fine suture line with a coagulant to keep it clean and dry, wiped the surrounding skin free of the skin paint that he'd used to sterilise the area, and the nurse handed Bridie some strips of gauze dressing to put inside her bra. "No stitches to remove," he said with a smile. "I'm a very good seamstress. When my brother operates and wants no scar along a bikini line, he calls me in to do it."

Bridie sat up. "I didn't feel a thing," she said in wonder. She looked in the mirror that the nurse held for her and, for the first time in her life, she saw no disfigurement, but just a faint line that matched one that occured naturally on the other breast. "It's wonderful," she said and was not self-conscious under the admiring gaze of the doctor and the nurse. "What do I do now?" she asked.

Dr Courtney laughed. "I prescribe a very pretty low-cut dress to celebrate. Go in for Miss World! Do anything that will make you happy and free. Go topless if that's what you want to do!" His eyes twinkled.

"I have just the dress," she said and tried to forget that even if she had it, she could see no future in wearing it again. She slid from the table and said goodbye and thank you to the doctors. The nurse helped her to dress carefully and asked if she'd like to stay on the chaise longue for a while or have a taxi to take her home.

"I'll go home now. I feel slightly numb, but otherwise I'm

fine." She gathered her things together and the receptionist rang for a car.

"Take it easy this evening. Have a catnap when you get home then eat and drink and be back to normal," the nurse suggested as she handed Bridie into the taxi.

The first cup of coffee was nectar and Bridie took the mild painkiller that the nurse had suggested in case the nerve endings came back to life and were uncomfortable, before settling back in an armchair with a book. It's over, she thought. It's over after all those years of waiting. But where was the elation she had expected to feel, the sense of freedom? She drowsed and was awakened by the telephone ringing.

"Bridie? I rang you in the office but you'd left early, then I rang you at home and you weren't there. What the hell is going on? I want you to do something for me." Carl sounded ruffled.

"Tomorrow? I have the day off tomorrow," she said, "Or I thought I had." She felt vaguely bemused, having dragged herself back from a deep pit of sleep that had done nothing to freshen her mind. How could she tell him that she'd already had the operation, after making sure that she had Friday off? In his present mood he'd take it for granted that she wanted time off for something more, maybe a date that she was keeping secret. He knows I'm off tomorrow, she thought. I can't say that I could be back at my word processor in the morning as if I had never made such elaborate arrangements to take the day off. He might even think that there was no operation and I'd used that as an excuse to take a long weekend away.

"Not tomorrow; tonight! You can't have any plans for this evening. Nobody makes arrangements the night before an operation, not even you who seems to dismiss this as something to treat very lightly and of no lasting importance." The bitterness was there again, sharp and wounding. "I haven't time to argue. Get into that dress; you know the goldy thing you wore at the banquet. I'll pick you up at nine for dinner. Be ready!"

"I don't understand," she said weakly.

"Oh, didn't I tell you? Maria has descended on me without notice, with Gesner of all people, and I have no intention of playing gooseberry to him! I need support." He laughed without humour. "Get ready. At least the condemned prisoner can have a decent meal before her execution tomorrow." His voice was without feeling, without concern and the line went dead.

Bridie stared at the silent phone. His laugh had been sad and almost desperate. Could the memory of his dead wife be constantly with him, magnified by the fact that he thought that Bridie was to have an anaesthetic? Was he reliving that event and now filled his spare time with frivolous evenings with whoever he could get to share them? It was goodbye, all over again, she decided. He hated her for reminding him and wanted to use her and make her pay. He didn't give me a chance to explain, she thought sadly.

"I can't go!" She sat before her mirror and saw the same Bridie who had been there before she left for the clinic. An exploratory touch of the scar was without pain. The suture line was stiff but more from the coagulant that protected it than from the incision. She changed into the brief featherlight bra that cupped her breasts and went with the dress and she could see no trace of the scar. The dress fell in soft folds about her body, the shoes lifted her back into fairyland and she saw a rather pale but lovely woman in the mirror.

The butterfly lay on the dressing table with one wing slightly bent. She had no need of it any more. There was no need to hide anything. The doorbell rang and she was ready. She picked up the shawl and draped it round her shoulders and made sure she had her key in the golden purse.

Carl was dressed in a lightweight dinner-jacket and black tie, as if going to a very sober dinner party with male colleagues. "You look . . . very good," he said, but didn't

211

smile at her. "I'm very sorry to ask you to do this, but there was no other suitable person available who knew the background to the Swiss week. I realise that it must be very embarrassing for you."

"Why embarrassing? I've met them several times and can meet them again," said Bridie lightly.

"But Gesner will be there! Don't you feel anything for him? Can't you feel any emotion, any hate or love for the man who—"

"The man who what?" asked Bridie coldly. "Just because he thought I was like Sandra and would be bowled over by his charm until he found out that I was immune, it doesn't make me embarrassed. He might well be, as it was worse for him. Men like that hate to be firmly repulsed by what they think is an easy conquest." She smiled grimly. "I managed to control him in the cable car when he tried to rape me, when we were quite alone and I was a bit scared, so I can cope easily with him when you are there, and he wouldn't want to upset Maria, would he?" She spoke slowly and very distinctly and watched his face as the full impact of her words struck him.

"It was rape?" His anger was mixed with a kind of relief.

"Attempted rape," she corrected him. "I don't need protection as I can manage quite well on my own. I was under the impression that you are the one who needs my protection tonight, at least for your pride! Is the beautiful Maria still keeping you both on a string?"

"But what about tomorrow? The operation? For God's sake tell me, Bridie. What is going to happen? I know it must be gynaecological. My wife had the same surgeon. After seeing that bruise on your arm and that . . . thing on your . . . Oh, hell!"

They had reached the taxi and the interested ears of the driver and Carl sat with his hands clenched at his sides and his mouth a grim line of tension.

Bridie sat back in comfort. "It isn't what you think. At least I think I know what went on in your mind about me. I am very

shocked that you jumped to the wrong conclusion, Mr Par-
terson," she added demurely, and found a great deal of
satisfaction in his complete discomfiture.

"Bridie," he began, then saw that the glass screen between
them and the driver was open. He sat back, suddenly helpless
to say anything while the cab took them through the busy
London streets. The driver gave a running commentary on the
lunatics driving in other cars, and the odd habits of foreign
visitors when it came to tipping.

From a deep recess in her mind, Bridie drew the beginnings
of a deep joy. Carl cared enough about her to be sad if she
died. It wasn't just the memory of his wife and lost love that
made him conscious of her situation; he really cared about
her, Bridie Mark, the girl he had bullied and kissed lightly and
almost driven mad with jealousy over his feelings for Maria.
She sighed. He might even love her a little, but there was
Maria and all that she could offer him.

Maria looked blooming and very beautiful. She made the
most of her snow-white plaster cast by having it resting in a
white silk sling against a stark-black velvet dress, as if it was
an amusing fashion accessory. Bridie gave her a genuine smile
as she couldn't help admiring her for her attitude to something that would make most women avoid being seen in a
smart public restaurant.

Anton clicked his heels formally, and inclined his head, but
made no attempt to kiss her hand, and Bridie wondered if his
hands might be sweating with uneasiness. He isn't sure how
much Carl knows about him and he certainly has no idea of
my reaction to him tonight, so he's not going to feel at his
charismatic best, she decided, and knew that she was going to
enjoy the evening! It must have been a shock for Anton to
hear that Bridie was to make up the party of four.

Maria eyed her intently. "You look a little pale, my dear,"
she said. She took Bridie's hand in her free one and squeezed it
with sympathy. "When I rang the office and asked to speak to

Carl, who as usual was not available, I asked to speak to you and was told that you had gone to see a doctor and wouldn't be back until next week." She gave Carl a mocking smile. "Such lack of security my darling! I can get anything I like out of most people if I say the right things. They think that we are cousins," she added with a tinkling laugh.

"Who told you personal details about a member of staff?" he said, frowning.

"Why should I tell you. I might need to use her again." Maria sighed. "You really must look after her, Carl. She is a little fragile tonight. You work all your girls far too hard and some go sick and some even turn to spying. Isn't that so?"

Anton said nothing but looked self-righteous as if he was shocked to hear it, and Bridie knew now that the temp had overheard most of her conversation with the clinic receptionist.

"I'm fine," Bridie said, firmly. As she sat down at the table, she slipped the shawl from her shoulders in the warm room and looked up at the gracious chandeliers and mirrored walls of the restaurant. One more glimpse of the good life before she put away the dress and could show her new image only in swimming pools and on sun terraces. She smiled as she remembered the high-cut black swimming costume that could now be thrown out for jumble. I can buy a really pretty bikini, she decided and was suddenly aware of two pairs of eyes . . . no three, staring at her low décolletage.

She looked down instinctively, half expecting the birthmark to have bloomed again, but there was nothing but a slight trace of the shiny sealant over the hidden scar.

Anton stared, first at her and then at Carl, believing that the blemish had really been a love bite and now it was gone, and Carl looked at Anton with a puzzled expression as Anton didn't look guilty, but almost accusing, as he faced the man he thought had beaten him to the girl he wanted.

Maria leaned forward to have a better view and said with the pleased expression of a woman who knows something that the others don't. "So you had it done." She looked pleased. "Monique said that you would make up your mind to have it done as soon as you saw yourself in her creation, but I wasn't sure if you'd have the courage." She ignored the two men who looked completely lost. "It's very good. Give me his name and address as I may have a nose job done some day and I think he might be careful."

"He did it today," Bridie said. "I suppose you saw the birthmark when the butterfly slipped, and of course Monique saw it and helped me to hide it for the banquet. I was to have gone in tomorrow but they changed the schedule and I had it done early this evening."

Carl pushed back his chair and came to her. "What the hell are you doing here? You should be in bed!"

She shrugged away his hand on her shoulder. "Please don't make such a fuss. It's all right. I didn't have an anaesthetic as there was no need. I had acupuncture and it was an almost pleasurable experience. I nearly dozed off!" She drew away further and he slowly went back to his chair and sat down, still staring at her until he couldn't face the clear level gaze she turned on him.

"The other girl who is being done tomorrow at the time for which I was originally booked, will have to stay for at least one night as she is having a termination of pregnancy, done by the other Dr Courtney who is, as you know, a gynaecologist and not a plastic surgeon. She will need rest, while this is literally, only skin deep."

"A birthmark?" Anton said.

"Of course. What did you think it might be?" Bridie looked from one face to another and gave a brittle laugh. "By your expressions anyone would think you believed it to be . . . a love bite or something equally ridiculous, as Monique thought at first when I fitted on this dress. She made me see how stupid I was to put up with it and so I came back determined to be free of it for ever, and not to have to cover it up." Her eyes were overbright and unhappy as she saw a kaleidoscope unfold before her. Carl thought that she was having an abortion because of Anton, Anton thought that she was Carl's mistress and so to him she must be untouchable, and Maria was softly laughing at them all.

Anton recovered first. He laughed. "And so, now you have no need to wear a butterfly to hide your beauty." A note of regret in his voice made Maria look sulky and he saw her change of expression. "Good!" he said. "It is less distracting, so, as every man wished to see what was concealed under the butterfly but now we know, it loses it's mystery and we will no longer be curious." He turned to Maria and kissed her hand, making her smile again.

"Wine, sir?" The sommelier hovered with the wine list and Carl turned away to give it his attention, as if waking from a dream. The food was well-served and Bridie knew must be delicious as she ate and drank and said all the right things as a perfect guest should do, but she tasted nothing and was aware of a smouldering volcano by her side.

Carl was attentive and courteous, glancing at her from time to time to make sure that she wasn't tired or fraught, and on the surface it was a very successful dinner party, with Anton and Maria announcing their intention to marry as soon as Maria was free of plaster. Bridie wondered how deeply hurt Carl must feel to see Maria discarding him for a man he despised. I know now that he couldn't have dined with them alone, having to hear such news without a partner with him, to look as if he too had female company when he needed it. She felt like a girl from an escort service, who would be given a good evening and then sent away, her work finished.

She stifled a yawn. At least this girl wouldn't have to give other services tonight if asked. Did they in fact, sleep with their hosts for the night? It was another grey area like massage parlours. That at least was not on the agenda, however much she longed to be held in his arms and loved with all the latent passion she knew he possessed.

Bridie shook her head when offered coffee. It would be

better to drink some in her room and then sink into bed.

Carl stood up. "I'm taking Bridie home," he said. "She may be brave and says she isn't tired, but the operation must have been trying, to say the least."

"But Carl, darling, I've only just got to know her," protested Maria.

"Invite her to the wedding," he said, and draped the shawl over Bridie's shoulders and took her hand. "It's late," he said, and Bridie gave him a grateful glance. It was wonderful to be treated like a fragile girl for a change and not the efficient machine he usually seemed to think she was, but she was soon shocked out of her dream.

He went to reception and the porter pointed down a long corridor and gave him a key. "Everything you need, sir. But please return the door key to the desk when you've finished."

"Come on," Carl said. "I have to send a fax."

Bridie followed him and leaned against the wall while he opened the door to the empty office. Work, after such a lovely evening? Had the man no sensitivity after all? She heard the hum of the various electronic machines and he closed the door. He sat her at a low table and handed her a slim notepad and a gold-plated pen. She looked up and was very conscious of his nearness as he bent over her. She held the pen poised. "This is just an outline?" she asked.

"It will need revision, refinement, much practice and will take time," he said. "First, make this an abject apology, to Bridie Mark, of the manse." Was that warm lips on the nape of her neck as she inclined her head? She shivered. "Then an avowal to do better in all things, to think only beautiful thoughts and to love someone who made me crazy for her since she appeared in a golden dress with a ridiculous butterfly; an extremely sexy butterfly, just there, where any man in his right mind would want to kiss." He bent his head and her hands brought him lower, to kneel beside her, so that his eager mouth might kiss her eyes, her lips, her throat and the tender line of the scar.

"Two weeks should be enough to make sure you are all

217

completely healed up," he murmured. "Two weeks and we can get married in Lucerne if that pleases you? Please?" he asked as if even now she might refuse him.

"I didn't get all that, sir," she replied softly. "I need that message again."

He was gentle with his caresses and reluctantly let her go to last. He sent a fax to himself at the office, congratulating him on his latest great success, just to show that he used the room for what it was intended and kissed her again. "Happy?"

She nodded shyly. "I've found everything that my Calvinistic upbringing told me was not for me."

"Not everything. The best is in the future. In Lucerne in two weeks' time we'll climb your clouded mountain together."